But Cats Don't Talk

a novel

LYNNE HEINZMANN

But Cats Don't Talk

LYNNE HEINZMANN

woodhall press
Woodhall Press | Norwalk, CT

woodhall press

Woodhall Press, 81 Old Saugatuck Road, Norwalk, CT 06855
WoodhallPress.com

Cover design: Danny Sancho
Layout artist: L.J. Mucci

Library of Congress Cataloging-in-Publication Data available

ISBN 978-1-954907-76-8   (paperback: alk paper)
ISBN 978-1-954907-77-5   (electronic)

First Edition
Distributed by Independent Publishers Group
(800) 888-4741

Printed in the United States of America

*This novel is dedicated to all piano nerds
and uniquely talented people everywhere.
Let the world hear your beautiful music.*

Table of Contents

The Seventh Beethoven Sonata Concert

Backstage at the Courthouse Center for the Arts, I lean forward on the piano bench and whisper in BC's furry ear, "I wish you could say *something*—wish me luck, tell me to chill...*anything*. Don't you know that's what best friends are supposed to do?"

Instead, BC does what he always does: sleeps in his cat bed on the top of the grand piano, while I do what I always do: perch on the very edge of the bench and suffer a minor bout of stage fright as I wait for the curtain to go up. I know I'm going to play well—I always do—but I still get nervous beforehand. Probably just an adrenaline rush.

"Mom, why do I agree to perform these stupid concerts?" I whisper-whine. "The audience is going to *hate* me." Beads of sweat trickle down inside my new black satin gown.

Mom—looking ridiculously calm and unbelievably gorgeous in her matching mother-of-the-bride dress—slides onto the padded bench beside me, wraps an arm around my shoulders, and hugs me

1

so close I catch a reassuring whiff of her Coach perfume. "Rebecca O'Sullivan," she says with a smile, "why do we have to go through this drama routine before every performance?" She pulls out one of her lace hankies and gently blots my face, neck, and back, careful not to smudge my stage makeup. "You know the audience is going to love you. They always do. You look gorgeous, you're amazingly talented, and you play beautifully. What's not to love?"

"But why do I have to be here at all?" I ask. "*Gone with the Wind* is on TCM tonight. Right now, BC and I could be sitting on the couch with a huge bowl of popcorn, enjoying our favorite movie."

Mom shrugs. "You're the one who says she wants to be a world-famous pianist. As far as I know, they don't award national touring contracts to seventeen-year-old girls who sit on sofas with their cats, eating popcorn and watching Atlanta burn to the ground for the twentieth time." How does she always know just the right thing to say? She and Grandpa . . .

My eyes brim with tears as I point my chin toward the audience on the other side of the blue velvet curtain. "I still have to remind myself that Grandpa won't be out there when the curtain opens. I can't believe I've played almost an entire season without my number-one fan."

Mom squeezes my shoulder. "You know he's here with you—in spirit."

I don't want Grandpa here *in spirit*; I want him here *for real*. Stupid cancer killed him on New Year's Eve, and now it's the day after Thanksgiving, almost a year later. He wasn't that old—only sixty-nine. No way he should have died yet.

Grandpa always said he was a corn farmer and didn't know much about classical piano music, but I could tell he loved hearing me play by the way his face lit up whenever he'd tell anyone who'd listen, "That's my granddaughter. Isn't she something?" He came to every one of my concerts and sat right next to Mom, all duded up in his brown three-piece suit—the only suit he ever owned. He'd even gotten married to Grandma in it. I always looked forward to him hugging me after my shows so I could press my nose into his suitcoat and smell pipe smoke, hay, and Old Spice aftershave. All the scents of Grandpa.

But there will be no Grandpa hug today.

A wave of sadness makes me feel heavy and empty at the same time. I take the hankie from Mom and dab the corners of my eyes. "Hey, maybe my *dad* will come to the show," I say sarcastically, repeating a long-standing joke between us.

"You never know," she says with a raised eyebrow.

"Wait...what?!" For just a moment, I forget my nervousness.

Then Mom waves a hand dismissively, completely stopping any further discussion about Dear Old Dad. Typical Mom behavior—always in control of every situation. One of these days, I'm going to get her to talk about my father. I mean, I have a right to know who he is.

She changes the subject. "Aunt Cassie told me she'd be here tonight. I left a ticket for her at the box office."

"If she's not too drunk to find the theater."

"Hey, she's been doing a lot better lately." Mom always defends her little sister. Maybe she doesn't see how screwed up Aunt Cassie is. I mean, I love the woman, but she is a hard-core alcoholic.

"So, maybe I'll know one person in the theater," I say.

"This is Rhode Island, honey. You'll know everyone: Mrs. Fox, my piano students, their families, your friends from your high school."

"You mean the friends who think I'm a piano-playing freak? Yup, I'm sure they're out there in the audience right now, holding their breath, just waiting for me to start the show." I stroke BC's soft fur and he rewards me with a gentle head butt. I can always count on him, too. BC and Mom—my small but powerful posse.

Mom shoots me a frown. "You and I need to talk about that attitude, young lady. Ever since your birthday party last year, you've been avoiding your friends, and I don't understand why. I always got the impression that Olivia, Hayley, Chelsea, and most of your other friends thought your concert career was cool."

"I think you have that wrong, Mommy Dearest. Most of my supposed friends think I am a complete nerd. Thank God for homeschooling."

"I'm still not sure if I should have let you get away with that. And for your senior year, too." She shakes her head. "We can talk about that another time." She rises gracefully. "Are you ready to perform, milady?"

I roll my eyes. "Sure. Let's get this over with."

Mom gives me one last squeeze and then walks to the soundboard where stage manager Dave Morales stands waiting. Tall, cute for his age—mid-thirties, like Mom—and well-built, Dave looks like he should be appearing *on* the stage at the Courthouse Center, instead of being its manager, especially when he's wearing a tux like he is now.

A few seconds later the house lights flicker once, twice, and then dim. Behind me, three potted trees sparkle with tiny lights and the scrim glows russet and brown to make the stage look more interesting, and to commemorate Thanksgiving, which was yesterday.

I see Mom slip through the stage door to join the audience. I know when the curtain opens, she'll be where she always is. Because no matter where I perform—the Courthouse Center, Boston's Symphony Hall, or even Carnegie Hall in NYC—Mom always makes sure she sits in the front row, middle seat. She writes it into every one of my contracts. She says she wants me to always see her face first thing at every show so I remember she loves me and is rooting for me with all her heart. She really is a cool mom, even if she is a bit of a control freak.

Time for my preshow rituals.

I jostle BC in his bed and whisper, "Where's middle-C?" As I press down the silent pedal with my foot, he slowly stands, stretches, hops down onto the keyboard, struts over, and calmly bats middle-C, the white key in the center of the piano's keyboard, looking up at me

4

with pride in his accomplishment showing in his beautiful yellow eyes. I smooch him and tuck him back into his bed, glad he'll be right there with me for the whole performance. Weird, I know, but BC is my best furry friend, security blanket, and good luck charm all rolled into one, and I need him right there with me at all my shows.

I stand, smooth the back of my gown, sit, brush out the wrinkles across my lap, and then stretch my legs to position my black ballet flats on the piano's shiny gold pedals. I know I should walk out on stage after the curtain is already raised like most concert pianists do—making a grand entrance to the sound of thunderous applause. But, since I don't take after my graceful Mom and am a complete klutz—Is Dear Old Dad a klutz, too?—I am already seated on the piano bench when the curtain opens so I don't need to worry about tripping and falling on my face or doing anything else totally embarrassing like that. Three deep breaths and I'm ready to go.

Dave catches my eye from his position stage right and smiles kindly. "All set?" He really is a nice guy. Mom should go for him, especially since he's been so into her for years, despite her lack of encouragement.

A shiver of anticipation runs down my back as I nod.

"Then, here we go," he says, clicking on the microphone and walking out in front of the curtain. "Ladies and gentlemen." His deep voice booms over the auditorium speakers, sounding like the voice of God. "The Courthouse Center for the Arts welcomes you to this evening's presentation of Beethoven's piano sonatas, numbers twenty-five through twenty-eight. We are proud to present tonight's concert, performed by our very own award-winning concert pianist, Rebecca O'Sullivan, who hails from just down the road, in Exeter. As many of you know, this season Rebecca is attempting to become a member of the exclusive B32 Club of pianists who have performed all thirty-two of Beethoven's sonatas in one season. Tonight's show is Rebecca's seventh in a series of eight. If she completes this challenge by performing the final four sonatas at her show next month, she will be the youngest concert pianist in the world ever to do so and will be awarded a Guinness World Record. So, please plan on coming back on Saturday, December 21, to see that final concert.

"Tonight, we are pleased to have a special guest in the audience: Krystian Zelinski, the world-renowned concert pianist. At the age of eighteen, Mr. Zelinski won the prestigious International Chopin Competition, and ever since then, he's enjoyed an amazing concert career, performing with premier orchestras all over the world. Last year, he also played all thirty-two of Beethoven's sonatas in one season. Mr. Zelinski, would you please take a bow?"

From my seat behind the curtain, the applause sounds muffled, like a rush of wind through some pine trees. I imagine Mr. Zelinski—who I haven't met in person yet—standing and smiling graciously, and I realize *he's* the one to blame for me being unable to watch my favorite movie tonight since he's sort of responsible for me trying to become the youngest member of the B32 Club.

About a year ago, Mom showed me a notice about Krystian Zelinski performing all of Beethoven's sonatas and asked me if I'd be interested in trying to do the same. When she managed to get Guinness World Records to sponsor the eight concerts and award me a national touring contract if I succeeded, I *had* to go for it. And then when Mom heard Mr. Zelinski would be in town tonight, she practically *begged* him to come to my show and was thrilled to death when he accepted. When I asked her why she was so interested in Mr. Zelinski, she wouldn't explain. Typical Mom behavior.

Over the PA system, I hear Dave inform the audience where the auditorium exits are located, ask them to turn off their cell phones, and then suggest they sit back, relax, and enjoy the show. Dave clicks off the microphone as he steps back into the wings. He flashes me another encouraging smile and then, as the audience claps in antic-ipation—sounding like another rush of wind—he hoists the velvet curtain, releasing dust particles that sparkle like tiny snowflakes in the blue, red, and white stage lights and the blinding spotlight pointing at me center stage. Every muscle in my body stiffens, while BC, unfazed by the bright lights and the loud applause, snoozes peacefully atop the piano, a low, rumbly snore accompanying his every exhale.

I shoot a glance at Mom's smiling face in the first row, close my eyes, and try to remember everything she taught me about the opening of the first piece. The auditorium becomes completely silent, like someone holding his breath in anticipation of something amazing. I fill my lungs, place my fingers on the gleaming black and white keys, and launch into the lightning-quick eighth notes and arpeggios of Beethoven's *Sonata No. 25*. Thirty seconds later, I've become part of the melody, soaring up and down like a hawk catching ascending and descending thermals over the cornfields surrounding our farmhouse, flying with the music I love.

To qualify for the world record, I have to play all of the sonatas by heart, without the music in front of me, which is how I prefer to perform anyway. Long ago, Mom and I figured out that the best way for me to do this is to picture vivid scenes in my mind while I'm performing—kind of like playing along to one of my favorite silent movies, providing its soundtrack.

For my first piece tonight, *Sonata No. 25*, I fill up its eleven minutes imagining beautiful yellow, black, and white goldfinches, calling back and forth, singing to each other. They take to the air, crisscrossing paths as they fly high and then swoop low, over and over again. I hope the audience can hear the birds and picture them flying, too.

Sonata No. 26 is nicknamed *Les Adieux* or *The Farewell*, and I play it like one long, sad goodbye, much slower than the first piece. For this one, I spend seventeen minutes picturing Lara and Yuri in scenes from *Dr. Zhivago*, leaving each other over and over again. I try to make myself weep through my fingers. When I see a woman in the second row with tears in her eyes, I know I've nailed it.

After a fifteen-minute intermission, during which I gulp down three glasses of water while Mom repairs my makeup, I play *No. 27* very dramatically. For fourteen minutes, I imagine a ballet performance where two handsome male dancers are fighting over a beautiful ballerina who can't decide which of them she loves more, and so, in the end, she dies of despair. For some sections of the piece, I play loudly, stomping my foot on the sustain pedal and crashing my fingers on the keys. Toward the end of the first movement, I play with such force that I manage to startle BC, who opens his eyes wide and sneezes but then settles back into his comfy bed. A few minutes later, I end the piece quietly, almost in a whisper, as the ballerina sinks to her death on the stage in my imagination.

I play *Sonata No. 28* while picturing two kids—a brother and a sister—romping around outdoors. For twenty-two minutes, I imagine them jumping rope, swinging on a wood-seat swing, and playing hide-and-seek in a forest. In my mind, the piece ends with them running home to their mother as the sun sets behind the trees.

Two hours after the beginning of the concert, I stand and bow as the audience's enthusiastic applause fills the hall. I'm sweaty and tired, but really happy because I played very well, a fact confirmed by Mom's proud smile beaming at me from the first row.

As soon as the curtain closes, I scoop BC into my arms, hug him tight, and breathe in his dusty smell. His silky fur sticks to my sweaty chest. With my arms trembling slightly from exertion, I carry him through the labyrinthine backstage hallways to my dressing room, while at the same time trying to psych myself up to sign autographs and receive congratulations, my least favorite parts of performing. Trying to come up with the right things to write and say makes me feel even more awkward than usual. I mean, just because I play the piano well doesn't mean I have any brilliant observations about life in general. I spend four to six hours a day practicing. I really don't know much about anything else.

Still dressed in my sweaty gown, I take off BC's bow tie and wait for my first autograph seekers. My fur baby is purring in my lap as I slowly swing back and forth in a dressing room chair—one of the best features of the Courthouse Center. They're red, vinyl, swivel chairs with chrome footrests and bases, like the ones found in old-fashioned barbershops. I've spent many hours swinging and spinning around in them, before and after every performance I've done here. Sitting in them always makes me feel special, like a princess on a throne.

The first time I sat in one of these chairs was also the first time I performed at the Courthouse—the first time I performed *anywhere* as a soloist. When I was eleven, I was one of three winners of the National Orchestra Student Competition—a pretty big deal. As part of our prize, the winners were invited to play a series of concerts, including one here. That night, together with our mothers, we were ushered into this same dressing room by Dave Morales, who's been the stage manager here *forever*. Mom laughed with me as I spun around in one of the cool barbershop chairs, but when the two boys tried to copy me, their moms frowned and snarled at them to stop fidgeting. I felt sorry for the boys for missing out on the fun.

Tonight, the first person to walk through my dressing room door is none other than Dave Morales, followed closely by Aunt Cassie. He says, "I found this pretty lady wandering around backstage looking for you." He flashes a friendly grin that makes him look very cute and makes me think again that Mom should *seriously* consider going out with him sometime.

Aunt Cassie slumps against one of the green concrete block walls. She's wearing a velveteen dress that probably was a pretty midnight blue at one time but has since faded to a muddy shade of denim. It's crumpled and two sizes too big for her, and looks even worse due to the random assortment of earrings—five in each ear—and neck-laces—two silver and one gold—she's currently wearing. As usual, I feel a little embarrassed about her.

She says, "I would've found you myself eventually. I just get turned around, with all of these stupid hallways." She drops a bunch of plastic-wrapped, supermarket pink carnations on the dressing table in front of me and scrunches her face into an exaggerated look of regret. "I've gotta bounce, kiddo. I've got the late shift at the pub tonight. But I wanted to see you first and say congrats. You done good." When she leans over to hug me, I catch a strong whiff of beer and weed. As she straightens up, she overbalances and tips over backward.

"Whoa there." Dave catches her and sets her back on her feet. "You aren't planning on driving yourself over to the pub, are you?"

"Nah. Jimmy is dropping me off, 'cuz we're going out afterward."

"Good thing."

She narrows her eyes at him. "What do you mean?"

Dave shakes his head and then smiles at me. "Great performance, Becca. I especially liked that third one, *No. 27*. That's a raucous piece, and you *nailed* it."

"Thank you. And thanks for helping my aunt find me." I feel my cheeks grow warm. I love Aunt Cassie and I know she loves me, too, but sometimes...

"No problem." Dave shoots me a grin and then guides Aunt Cassie toward the exit, both of them stepping around the white-haired woman in the doorway.

"Mrs. Fox!" I say, and give her a one-armed hug with BC squished between us. He doesn't seem to mind, though, especially when she slips him a yummy cat treat, an after-show tradition. Mrs. Fox is Mom's old piano teacher and my pseudo-grandma, the only grandparent of any sort I have left now that Grandpa's gone.

Mrs. Fox is also the person who confirmed Mom's early assessment of my piano-playing abilities. One morning when I was six years old, she stopped by the house and heard Mom giving me a lesson. I'd been playing for a little over a year. Mrs. Fox told Mom, "You know,

I believe she's even better than you were. And she's younger, too." Mom's face glowed with pride.

In my dressing room now, I tell Mrs. Fox, "I was hoping you'd make it tonight."

"Oh honey, I wouldn't miss one of your shows for anything in the world. As long as I can find someone to take care of Howard for me for a few hours."

"And how is Mr. Fox?"

"Oh, as you know, he has his good days and his bad days." She chuckles. "Today he was convinced that he was Agent 007, James Bond, and that he had thwarted an attempted coup of the United States government, so I guess, as far as he was concerned, this was a *very* good day." Mrs. Fox could teach me a thing or two about maintaining a positive attitude.

Biting my lip, I ask, "And what did you think of my show?"

From her oversized purse—I often tease her that it looks like Mary Poppins's carpetbag—she pulls out a green tissue paper–wrapped florist's bouquet of a dozen red roses and hands them to me. "Beautiful flowers for a beautiful performance by a beautiful young lady."

"Thank you. That means a lot, coming from you." I inhale the flowers' sweet aroma and then carefully lay them in a special place at the end of the dressing room table.

"I taught your mother to play the piano and then she taught you, so the way I see it, you are essentially a pupil of mine, too. When you get older and retire from performing, maybe you'll teach students of your own to continue the tradition."

Gently squeezing her soft but strong hands, I laugh and say, "I can't imagine trying to teach a bunch of squirmy little kids."

Her crinkly lips pinch in disapproval.

"By the way," I say, deliberately changing the subject, "you look particularly gorgeous tonight." She's dressed in a glittery red gown, and her hair is freshly styled and tinted a unique shade of gray-pink.

She's on the board of trustees at the Courthouse Center and seems to make an effort to look the part.

Mrs. Fox giggles like a young girl. "These days, I don't get many chances to get all dolled up, so I need to take advantage of them when they come up." Looking around the dressing room, she says, "I suppose I'd best be getting back home to Howard, but I was hoping to see Maggie..."

"Mom's still backstage, probably making arrangements with Dave Morales for next month's show."

"Well, please tell her I say hi, and ask her to give me a call about tomorrow."

I frown quizzically.

Mrs. Fox laughs. "Only you would forget about your own eighteenth birthday party." She pats my cheek. "See you tomorrow at lunch."

I sigh. My eighteenth birthday party. After that disastrous sleepover party with Olivia and company last November, I'd stopped talking to my friends, so this whole birthday party thing tomorrow is going to be pretty lame: only Mom, Aunt Cassie, Mrs. Fox, and me. Not exactly a *party*. I tried to talk Mom into skipping it altogether, telling her it wasn't important, but she insisted that we celebrate in some small way at least. She *loves* birthdays and always makes a big deal over them.

Growing up, Mom never made me go to school on my birthday. Every year, from the time I woke up in the morning until I went to bed at night, Mom had activities planned for me. When I was eight, we spent the whole day in our pajamas, reading princess fairy-tale books and then acting out scenes together. Another year, we went to a *Star Wars* marathon, watching three movies in a row and stuffing ourselves with greasy theater popcorn. Mom always ensures that every birthday is special: mine, Grandpa's (when he was alive), Aunt Cassie's, and even her own. There is *no way* she'd ever let me ignore my eighteenth birthday.

As Mrs. Fox totters away, a steady stream of other people bearing flowers appears in my dressing room, offering congratulations and requesting autographs. As usual, I'm embarrassed and act super awkward. Fortunately for me, most of the visitors are Mom's piano students and their families, so I'm able to get by with mumbling lame things about the sonatas I'd just played. For the younger kids, I let them pet BC while I draw stick figures of cats and sign my name on their programs, and they're happy.

One little girl—around seven or eight years old—shuffles into my dressing room, hiding behind a man's leg. He shakes my hand, congratulates me on my performance, and then gently pulls the girl in front of him. She's wearing a sparkly blue dress and is staring down at her matching glittery shoes. What a cutie!

The man says, "Rebecca, I'd like you to meet my daughter, Alexandra. She's been taking piano lessons for a few years now and is about to participate in her first local competition in January. I wanted her to meet you, a talented *woman* pianist."

The girl reminds me of myself at that age—afraid of the world. I slip off my chair and kneel in front of her, still cuddling BC. "Alexandra, would you like to pet my cat?"

She nods and gently strokes BC's head with her little hand.

"His name is Beethoven the Cat," I say. "BC, for short. I named him after the composer, Ludwig van Beethoven. Do you know who that is?"

Her eyes light up and she nods rapidly. "I'm playing his *Minuet in G* for the competition."

I smile. "That's the first piece I ever played for a competition, too." I lean forward and whisper loudly, "I won—and I beat *all* the boys."

She giggles.

I nab a black-and-white stuffed-animal cat off of my dressing room table—a gift from one of Mom's piano students—and give it to Alexandra. "I want you to take this and put it on your piano at home. And whenever you see it, remember that if you work hard, you can do anything you want."

She looks up at her dad, who nods his permission, and then she tentatively reaches out and takes the toy cat from me. "Thank you."

"You're very welcome. Come see me again and let me know how you do in the competition. Okay?"

She nods and then follows her father out the door.

As I watch them leave, I hope to read an internet post soon about a girl named Alexandra from Rhode Island becoming a nationally-ranked pianist.

The last person in line is a tall, dark-haired guy my age, who smiles at me with a cute grin full of very white teeth. He looks kind of familiar. But what's up with his sneakers, khakis, and polo shirt with a grocery store logo on it? Way too casual for a classical piano concert. One more reason not to hang around with kids my age: no respect for traditions.

Pointing toward the pile of flowers behind me, he says, "I'm sorry I didn't think to get you any of those, but from the looks of it, you don't need any more."

Is that supposed to be a cut? I raise my chin and say, "My mom and I drop them off at the hospital on our way home, for patients who don't get many visitors."

"Wow. That's cool."

"It makes me feel less guilty about the death of all these flowers," I say, hugging BC to my sweat-salty chest, appreciating his warmth and heaviness.

"Let me guess... You're a vegetarian?"

I nod, aggravated that he figured that out in just a few seconds.

He points to my lap. "Who's this?"

"Beethoven the Cat—BC for short. He comes with me to all my shows and, well, everywhere." Why do I feel so awkward around this guy?

He gently scratches BC behind the ears, waking him up just enough to purr. "I'm Dak Ronen, by the way. I don't think we've met. I just signed up for piano lessons with your mom."

"Nice to meet you. Have you played before?"

"Not piano. I plan to study guitar at URI next fall, but for admission they're making me play piano, too, so your mom's going to help me get ready for an audition this spring."

"How long have you been playing guitar?"

"Long time. I'm in a band with a couple of buddies. Maybe you've heard of us: the Hep Cats?"

I shake my head. "Are you any good?"

"We have fun."

"Yes, but are you good musicians?"

He shrugs.

"What type of music does your band play?" I ask.

"Rockabilly, mostly. Actually, we have a gig tonight down at the Pump House in Wakefield. If you're not doing anything later, you should stop by." Dak flashes me another one of his crooked smiles, and I notice that he has the darkest brown eyes I've ever seen—practically black.

"Sorry," I say. "I have to go out to dinner at the Coast Guard House Restaurant with Krystian Zelinski, his wife, and my mom."

His grin broadens. "You *have* to?"

Is he mocking me? "Mr. Zelinski has all sorts of international connections. Mom says knowing him could help my career."

"You know, there are more important things than fame and fortune."

Why is this bozo trying to give me life lessons? I didn't ask for his opinion. "It takes a lot to make it in the world of professional classical music. Opportunities like meeting Mr. Zelinski are rare. I really have to make the most of them."

"Or you could have fun going to our gig."

"Like I said, I already have plans." I hate it when people try to tell me how to have fun. As if I can't figure it out for myself. My idea of what's fun might be different than theirs, but that doesn't mean they're right and I'm wrong. "What sort of name is *Dak* anyway?" I ask out of spite.

"My full name is Dakota, which means *friend*, by the way. And I'm sorry if I got you mad. I wasn't trying to."

"What exactly *are* you trying to do? Do you want an autograph or something?"

He raises his palms. "Hey, I just wanted to tell you that I liked your performance. You looked so into it, and that makes me psyched to learn to play the piano."

"Thanks." I deliberately look at the doorway.

He chuckles. "Okay. See you around." He strides into the corridor, and a few seconds later I hear him say, "Hey, Ms. O'Sullivan. See you at my lesson next week."

"Hello, Dakota. Wednesday at four-thirty, right?" Mom says. "See you then."

A moment later, she swishes into the dressing room, her black satin gown rustling as she walks. She stops with her hands clasped over her stomach and a pinched look on her face. "Aren't you changed yet?"

I jump to my feet. "It'll only take me a second." I plop BC into his pet carrier, Mom unzips me, and I slide out of my black gown and into a blue dress she picked out especially for this dinner. As I slip on a pair of black heels, I see Mom wince as she gingerly sits in one of the swivel chairs. "Is your stomach still bothering you?" I ask. She's been complaining of indigestion all day, which is strange because she is *never* sick.

"It's nothing. Maybe a touch of the flu."

"Do you want to skip going out to eat?" I ask hopefully. To be honest, I'm not really looking forward to dining with someone as famous as Mr. Zelinski.

"I told you, it's nothing." She peers into the dressing room mirror and savagely rips a brush through her curly hair. Red, just like mine. She dumps out her black beaded purse next to the mound of flowers and paws through its contents. Using some bobby pins she finds, she stabs them into her hair, fixing it into a fancy twist, only to pull them out immediately and style her hair into a bun, muttering to herself all the time—very unusual behavior for my typically Zen mother.

"Mom, what's with all the different hairdos?"

She pivots away from the mirror, her brown eyes wide. "Why? Don't you like the bun? Does it make me look too old?"

"No. It looks great. But so did the twist."

"Oh, you're no help," she huffs. She yanks out the bobby pins and fashions a reverse twist.

She seems angry or worried...or disappointed. "Hey, Mom, do you think I played the sonatas badly or something? I know this Zelinski guy's a bigwig virtuoso and all." There's nothing in this world I hate more than disappointing Mom.

Dropping her hairbrush on the countertop with a loud clack, she says, "Oh Becca, I'm sorry. You played beautifully tonight. I should have told you that before."

I slide my arms into my faux-fur jacket.

"I especially thought you did well with the Allegretto section of *No. 28.* Just the right combination of speed and lightness. Your interpretation sounded like children running through the woods, exactly the way we planned it." She waves a pad of paper from her purse pile. "I have notes for you on the entire concert, but we can go over them tomorrow. You did well, though. Very well. I'm sorry I didn't say that first."

Relieved, I ask, "So, what's wrong? Why are you so nervous?"

Mom laughs and slumps in a chair, hooking the heels of her shoes on the chrome footrest. "I am acting ridiculously, right? I'm sorry. It's just that I used to know Krystian Zelinski a long time ago, back when I went on that tour with the college orchestra. And I want us both to make a good impression on him tonight...and his wife." She takes up the brush and works on her hair again.

I can tell there's something special about this Zelinski guy as far as Mom is concerned, but I don't know what it is. She and I never keep secrets from each other, which makes this whole thing even more confusing. I check my hair and makeup in the mirror and brush on some lip gloss. "Was that tour the last time you saw him?" I ask.

She nods. "It's been almost nineteen years."

"Before I was born, then?"

"Yes." She looks like she's about to say more, but then presses her lips together instead.

Maybe if I keep asking her questions..."How'd you meet him, again?"

"He created the Polish Festival Orchestra to celebrate the one hundred and fiftieth anniversary of Chopin's death, and I performed with them when I was in Warsaw."

"And was he already married to his wife?"

"Why do you ask?" Her voice is sharp.

So much for asking her questions. "I thought maybe he was your boyfriend or something."

"He was much older than I was—and he was married." She pops a couple of antacid tablets into her mouth and chomps down hard on them. "Are you ready?" She stuffs her things back into her little black purse, ending the conversation. Typical control-freak Mom.

"Yes, ma'am." I pick up BC in his carrier and stand, waiting.

"Don't you dare *ma'am* me, young lady!" she says with a smile as she scoops up the bouquets and ushers me out the door.

The heels of our shoes click in unison as we walk down the hallway. We hand off the flowers and BC to Dave—on his way home, he's going to drop off the bouquets at the hospital and the cat at our farmhouse—and then Mom and I step out into the frigid November night.

Dinner with the Zelinskis

When we arrive at the Coast Guard House in Narragansett, Mom insists on having the restaurant's valet service park our car. "That way I won't have to worry about the Goat getting dinged up." The Goat is her royal blue 1967 Pontiac GTO convertible she and Grandpa painstakingly restored when she was in high school. "And besides," she adds, "we're already twenty minutes late for dinner."

I can't remember the last time my frugal mom paid for valet parking, just like I can't remember the last time she was late for *anything*. Mom's usually ten minutes early for everything, even church. But she spent so much time fussing with her hair and obsessing about this dinner with the Zelinskis that she made us late. I consider chancing another question about Mr. Zelinski but then recognize the valet driver as a kid from my eleventh-grade economics class who once teased me about being in love with Mozart. I tuck my chin into the fuzzy collar of my jacket, duck behind Mom, and follow her inside the restaurant.

Krystian Zelinski rises as we approach the corner table that over-looks Narragansett Bay, glittering in the moonlight. He looks just the way a world-famous male concert pianist should: stately and slender, with snow-white hair, beard, and mustache, and long, graceful hands. He kisses Mom on both cheeks and then does the same with me. Pulling out a chair for Mom, he says, "Thank you for inviting us to join you for dinner this evening, Margaret. You remember my wife, Maja?" He places his hand on the shoulder of the attractive blonde woman seated next to him, who smiles broadly and nods to both Mom and me.

"Yes, of course," Mom says with a tight smile. "And this is my daughter, Rebecca. But of course, you know that, because you just came from the concert, and..." Her voice trails off into the din of the restaurant and she sits down abruptly. *Not* typical Mom behavior.

"Very nice to meet you in person finally," Mr. Zelinski says, shaking my hand. "And please allow me to say I was impressed with your performance this evening. You exhibited a level of sophistication well beyond your years."

His wife says, "I'm not sure Krystian ever played those sonatas with as much emotion as you did tonight."

"Very well done indeed," Mr. Zelinski adds.

I swallow hard, overwhelmed. "Thank you—both."

Mr. Zelinski turns to Mom. "Margaret, am I correct in assuming that you are the one to be congratulated for training Rebecca so well?"

Mom's cheeks turn almost as red as our hair. Wrapping her arms tighter around her waist, she says, "Thank you. You are very kind."

We sit in silence for several moments. I keep expecting Mom to say something—she's usually an expert at small talk—but she's suddenly mesmerized by the cloth napkin in her lap.

Our waiter arrives and we place our orders. Mom gets the fancy macaroni and cheese for herself and orders a mushroom risotto and a green salad for me.

"Mushroom risotto and a salad?" Mr. Zelinski says, closing his menu. "Please bring me the same."

Mrs. Zelinski selects the salmon, the waiter leaves, and we settle back into an awkward silence. After our drinks are delivered, Mr. Zelinski finally says, "Rebecca, I assume you're aware that by the time Beethoven composed the last of his sonatas, he was completely deaf." His voice is soft and warm and easily understandable, despite his Polish accent.

I nod. "For one of my homeschooling classes this year, Mom had me write a research paper on Beethoven."

Mr. Zelinski smiles and I see he has bright blue eyes. Just like mine.

He asks me, "Have you ever wondered how Beethoven heard the music—how he knew what he was composing?"

"Yes, I have actually."

"Me, too, so I did some research at Beethoven-Haus, a museum in Bonn, Germany, and found out the maestro composed while holding a wooden rod between his teeth, which he pushed against the piano's soundboard. As he composed, the vibrations traveled from the piano, up the rod, through his teeth, and vibrated his skull. Thus, he was able to hear—or feel—the notes he played." He chuckles. "Before I played my season of Beethoven sonatas last year, I wanted to re-create the composer's experience, so I bought a rod to hold in my teeth and covered my ears."

Mrs. Zelinski laughs. "I went into Krystian's studio one day and there he was, wearing earplugs and a motorcycle helmet, clenching a stick in his mouth, and playing all hunched over the keys, like this." She mimes the scene. "I thought my husband had gone crazy." We all laugh, but none louder than Mr. Zelinski.

"And did you know historians have recently discovered two more sonatas supposedly composed by Beethoven?" he asks me.

"Oh, no!" I say. What would that do to my world record? I'm supposed to play *all* of his sonatas in one season.

Mr. Zelinski holds up a hand. "Don't worry. Their authenticity has not been completely verified yet, so for now, we only need to contend with his original thirty-two."

I puff a sigh of relief. I like playing Beethoven, but this past year has been *brutal*, trying to bring original interpretations to so many of his pieces. And all without Grandpa to provide his regular doses of encouragement. I'll be very happy to finish the last of my sonata concerts next month.

The food arrives and I do my best to use the correct fork and not spill my water. I notice Mom just picks at her mac and cheese, breaking off bits and then pushing them around her plate. Is she feeling sicker, or is she too freaked out about the Zelinskis to eat? I can't catch her eye to ask her.

During coffee and dessert, Mom finally speaks. "Krystian, I understand that you will soon be working for the University of Rhode Island?"

"Yes. I will be the music department chair there for three years, starting in January. Maja and I are in town this week, looking for a house to live in. But we just found out that one of the university professors has accepted a long-term position in Poland, so we'll be able to simply trade homes. Isn't that a stroke of good luck?"

Mrs. Zelinski adds, "And the house here has a beautiful sunroom on its south side, overlooking a tree-filled backyard. It will make a perfect painting studio for me."

Mom asks, "What type of painting do you do?"

"I work in oils and paint still lifes—flowers, mostly. I've painted all my life, with more or less success."

"She's being modest," Mr. Zelinski says. "Her one-woman show in Kraków last month was widely praised by several major art critics. She sold over a dozen pieces and received commissions for a dozen more." His eyes sparkle with pride.

Mrs. Zelinski laughs. "Well, it gives me something to do while Krystian works his magic overhauling outdated curricula at universities all over Europe, bringing them into the twenty-first century."

The two of them certainly sound like a happily married couple.

Mom asks Mr. Zelinski, "Why have you decided to come here to the States now, and to such a relatively unknown school as URI?"

He smiles. "After working with European schools for so long, I wanted to try my hand at transforming the way an American university trains its classical musicians. And I enjoy taking a relatively unknown program like URI's and molding it into a cutting-edge music curriculum. I find it to be a welcome challenge."

"URI is lucky to have you," Mom says, blushing. I've never seen her behave like this before.

He nods his thanks for the compliment and then looks at me. "What about you, young lady? You must be finishing high school this spring. What are your plans after that?"

I glance at Mom, but she's back to staring at her napkin. "Umm... well, actually, with Mom's help, I already graduated high school this winter, six months early."

"Smart girl," he says.

"Thank you. So, after my concert next month, when I become the youngest B32 performer, Guinness World Records has agreed to sponsor me in a twelve-city national concert tour. We're hoping that will lead to an international tour with a major orchestra or symphony."

He says, "That sounds wonderfully exciting. But what about studying at university?"

"To tell you the truth, Mr. Zelinski, I didn't enjoy high school very much, which is why Mom ended up homeschooling me this past year. Other kids don't understand my passion for playing music, and that makes me...uncomfortable."

"But don't you think college would be quite different? You'd be with other like-minded students, all working toward careers in music."

I look over at Mom, who's now staring at me, eyebrows raised. "That's exactly what Mom says," I admit.

"Several of the best music schools—such as the Curtis Institute, Juilliard, and the Peabody Institute—have contacted Rebecca with scholarship offers," Mom says. "A few of them are sending recruiters to her final Beethoven concert next month to entice her to join their programs."

"I'm not surprised," he says. "As the chair of URI's classical music department, I would love to recommend you for admission there. Having a musician of your caliber would be a major boon to the program. I'll be mentoring a few pianists, too, so perhaps I could provide you with some personal instruction, to augment the excellent education you've already received from your mother."

"Thank you, Mr. Zelinski. That's an amazing offer," I say, but I'm still full of doubts. I felt like such a freak in high school. Would it be that much different in college? And what about the party-hardy crowd, people like Aunt Cassie? I've never had a drink in my life. How would I fit in with them? But studying piano with Mr. Zelinski would be *amazing*. "I'll certainly think about it."

"You do that," he says. Looking at Mom, he asks, "Speaking of schools, Margaret, what did you do professionally after you left Warsaw that year we met? We spoke briefly by phone that one time..."

His comment is followed by a strained silence, with him, Mom, and Mrs. Zelinski all looking awkward. What's that about?

"I made inquiries," he continues, "but couldn't find any information about your career after that."

Mom pats her mouth with her napkin, which is completely unnecessary since she hasn't eaten a single bite of her dinner. Is her stomach still bothering her? Didn't those antacid tablets help at all? How sick is she?

She says, "Well, I finished that tour with the Juilliard Orchestra—we were nearly done when we performed with you in Warsaw—and then I came home to Rhode Island. When Rebecca arrived, I left school and the two of us moved back into the family farmhouse with my dad."

Mom had returned from the tour pregnant with me, offering no explanation to anyone. Hearing her talk about it now makes me wonder if Mr. Zelinski might know something about Dear Old Dad. Or maybe... I shake my head. No way. Mom would have told me.

"Ah, yes," Mr. Zelinski says. "I remember you speaking fondly about your dad. He's a corn farmer like my father, I believe?"

"He *was*. Unfortunately, he passed away last winter. Cancer."

"Oh, I'm sorry to hear that. And your mother?"

"She died when I was in high school."

"Yes, now I remember you mentioning that in Warsaw. Tragic for a girl to lose her mother so early."

Mom nods. "When Rebecca was three, Mrs. Fox, my former piano teacher, retired and turned over her business to me. Since then, I've been concentrating on being a mother, helping to run the farm, and teaching piano lessons—especially to this young lady here." She looks over at me and winks. "It's been wonderful."

"Well, if Rebecca's any indication of your talents as a teacher, you have certainly chosen the perfect profession for yourself," Mr. Zelinski says.

Mom beams with her first genuine smile since arriving at the restaurant.

⁓

A half-hour later, we say goodbye to the Zelinskis. They're returning home to Poland in the morning; he has to finish a concert tour there before they move to Rhode Island in mid-December. Mom and I trudge through the snow and ransom the car from the restaurant's valet service—*twenty bucks!*—and head home to the farmhouse through lightly falling snow.

Halfway there, I glance over at Mom and see that she looks even paler than she had at the restaurant. "You okay?"

She nods and pats her belly. "My stomach is still bothering me. I guess I might have the flu, after all. No big deal." She smiles. "It sure has been a good day, though. Hasn't it?"

The Goat's massive wiper blades scrape the snow into arcs at the edges of the windshield.

"Mr. Zelinski seems like a nice guy for a virtuoso pianist," I say. "He isn't stuck-up or anything."

Mom nods. "And his wife is nice, too. And pretty. They seem very happy together. And they both said some very nice things about your performance."

"And your teaching."

She holds up her palm. "Put it there, girl."

We high-five.

Since she's in a good mood, I say, "I was wondering—what was the deal with you and Mr. Zelinski back when you were in college?"

"What do you mean?" We pass our unlit farmstand and she turns into the long, gravel driveway that leads to our house.

"When you met him, he was already a bigwig pianist. You were just a kid, like my age, but you played as a soloist with his orchestra in Warsaw. And he clearly remembers you, too. Did the two of you connect somehow?"

She wipes a hand across her forehead. "I don't want to go into that with you right now. Maybe later, when you're older."

"I'll be eighteen years old in a few minutes."

"Later."

"Fine." Shut down by Mom, *again*. I wish she wouldn't treat me like a little kid. I know she does a lot of stuff for me—teaching, managing, cooking, cleaning—stuff that I'm not sure I could handle on my own. So, I guess I have to take the good with the bad, but it's frustrating.

It's close to midnight as we drive up to our white farmhouse. Covered with snow, it looks positively haunted in the car's headlights. Dave Morales appears in front of the Goat like a ghost, wearing a headlamp and carrying a shovel. He waves.

"Dave sure is a nice guy," I say. "And he seems to like you."

Mom smiles tiredly and waves back at Dave through the windshield. "Maybe I should go out with him sometime."

"Really? That would be great. What made you change your mind about him all of a sudden?"

She shrugs. "I have a feeling that things are going to be different now."

"Different? How? Why?"

Of course, Mom shakes her head and doesn't answer me.

I climb out of the car and call out, "Hi, Dave."

"Hey, Becca. How was dinner with the Zelinskis?"

"Great."

"Did you bring me any leftovers?"

"No. Sorry."

"Next time."

"Okay." In my high heels, I carefully pick my way across the driveway and up the still-snowy porch stairs. When I turn to hold the door open for Mom, I see her kiss Dave on the cheek, presumably as a thank-you for shoveling our driveway. Seems like some things *are* going to be different around here. *Good* different, I hope.

Inside the house, I jog up the stairs and immediately snuggle BC, who is waiting for me in his usual spot on my bed. His deep purr makes me feel all warm and happy. My furry friend for almost thirteen years, now. Back downstairs in my comfy flannel pajamas, I grab the bowl of popcorn Mom makes for us and curl up with BC on the parlor couch to watch the last few minutes of *GWTW* as Scarlett O'Hara makes a fool of herself over Ashley Wilkes once again. I'm glad that some things are *always* going to remain the same.

My Birthday and the Worst Day Ever

The next morning, I get up at my usual six a.m., stuff myself into my farm clothes, winter coat, muck boots, and heavy work gloves, and shuffle through the snow to the barn to do my morning chores, missing Grandpa more than ever.

Mornings used to be our special time together. From the time I was four years old right up until a few weeks before he died, Grandpa and I would get up early every day and head out to the barn together while pulling on thick work gloves—to "protect our valuable piggies," he'd say, twinkling his fingers. In the barn, I'd muck out the stalls, milk Bessie (the cow), feed Snowy (our horse), and collect the chickens' eggs while he'd putter around with the farm equipment, getting ready for whatever field work he planned to do that day.

Afterward, we'd head back to the farmhouse kitchen for our special breakfast together: big bowls of oatmeal, toasted slabs of homemade bread slathered with peanut butter and raisins, and tall mugs of steaming coffee with lots of milk and sugar. When I was young—like four or five—my coffee was mostly milk and sugar, but as I got older, it grew darker brown and significantly less sweet. BC would join us for breakfast, too, lapping up the bowl of fresh cream Grandpa set on the floor for him.

Then, every morning as BC snoozed in a patch of sunshine, Grandpa and I would sit together at the kitchen table for a half-hour or more, discussing things. Important things. He was the only father-type I ever had, and my go-to advisor whenever I couldn't talk to Mom about something. When I was really little, Grandpa and I would discuss silly stuff, like our favorite flavor of ice cream (Rocky Road, *of course*), or the best pro football team (*obviously* the New England Patriots). But as I got older, our talks grew more serious, and he helped me figure out some major things. Like, he was the one who got me to recognize real friends as being the ones who thought my playing piano was cool. And he did that in just a single morning breakfast talk.

In fifth grade, Olivia, Hayley, Shayla, and I decided to do a ballet number in the end-of-the-year talent show at school. We'd all been taking classes for a while at Rhode Island Ballet Arts in town and owned matching recital costumes, so Shayla figured this would be the perfect chance for us to show off our moves. At eleven years old, she was tall, graceful, and a very good dancer, so she picked herself to be the star of the number. Being the klutz I've always been, I *hated* dancing in front of other people but agreed to back her up with the other girls because Olivia said that's what friends do. We practiced for weeks in Shayla's family room and managed to come up with a routine that looked pretty good, I thought.

By fifth grade, I'd already been playing piano for six years, so Mom convinced me to sign up to play a short piece in the talent show, too. "It'll be an ideal opportunity for you to perform in front of a friendly crowd," she said. Then, the week before the show, I won the National Orchestra Student Competition, and my life changed drastically overnight. Newspaper and magazine reporters called me for interviews; I was on two nationally televised morning shows; and I was scheduled to go on a concert tour as soon as school let out for the summer. By the evening of the talent show, I was a bona fide local celebrity. Several local television stations sent crews to film me playing my Bach piece—an excerpt from the one I'd played for the competition—and reporters followed me around the auditorium, asking me questions and snapping my picture. Our school principal moved my piano performance to the last spot on the program, "So we can end with a bang!" I was a little dazed by all the attention but had to admit it made me feel pretty special.

Shayla *hated* that I was in the spotlight at the talent show. "Why is everyone taking your picture?" she asked. "All you do is play the stupid piano. Anyone can do that. I know how to stand on my toes, and that is *way* cooler." Just before we were scheduled to go onstage together, she shoved me out of line. "I've decided you're not doing the number with us."

"What? Why not?"

"Because...you're a bad dancer."

I rubbed my shoulder. "I practiced hard and I know the steps."

"Yeah, well, we don't need you." She went back to the front of the line.

"Oh, come on, Shayla," Olivia said. "You're just mad because everyone's paying attention to Becca and not you."

"Whatever," Shayla said. "I'm the star, and I say she's out."

"Fine," Olivia said. "Then I'm out, too."

Shayla shrugged. "If that's the way you want it. Hayley and I can do it just fine without you. Probably better."

Olivia took my hand and led me toward the dressing room.

"You don't have to quit the show just because of me," I said.

"I didn't want to dance with Shayla anyhow. She shows off too much." She helped me change into my black dress for my piano piece.

After the talent show, and after I'd finished the last newspaper interview of the evening, Mom, Grandpa, Aunt Cassie, and I went out for ice cream—Rocky Road, *of course*—with Olivia and her mom. I had fun, especially when Olivia imitated the way Shayla had tripped over Hayley during their number in the show, with both of them crashing to the stage, embarrassed but not hurt.

The next morning at our breakfast table, I cuddled a sleepy BC and asked Grandpa, "Why was Shayla so mean to me? Why did she cut me out of our ballet number?"

"I suspect it was jealousy, pure and simple, just like Olivia said."

I sipped my light tan coffee and thought about this. "Do you think I should stop playing the piano? Or at least stop telling the other kids about it?"

"Why would you do that?"

"So they don't get mad at me like Shayla did. And so they don't think I'm a weirdo. I mean, I don't want to lose all my friends."

Grandpa nodded several times while stirring his oatmeal. "What does Olivia think about you playing the piano?"

"She thinks it's pretty cool. She was all excited when I won the competition. She even got me a congratulations bear...and a mini one for BC."

He nodded a few more times. "Seems like the kind of reaction you'd get from a true friend."

As I ate my peanut butter toast, I mentally compared my friendships with Olivia and Shayla. Brushing my crumbs into BC's empty milk bowl, I decided, "I'll be friends with nice kids, like Olivia, who think my piano playing is neat, and I'll talk to them about it. But I'll ignore grumpy people, like Shayla."

Grandpa slapped his knees and beamed a smile at me. "Sounds like a good plan."

And that's the way he worked. He'd give me good advice, but make me think I'd come up with it myself. I finally caught on to his wonderfully devious ways a few years ago, but never called him out on it. He was an *awesome* grandpa.

The morning after my Courthouse concert, I finish up my chores and then eat my usual breakfast of oatmeal, toast, and coffee, now made by—and shared with—Mom. I love being with Mom, of course, but most days we eat breakfast in silence or spend the time reviewing my schedule for the day. It's not the same as my special mornings with Grandpa. On the floor, BC slowly laps up his cream. I think he misses Grandpa, too.

Even though it's my birthday, as soon as I finish eating, BC and I head to the Yamaha baby grand in our piano parlor to get in a few hours of practicing before my lame party, scheduled for noon. Because ever since I won that first major piano competition at the age of eleven, I've been determined to become a world-famous concert artist. I know part of my obsession is due to the feeling that I need to pay Mom back for giving up her performing career to become my mother. But most of it is because I love playing classical piano music. I'm not very good with most people, I stink at sports and dancing, and I completely froze the only time I tried acting in a play, but I am a *great* concert pianist. When I get up on that stage and my *little piggies*—as Grandpa called them—hit those keys, I forget all about everything else and soar with the melodies. I am never so alive as when I'm performing.

Today, BC and I are preparing for my next concert, which is at Mohegan Sun Casino in Connecticut in two weeks. It's a practice performance for my final Beethoven sonata show, scheduled for one week after that. BC is a big part of my concert preparations...and my life. Always has been, ever since I was five.

⌒

When Mom saw me spending hours playing the piano every day—even at that young age—she said I needed someone soft and fuzzy to keep me company. So I was excited when we were out doing errands in Grandpa's beat-up pickup truck one warm Saturday and we turned into the driveway of the town's animal shelter. I trotted behind Mom as we entered the reception area, full of wonderful animal sounds and smells.

A *very* old woman smiled up at us from the dented desk. Every square inch of her face contained a wrinkle or spot of some kind. At first, she kind of scared me, reminding me of the witch in one of my favorite picture books. But then I started mentally connecting the dots and lines of her face to form astronomical constellations: Orion, Ursa Major, Taurus the Bull—many of the same formations Grandpa and I had seen through my telescope the night before. Recognizing the Big Dipper on her forehead made her seem much less scary.

"May I help you?" she croaked.

Mom rubbed her hands together. "Yes. We'd like to see your kittens."

"We are going to get a kitten?" I gasped. "It's not even Christmas!"

Mom nodded.

"What are your names?" the woman asked, jiggling her computer's mouse.

Mom tucked her long, red hair behind her ears—she looked so pretty—and said, "I'm Maggie."

"And I am Rebecca Elizabeth O'Sullivan, but you can call me Becca," I informed her. "What's your name?"

"Dorthea Rosetta Jones, but you can call me Dot." We shook hands. "Well, Maggie and Becca, let's go see the kittens."

Moving very quickly for such an old lady, she led us through two rooms full of barking dogs to a large room in the back that was lined floor to ceiling with cages of cats. Big ones, small ones, white ones, gray ones. Ones with short hair and long hair, and some with almost no hair at all. I'd never seen so many cats in one place before. And so many of them were meowing, each with a different tone and voice. "It's like a cat *orchestra*," I whispered.

Mom smiled and squeezed my shoulders.

Dot pinched the latch of one wire cage door and swung it open to reveal a pile of fuzzy kittens tumbling over each other. "This is our latest litter," she said. "Just got them in the day before yesterday. But the vet already checked them out and gave them their first shots, so they're ready for adoption." She reached in and scooped up a tiny black-and-white kitten with golden eyes. Turning to me, she asked, "Would you like to hold him?"

I looked at Mom, got a go-ahead nod, and so cupped my hands in front of me, nervous but excited. I'd never held a baby cat before.

Dot gently slipped me the kitten and encouraged me to cuddle him underneath my chin where he immediately began to purr. "That one's very friendly, she said. "We call him *Tux* because of his markings. Kind of looks like he's wearing a tuxedo, don't you think?"

I nodded and closed my eyes, inhaling the kitten's scent.

After a minute, Dot asked, "Would you like to see a different one?"

I shook my head.

"How about that orange-and-white tiger? She's a girl."

"I want this one."

Mom laughed. "Becca generally knows what she wants."

"I can see that." Dot scratched the kitten under his tiny chin. "Well, Tux, it looks like you've just gotten yourself a new home with a girl who already loves you."

"His name's not Tux," I said.

"It's not?"

I shook my head. "It's Beethoven," I said. "Beethoven the Cat."

"That's quite a mouthful, but I guess you can call him *BC* for short." She smiled and shut the cage door. "If you're sure...?"

I nodded and Mom nodded, too.

"Then let's bring BC to the office and fill out his adoption paperwork."

And just like that, I gained a best furry friend who has done everything with me for the past thirteen years. He sits on the piano whenever I'm practicing, listens to Mom when she teaches me lessons, and goes with me to every one of my competitions and performances, wearing a black silk bow tie Mom bought him, just for such special occasions. He cuddles me when I'm sad, plays with me when I'm happy, and even finds middle-C for me on the piano, a trick I started teaching him the day we brought him home from the shelter. I love BC with all my heart. Sometimes, I wish he could talk, because I'd *love* to hear what he'd have to say.

⌒

The morning after my seventh Beethoven concert, with BC in his usual spot, snoozing away atop the piano, I do my warm-up exercises and then launch into the first sonata for the next concert, *No. 29*. But just a few minutes after I start practicing, Mom comes into the piano parlor, sits down, and pats the sofa cushion next to her. "Becca, come here, please. I need to talk to my favorite daughter slash birthday girl."

Did I do something wrong? I scoop BC out of his bed and join Mom on the sofa. She's very pale and her eyes are pinched with pain. Did she look this bad at breakfast? I hadn't noticed. "Are you still feeling sick?" I ask. "Should you go see Dr. Miller?"

She wraps her favorite quilt tighter around her shoulders and shakes her head.

"I'm sure I've just got the flu. Probably from one of my germy students. Good thing you've had your flu shot."

"Didn't you get one, too?"

She shakes her head again. "You know how I feel about shots." Mom's always been one of those earthy-crunchy, no-medicine-please kind of people for herself, even though she's always made sure that I'm up-to-date on all my shots. Beads of sweat decorate her hairline like a crown.

"Are you running a fever, too?" I ask, reaching for her forehead. It's warm and damp.

"Maybe a teensy one. If I take it easy this weekend, I'm sure I'll be fine by Monday. Now stop asking me pesky questions and listen up, because I want to talk to you about a few things."

I tuck BC, who's purring softly, under my chin and snuggle up to Mom. She feels *a lot* warmer than usual.

"For a while now," she says, "I've been thinking about you growing up, and what we should do about it."

I laugh. "As far as I know, it just kind of happens, Mom. There's not much you can do to stop it."

"I know that, Miss Smarty Pants. What I mean is, I feel like I should do more to encourage you to be more independent...of me." She smiles. "I'm afraid I've been guilty of being one of those helicopter moms, hovering around you and doing way more than I should."

"I wouldn't say that." She does do a lot for me—probably more than some other moms would—but I don't mind it. *Most* of the time.

"Well, I think we should switch things up a bit, especially with this being your eighteenth birthday and all." She coughs and then winces. "I keep taking Tums and Tylenol, but this gas pain just won't go away. Must be a real nasty strain of the flu." She presses a pillow to her stomach and sighs. "Anyhow, ever since you were five and decided you wanted to be a concert pianist, I've tried to help you with your practicing and performing—"

"And I really appreciate all you've done."

She holds up a hand. "I know you do, hon. I'm not complaining. Honest. I'm just afraid I might have gone a bit overboard. You haven't learned some of the basic stuff a young woman your age should know. Like how to cook a meal, or how to do laundry, or even how to deal with friends sometimes." Mom wraps her arms around my shoulders and pulls me even closer to her. "I'm not criticizing you, Bec. I'm just saying I plan to stop doing some of these things, to let you be your own person more."

I frown. "But I like things just the way they are. I don't see why we need to change anything."

"And for the most part—for the stuff that matters—things won't change. I'll still be your teacher and your manager and your mom." She squeezes me hard and I squeeze back. "It's just some of the other stuff, like..." She digs her hand into her jeans pocket and pulls out a keychain decorated with a shiny black musical eighth note. "These are for you."

"I already have house keys, and I certainly don't need a second set, since we never lock the doors anyhow."

She puts the keys in my hand. "Look at them."

Now that I'm holding them, I can see the two worn silver keys on the ring are bigger than our house key. They're more the size of... "*Car keys?*"

Mom nods. "As of now, the GTO belongs to you. Happy birthday."

"What? No way! You can't give me the Goat! You and Grandpa worked on that car for two years!" I thrust the keys back toward her.

She holds up a palm, refusing to take them. "I'm way too old to be driving around in a big muscle car like that."

"I don't even know how to drive!"

"You'll learn. We'll sign you up for driver's training on Monday."

"But you can't give me your car! How are you going to get around?"

"I'll use Grandpa's pickup truck until I buy myself another car, something more suitable for a woman my age."

I giggle. "I can just imagine you driving around in a minivan or an SUV."

She smiles devilishly. "Hey, you never know. Maybe I'll buy myself a Porsche or a Beemer."

"Yeah. Like we could afford one of them."

"Don't you worry about what we can afford. You just concentrate on learning to be the best driver you can be because I don't want to see any scratches or dents on the Goat. And you need to take good care of her, too. She requires extra maintenance—like buying high-octane gas and adding the marine additive and lead substitute, as you've seen me do. They don't make engines like that one anymore, so you're going to have to treat her right."

I shake my head. "I don't know, Mom."

"Well, I do, and that's *final*. The Goat is yours. Now, let's talk about some other things that are going to change around here, like—"

"Hello! Anyone home?" Aunt Cassie's voice calls from the kitchen.

"Good morning, sis," Mom says loudly. Turning to me, she says, "We'll continue this conversation later, after the party, while we decorate the house." Mom's favorite season is Christmas, and she always insists we go all out trimming the house, starting the weekend after Thanksgiving. By the time the actual holiday rolls around, the place will be twinkling with *thousands* of miniature lights and entirely covered in red, green, white, and silver decorations.

39

I follow Mom down the hall, carrying a snoring BC. In the kitchen, we find Aunt Cassie flopped into one of the wooden chairs with her head resting on her forearms. Her clothes are wrinkled and her bleached hair is pulled into a messy bun on the top of her head.

"How're you doing, Aunt Cassie?" I ask, knowing from experience to whisper.

She groans as Mom loudly smacks a mug on the table next to her head, splashing coffee on her sister's arm. "You really should lay off the booze," Mom says.

Aunt Cassie raises her chin just enough to take a sip. Squinting her bloodshot eyes at Mom, she says, "Yeah, well you don't look so hot, either. You tie one on with the Zelinskis last night?"

Mom folds her arms across her swollen stomach. "I only had one glass of wine, but apparently, I've managed to catch the flu. Which reminds me—did you get a flu shot this year?"

Aunt Cassie nods. "Ed, our manager, makes everyone at the pub get them. He doesn't want any of us to miss work and mess up his schedule."

"That's a good thing," Mom says. "I'd hate for either of you to catch this from me." She arranges flour, sugar, eggs, and other baking ingredients on the kitchen countertop. BC rubs up against her leg and she bends to scratch him under his chin. "Come on, girl," she says to her sister. "This cake isn't going to bake itself."

Aunt Cassie groans again. "I don't know why you need me to do it. You know perfectly well how to bake a cake."

"I know how to bake a *regular* cake, but you know how to create a *masterpiece*. And we have to have a masterpiece for my girl's eighteenth birthday." Mom hugs me tightly, and even in the cold kitchen, I can feel waves of heat radiating from her body.

"Hey, Mom, you should go lie down," I say.

"Later."

She never lets me—or anyone else—take care of her.

Aunt Cassie pulls out our big KitchenAid mixer and expertly cracks some eggs into its stainless-steel bowl, one-handed.

Mom chuckles. "You know, even hungover, you're still fun to watch when you're baking."

"I'm glad I can provide you with some entertainment," Aunt Cassie grumbles while adding butter, sugar, and other ingredients to the bowl.

"Any progress on your application to Johnson and Wales's culinary arts program?" Mom asks her. "You know, Dad and I saved up a full four years' worth of tuition money for you. It's sitting in the bank, just waiting for you to use it. If you apply now, you could start classes in January."

I pull BC into my lap and settle in to watch them have this conversation for the *hundredth* time.

Aunt Cassie grimaces. "Why would Johnson and Wales want me?"

"Because you're a fantastic pastry chef and they'd be lucky to have you."

"Yeah, but I'm, like, twice the age of a normal student."

Mom sighs, and I notice she has bags under her eyes. *Not* typical. To her sister, she says, "As I've said before, they don't care how old you are, as long as you can cook, and you've won a dozen awards that say you can cook up a storm."

"Yeah, I've won the North Kingstown Grange Apple Pie Contest and the Washington County Fair Brownie Bake-Off and all sorts of very *prestigious* competitions like those." Aunt Cassie crosses her eyes and sticks out her tongue. "I'm sure that's going to impress the hell out of those fancy-ass instructors at Johnson and Wales."

Mom shrugs. "You'll never know until you apply."

Just like every other time I've heard them have this conversation, I can't figure out why Aunt Cassie doesn't just fill out the application. Grandpa and Mom already saved up the tuition money. And she obviously loves to bake and is *really* good at it. What does she have to lose? It's almost like she's afraid of failing before she's even tried—which makes no sense to me.

In my lap, BC lazily rolls onto his back so I can scratch his round belly.

Mom retrieves carrots and celery from the refrigerator, scrubs them, and starts chopping them into sticks, pausing to clutch her stomach.

"You okay there, sis?" Aunt Cassie asks with a frown.

"Just some gas pains," Mom says. Looking at her sister, she asks, "And what about moving back in here with us? You don't honestly want to be living with that deadbeat boyfriend of yours, do you?"

"Jimmy's not *that* bad."

"You could do better," Mom says.

I silently agree. Jimmy drinks too much, gets into too many fights, and doesn't treat Aunt Cassie very well. As smart and nice as she is, I can't understand why she doesn't get herself a nicer boyfriend. I know she drinks a lot, too, but if she found a good guy, maybe she'd be motivated to stop. Of course, I'm probably not the one to offer her dating advice, since I've never had a boyfriend. Pretty pathetic for a seventeen-...er, eighteen-year-old. I've gone on exactly one date—sort of—and it was an absolute disaster.

⁓

Carl Solly, a talented pianist from Worcester, Massachusetts, who's two years older than me, was expected to win first place in the American Pianists Awards last year. Just before we took the stage, he swaggered up to me and asked if I would like to have dinner with him in the hotel restaurant after the competition. Never having been on a date before, I shot a panicked look at Mom, who was standing behind Carl. She nodded emphatically, so I said, "Umm...er...yeah, sure," and then mentally smacked myself in the head for giving such a *lame* response.

He didn't seem to notice. He tossed his head, swishing his too-long hair away from his eyes, and said, "Great. I'll see you after the trophy ceremony." He strutted away, acting like he thought I was watching him—which I was.

Then *I* won the competition.

Afterward, in the restaurant, I saved an empty seat next to me at the table where I sat with Mom and Grandpa, receiving warm congratulations from dozens of other piano teachers and students. When Carl finally came over, I smiled at him and took my sweater off the spare chair, inviting him to join us.

Instead, he curled his lip, shook his head, and pointed to a table across the room. "I'm sitting over there with my *friends*," he said. His voice sounded sharp and mean.

"Oh," I said, "I thought we had a date."

He twisted his face into a grimace and snorted. "A *date*? Where'd you get that dumb idea?"

"You said we'd eat dinner together."

"That was before."

"Before what?" I asked.

"Before you cheated to win the competition."

"Cheated?"

He snorted again. "Wearing that slutty dress just to impress the judges. Everyone knows you're one of the few girls at this level of competition, so you deliberately show off your boobs to get their attention. Are you planning on having sex with them, too?"

I felt like everyone in the room was staring at me.

Mom jumped to her feet and pointed a shaking finger toward his table. "Carl, I think it's time for you to rejoin your friends. *Now.*"

"Gladly." He flicked his hair and strutted away.

I looked down at my simple black dress with its princess collar and below-the-knee hemline. With tears in my eyes, I asked Grandpa, "Do I look slutty?"

He handed me his handkerchief. "What do you think?"

I took a moment to breathe in Grandpa's scents from his handkerchief, wipe my eyes, and blow my nose. Taking a deep breath, I said, "He was jealous because I beat him, and he just said those things to hurt my feelings. Right?"

Both Grandpa and Mom wrapped me in a soul-warming hug that lasted forever, but not long enough. Back in her seat, Mom pointed to the menu. "I hear they've got terrific tiramisu here. How 'bout we all skip dinner and have two helpings of dessert, instead?"

Grandpa and I wholeheartedly agreed with her suggestion, thus officially ending my first and only date so far. Since then, I haven't been in a hurry to go on another one with anyone. No surprise there.

Back in the farmhouse kitchen, Aunt Cassie turns on the mixer and gradually adds flour to the bowl.

Mom squints at her. "Just remember how popular your cakes, pies, and other pastries have been at the farmstand. We sell them as fast as you make them. You are an amazing baker, which is all the more reason for you to dump Jimmy, move back in here with us, and go to school to learn to cook all kinds of other things, too."

"Mom's right," I say. "You've got a gift—just like my piano-playing. That strawberry rhubarb torte thing you make is amazing...and I don't even like rhubarb."

Aunt Cassie flashes me a smile and then looks at Mom. "But what about my job? How am I supposed to go to school and waitress six nights a week?"

Mom places a loaf of nutty-smelling homemade bread—she's a good baker, too—on a wooden board and carefully slices it evenly. "Your classes would be during the day. You could still work nights, but fewer hours, since if you were living here, you wouldn't have to make as much." Mom arranges the bread on a platter with slices of ham, cheese, tomatoes, lettuce, and other sandwich fixings. With a sigh, she drops the knife into the sink and rubs her stomach. "I'm still feeling pretty sick, so I'm going to go lie down until Mrs. Fox gets here for the party."

"If you're not feeling well, why don't we just cancel it?" I ask hopefully, stroking BC's soft fur as he continues to snore.

Mom's eyes fly open wide. "Cancel my baby's eighteenth birthday party? *No way!*" She forces a big smile. "Just let me catch a catnap and I'm sure I'll be good to go." Even sick with the flu, Mom's still in charge. Looking at her sister and gesturing around the messy kitchen, Mom asks, "You got this?"

Aunt Cassie shrugs. "Yeah, sure. Go lie down. We'll wake you up when Mrs. Fox gets here." She pours the cake batter into round pans and places them in the hot oven as Mom leaves the room.

Just before noon, I watch Mrs. Fox's tan Toyota Camry slowly crawl up the snow-dusted driveway and pull in behind Aunt Cassie's beat-up truck in front of the house. I throw on my coat and jog out into the brisk cold to offer Mrs. Fox a hand getting out of her car. I don't know exactly how old she is but my guess is somewhere between eighty-five and one-hundred-and-thirty.

"Oh, thank you, dear, and happy birthday," she says, handing me a plastic-wrapped fruit plate and an iridescent purple gift bag with pink tissue paper sprouting from its mouth. Mrs. Fox holds my elbow tightly as we inch our way across the driveway, up the porch stairs, and into our big white farmhouse.

BUT CATS DON'T TALK

I *love* our house. Everything about it, from the wide wraparound porch to the huge double-hung windows to the red front door with stained glass sidelights, says "home," welcoming me whenever I return, even if it's only from a trip to the driveway.

I help Mrs. Fox off with her heavy wool coat and she sinks into a kitchen chair.

Aunt Cassie kisses her on her cheek. "How are you doing today, Mrs. Fox?"

"Can't complain."

"And how about Mr. Fox?"

"Fair to middling. He didn't sleep very well last night—imagining an attack of killer bees—so I suspect I shouldn't stay out too long. He's apt to give Roberta, our home health aide, a run for her money today." She sighs but then immediately smiles again. "And how about you, Cassie? What have you been up to?"

"Making a cake for Becca's birthday." My aunt points to her just-completed creation in the center of the table: a smooth tower covered in chocolate frosting, decorated with delicate pink and white flowers, and wreathed with a vine of dark green leaves and stems.

"Oh my! That's *lovely!*" Mrs. Fox says.

Aunt Cassie grows an inch taller with pride.

Mrs. Fox smiles at me. "And where is your mother, dear?"

"She thought she might be coming down with the flu, so she's resting. We're supposed to wake her as soon as you arrive." I stand, but she waves me back into my chair.

"You just relax, birthday girl. I'll go get her." She resolutely hoists herself to her feet and trudges toward the stairs, her wet orthopedic shoes squeaking on the wood floor.

Aunt Cassie unties her apron and hangs it on the back of the pantry door. "Well, Becca, I've got some good news and some bad news. The good news is, your cake's done!" She strikes a Vanna White pose, gesturing toward the table.

"It's *amazing*, Aunt Cassie. Thanks so much for making it."

"You're welcome. Now for the bad news...While you were helping Mrs. Fox get out of her car, I got a call from the pub. They're short-handed for the lunch crowd and asked me if I could fill in." She shrugs. "I need the money, so I told them I'd be there."

Aunt Cassie *always* seems to need money. Beer must cost a lot.

She kisses me on the top of my head and hands me a copy of the *Rhode Island Division of Motor Vehicles' Driver's Manual*. "Happy birthday! Sorry I didn't have a chance to wrap it. I thought it was about time you learned to drive. You're eighteen years old, for Pete's sake!"

For Pete's sake. An expression Grandpa used all the time. Just hearing it now makes my heart ache and reminds me this is the first birthday of mine he's ever missed.

I hug Aunt Cassie. "Thanks. Mom was just talking to me this morning about signing me up to get a learner's permit on Monday." To be honest, I'm not sure how I feel about driving a car. On the one hand, I'm such a klutz I'm afraid I'll crash and hurt myself, or other people. On the other hand, I'd love to be able to go places without having to ask Mom for a ride. Not that I have anywhere to go...

Aunt Cassie asks, "Did she give you the Goat?"

I nod.

"Good. She said she was going to." She points to the driving manual. "Now learn how to drive it. It'll be good for you." She wraps a hand-knitted scarf around her neck several times, shoves her arms into a thick canvas work jacket, and gives me a huge bear hug. "Say bye to your mom for me when she wakes up, and tell her I'll call her later." She stomps out of the house in her black combat boots, and a few moments later I watch as her old truck rumbles down the snowy driveway.

"Rebecca," Mrs. Fox's voice calls from the top of the stairs. "Would you please come up here?"

I frown a question toward BC, who's lounging in a sun patch on the kitchen floor, and hurry up the stairs where I find Mrs. Fox standing in the doorway to Mom's room. She gently pats my shoulder. "Now, I don't want to frighten you, but, in an abundance of caution, as they say, I think we should get your mother to the hospital."

I jump slightly. "The *hospital*? Why?"

"Because she's a meddling old woman," Mom says from her bed, followed by a low moan. "Jean, you're a retired piano teacher, for Pete's sake! What do you know about sick people?"

Mrs. Fox purses her lips together but doesn't argue with Mom. Instead, she says to me, "As I mentioned, we're probably erring on the side of caution, but your mom is running a fever and seems to be in a lot of pain."

I suddenly feel disoriented, as if the edges of the room have gotten fuzzy. Mom . . . *really sick*? I can't wrap my head around the idea. I ask, "A fever? How high?"

"A hundred and one," Mom says. "No big deal. As I said, I'm sure it's just the flu."

"And you're probably right, dear," Mrs. Fox says, "but let's just find out, okay?" The wrinkles around her lipsticked mouth seem deeper than usual.

I ask, "So should I call an ambulance?"

"Absolutely not!" Mom says. "I am certainly not paying hundreds of dollars for an ambulance ride I don't need."

Mrs. Fox holds up her palms. "Fine. I'll drive you." She looks at me. "Why don't you go pack up the food, tell Cassandra what's going on, and then both of you come back up here and help me get your mother to the car."

"Aunt Cassie left," I say. "She got called in to work at the pub."

"Well, then I suppose you and I will have to manage."

"Oh, this is so absurd!" Mom huffs. "I'm telling you, all I have is the flu. Jean, if I promise to be a good girl and get my flu shot every year from now on, will you drop this whole thing?"

I walk over and squeeze Mom's hands, surprised at how cold they feel. I'm shocked by her appearance, too. Curled up under all those quilts, she looks like a sick little girl rather than her usual invincible self. I grimace a smile at her. "Come on, Mom. Let's go get you checked out—to make Mrs. Fox feel better."

She closes her eyes and moans, "Fine."

I hurry down to the kitchen where BC is still snoozing on the floor. When I grab the plates of bread and vegetables off the table and start shoving them into the refrigerator, he walks over to me and rubs himself on my leg, as if asking, "What's wrong?" I explain to him about Mrs. Fox's plan to take Mom to the hospital while I put away the rest of the food and place a cover over Aunt Cassie's beautiful cake. Just hearing myself say the words "sick" and "hospital" frightens me. So, I pick up BC, cuddle him, and ask, "You don't think they'll admit Mom, do you? Keep her there overnight? I mean, she's not *that* sick, is she?"

He looks at me intensely with his big yellow eyes but doesn't purr.

At the hospital, everything happens too fast. They hustle Mom into the emergency room, take her vitals, hook her up to several noisy machines by threading needles and tubes up her nose and into the veins on the backs of both hands, and then ask her dozens of urgent questions. But now, all of a sudden, Mom is completely out of it, letting herself fall asleep just when she should be totally taking control of the situation. Very *atypical* Mom behavior that scares me to death.

The nurses and doctor redirect their urgent questions to me. "When did she first start exhibiting symptoms? What are her primary complaints? When did she develop a fever? Has she been vomiting?" They go on and on.

With each question, I feel more and more panicked. After a few minutes, I can't answer any more of them—my mouth won't move. I stand against the far wall, with my arms wrapped around myself, wishing BC were here with me. I watch as Mrs. Fox steps in and answers the doctor's questions. *Thank God* she's here.

More hospital people appear and wheel Mom away for an ultrasound. An ultrasound of *what*? Mrs. Fox and I, still dressed in our winter coats, drop into chairs in Mom's now-empty cubicle to wait for her return. After twenty minutes or so, a nurse hands us two cups of coffee without milk or sugar, but at least the cups are hot and help keep us warm.

"Any word?" Mrs. Fox asks the nurse.

She shakes her head. "It shouldn't be too long now." She hurries back to the large desk in the center of the emergency room.

"Word of *what*?" I ask Mrs. Fox.

"The doctor thinks your mother may be suffering from appendicitis—an enlarged appendix. That's why they're doing the ultrasound."

"Appendicitis. That's not too bad, right? I mean, they can just give her antibiotics or take out her appendix or something like that, right?"

Mrs. Fox nods with a frown. "Hopefully that's all she needs, unless—"

Mom's doctor rushes into the cubicle, clipboard in hand. He blasts me with a string of sentences that assault my ears. I can only make out a few isolated phrases: "burst appendix," "critical condition," "emergency surgery," and "life-or-death situation." He finally stops talking but then thrusts the clipboard toward me, hands me a pen, and points to a blank line at the bottom of the page.

Mrs. Fox nods rapidly, so I sign my name, not knowing what I am agreeing to.

The doctor rushes off, saying, "Go to the waiting room outside the OR. I'll come to find you there after she's out of surgery."

"What's happening?" I ask Mrs. Fox. "What are they doing to Mom? Is she going to be okay?"

Before she can answer me, the nurse bustles into the cubicle again, this time pushing a wheelchair. She smiles at Mrs. Fox. "I thought you might appreciate a lift to the surgical waiting room. It's up on the second floor."

Mrs. Fox nods weakly. "Thank you. I am a bit tuckered out."

We end up seated near a half-dozen other worried-looking people in a windowless, airless area decorated with close-up photos of flowers. A television drones on in the corner, unheeded. The staff members in this part of the hospital wear head-to-toe surgical garb and hurry up and down the corridors, wordlessly passing us.

Mrs. Fox pats my hands, which makes me stop digging my fingernails into my palms. She asks, "Dear, do you have Cassandra's phone number? I want to call her to let her know what's happening with your mother."

Aunt Cassie—she should be here. "I'll call her." I pull my phone from my jeans pocket and dial her number. Repeated calls go straight to voicemail, so I leave her a message: "Please, call me." I try not to sound too desperate.

Now time ticks by in slow motion, each minute taking an hour, as we wait in the uncomfortable orange chairs. The monitor mounted high on one wall continues to report Mom's status as *In Surgery*. After two hours, a doctor enters the waiting room and I stop breathing. In my mind, I yell, "Tell us something about my mom!" But he continues past Mrs. Fox and me and delivers good news to another family waiting in other orange chairs. Wearing smiles of relief, they all follow the arrows toward *Recovery Room*. Why can't that be us?

More time passes—very slowly now. I memorize the composition of each of the flower pictures and the names of their photographers.

I try again to reach Aunt Cassie and leave her another message, this one sounding more desperate: "Call me. Now. Please."

At four-thirty, she finally calls back. "Hey, kiddo. I turned off my phone while I was at work, but I see that you called a bunch of times. What's up? How's your birthday party going? Did the cake taste all right?"

How should I tell her? I don't want her to get all upset and get into an accident on the way to the hospital. "So, you know how Mom wasn't feeling good this morning?"

"Yeah. She has the flu, right?"

"Well, apparently it's a little more serious than that."

"What do you mean?" Her voice sounds sharp and afraid.

"Mrs. Fox and I brought Mom to the hospital and—"

"The hospital? Why?" Now she sounds mad, as if she thinks we overreacted.

"It turns out that her appendix was—"

"Appendix? What are you talking about?"

I sigh because I realize there is no easy way to tell her. "Aunt Cassie, Mom's appendix burst and the doctor is taking it out. She's in surgery right now."

"Surgery? What?" Now, Aunt Cassie sounds like she's struggling to understand me. "I'll be there in fifteen minutes," she says and hangs up.

Mrs. Fox asks, "Is Cassandra coming?"

I nod. "She's on her way." I hope she's not drunk. I don't think I could handle that, too.

"I'm glad to hear that she's coming." Mrs. Fox slowly climbs to her swollen feet and hugs me. "I'm afraid I'm going to have to leave you here alone for a few minutes, Rebecca. I really must get home to Howard. Roberta has already stayed an extra hour for me. Will you be all right?"

I don't want to be alone, but I nod anyway because I see Mrs. Fox's normally perfect hair is pushed to one side and her lipstick is smudged. Today has been *a lot* for her to handle—too much, maybe.

"Would you like me to find a wheelchair for you?" I ask. "I'd be happy to push you to your car."

She shakes her head. "I can manage. You need to stay right here and wait for that doctor. But please call me as soon as you hear anything."

"I will." All of a sudden, I feel very small in that big waiting room.

"And I'll stop by tomorrow morning if you're still here in the hospital." She smiles shakily. "Who knows? In five minutes, the doctor may come out here and report that the surgery was a big success and that Margaret will be ready to go home in a few hours."

I force a return smile. "I sure hope that's the case."

She squeezes both my hands. "Me too, dear. Me too."

Forty-five minutes later, Aunt Cassie finally shows up carrying two Styrofoam carry-out containers and a couple of cans of Coke. She hands me one of each and flops into the chair next to mine. "How's your mom doing?" Her black waitress outfit is splattered with tomato sauce but she seems sober—*thank God*. I'm glad she's here.

"No word," I say.

"Really? How long has it been?"

I check my phone. "Over three hours, now. Do you think that's a bad sign?"

She shrugs. "Maybe the surgery was more complicated than they thought it would be." She snickers. "Or maybe Maggie's in there telling them what to do."

I laugh, too. "I wouldn't put it past her. You know Mom: Ms. Always-In-Charge." Except she didn't look very in charge when they wheeled her out of the emergency room. She looked really sick.

Aunt Cassie says, "If it was anything really serious, the doctor would have come and told you already." Does she know what she's talking about, or is she just trying to make me worry less? She pulls some plastic forks from her coat pocket and I pretend to eat eggplant parmesan with her, but really, I'm just waiting for good news.

An hour later, Mom's doctor slowly shuffles into the waiting room, blue booties on his shoes, mask lines indented into his stubbly cheeks.

I leap to my feet. "How's my mom? Is she okay?"

Aunt Cassie stands up behind me and grips my shoulders.

He says, "She made it through the surgery and is being transferred to the intensive care unit now."

"Intensive care?" Aunt Cassie asks. "Why?"

"There were complications."

"W-what does that mean?" I ask. I don't want *complications*. I just want Mom.

He sinks into the chair opposite mine and looks at me. "You're Rebecca O'Sullivan, Margaret's daughter?"

I nod and sit.

"And who are you?" he asks, glancing at Aunt Cassie.

"Cassandra, Maggie's sister." She perches on the edge of her chair and grabs both of my hands.

"I'm Dr. Baker, your mom's surgeon."

"Great to meet you," Aunt Cassie says with sarcasm. She's obviously not in the mood for small talk. "So, what's the deal with Maggie?"

"As I explained to Rebecca earlier, the ultrasound showed that Margaret's appendix had ruptured, so we performed an emergency appendectomy. Unfortunately, once we got in there, we discovered that the rupture had occurred several hours—maybe even as much as a day—before she came here to the hospital. Because of this delay, she'd already developed a severe case of peritonitis, which is inflammation of the lining of her abdomen, and that caused septicemia, which is bacteria in her bloodstream—"

"Doc, you're *killing me* with all these medical terms," Aunt Cassie says. "Please cut to the chase. What's up with Maggie?"

"If you'll just give me another minute, I'm trying to be as clear as possible."

Aunt Cassie nods, squeezing my hands even tighter.

"Margaret's body released chemicals to fight the infection, which triggered an inflammatory response throughout the body called sepsis. We put her on a high dose of IV antibiotics that should knock down the infection—"

"That's good, right?" Aunt Cassie asks.

Dr. Baker raises a cautionary palm. "Please, hear me out."

I don't like the way he's talking—like someone trying to deliver bad news in the gentlest way possible.

"As I said, we have her on antibiotics now, but she's in septic shock."

"What does *that* mean?" Aunt Cassie huffs.

"Her blood pressure is dropping fast. Unless we can stabilize her soon, she may go into multiple organ failure."

"That's ridiculous!" Aunt Cassie says. "Maggie was just fine this morning. I mean, yes, she was sick to her stomach and running a fever, but no big deal. Hell, she was even giving me shit for drinking too much last night. How does she go from that to *multiple organ failure* in a few hours?"

"She will get better, right?" I ask. "She *has* to."

The doctor says, "She's young and healthy, and we put her on a vasopressor and corticosteroid to help normalize her blood pressure, so she's got a chance. But septic shock...well, it can be fatal."

Aunt Cassie springs to her feet. "*Fatal*? What are you talking about? Is my sister going to live or not?"

"We're doing everything we can to help Margaret recover. Now we'll just have to wait and see what happens. I'm sorry I don't have more definite answers. I'll keep you updated on her condition, but right now I need to get back to her."

I can't believe her condition is as bad as Dr. Baker is making it out to be. After all, Mom's a health freak: she eats well, never smoked, rarely drinks, and jogs five miles a day, rain or shine. And besides that, I need her, so she *has* to get better. *Now.*

Dr. Baker looks from Aunt Cassie—who's still pacing—to me. "Do you have any other questions for me before I go?"

I ask, "May we see her?"

He nods. "She's being transferred to the ICU now. Go up to the waiting room on the third floor and I'll have them come get you as soon as she's settled—probably in about an hour. She should be coming out of the anesthesia by then, too." He stretches his back and neck as he stands. "I'll go check on her now."

I just know if Mom sees me and talks with me, she'll get over her septic shock—or whatever it is. No way she'd let a burst appendix stop her from being my mom.

As the doctor disappears through the double doors at the end of the corridor, Aunt Cassie stops pacing and drops into the chair next to me. "I know this is supposed to be a good hospital and all, but I'm starting to wonder. I sure hope these bozos know what they're doing."

"Mom didn't seem that sick to me."

"I know, *right*?" She checks the time on her phone. "I'll run back to the farm to feed the animals and milk Bessie, and then meet you in the ICU waiting room. Do you want me to feed BC, too?"

I nod. "I wish you could bring him back here with you."

"No way they'd let a cat in the hospital, kiddo. Especially not in the ICU. But I'll give him some of his special treats. Okay?"

"Thanks." We walk together to the elevator.

Aunt Cassie hugs me so tightly that I can feel her heart beating. "Your mom's a tough cookie, Becca. She's going to pull through this just fine."

I hope she's right.

On the third floor of the hospital, I discover a chapel next to the ICU waiting room. It has obnoxious green carpeting and ugly stained glass windows, and it smells like disinfectant. It's not a place I'd choose to pray, but it does have a good-quality Baldwin upright piano in it. I try a few warm-up scales and discover the piano is slightly out of tune but has decent key action. Within a few minutes, I'm halfway through Liszt's *Feux Follets*, one of Mom's favorite pieces. My right hand races up and down the keyboard, playing the complicated melody, and my left hops back and forth, playing the piece's unusual chords. I picture a mad doctor reviving dying patients with injections of a miracle drug and then forcing them to dance for him—not my usual mental images for this piece. I stop in the middle of a run of thirty-second notes and start the étude again. But this time I deliberately play it as loudly and as badly as I can. With the chapel door open, the music will carry down the hall to the ICU rooms. Maybe if Mom hears me, she'll get angry enough to come to correct me.

I'm still banging away on the Baldwin a half-hour later when Dr. Baker walks in and tells me Mom's organs are shutting down and she doesn't have much time left to live. He tries to place a consoling hand on my shoulder, but I jerk away from him.

"What are you talking about?" I hiss. "I *need* her. She can't be..." I can't even say the word.

"I know this is a lot for you to take in. Probably too much to handle alone, especially at your age. How old are you?"

"Eighteen. Today's my birthday."

"Oh. I thought you were younger. Is your aunt still here?"

"No. She went home to feed the animals."

"Can you call her? Or is there someone else who could come here and be with you?"

I try to make sense of his words, but I can't. Mom *can't* die. That just isn't possible. She *has* to get better.

"Rebecca, I hate to rush you, but you need to move. *Now.* Your mom is awake and she's asking for you. I don't know how long she's going to remain conscious. If you want to say goodbye to her, this is your chance."

I jump off the piano bench and dial Aunt Cassie as I rush down the hall with Dr. Baker.

"Hey, kiddo," she says. "I'm just pulling into the hospital parking lot right now. How's your mom doing?"

"Dr. Baker just told me that she's *dying!* Get up here now—third floor, ICU!"

"Oh my God! I'll be there in two minutes. And I'll call Mrs. Fox."

"Hurry!"

By the time Dr. Baker and I reach the ICU nurses' station, Aunt Cassie is rushing off the elevator. The doctor has us put on sterile paper suits and then ushers us into Mom's glass room. She's lying on her back with a white cotton hospital blanket pulled up to her armpits. Her hands are clasped together, resting on her stomach. Her eyes are closed. She looks way too much like Grandpa did in his coffin. I'm horrified by the tubes and wires projecting from her body that make her look more like a failed robotics experiment than my mother. One machine near her left shoulder emits an off-pitch beep every three seconds and another one near her head whooshes continuously. Aunt Cassie stands on one side of Mom's bed while I stand on the other, willing Mom to open her eyes. Her skin—usually quite fair, like mine—now looks positively transparent. When her eyes finally do flutter open, I notice dark purple bruises have formed beneath them. She looks *awful*.

Mom feebly pulls the plastic oxygen mask off her nose and mouth and puts it down on her neck. "Hold my hands. Please." Her voice is thin and reedy.

We each take one of her cold hands. Even her pink nail polish, which matches mine, looks faded. My superhero mom suddenly seems way too human and very frail.

"This stinks, right?" she asks with a tiny chuckle.

"Mom, you've *got* to fight this and get better," I plead. "For me. I need you."

She takes a few labored breaths and faintly shakes her head. "Not looking good, kiddo."

"Don't say that!"

She closes her eyes and I'm afraid she's going to go to sleep—or worse—so I squeeze her hand. Hard. I'm relieved when her mouth twitches into a small smile and she opens her eyes. She says, "We need to talk." Every word she utters seems to sap her strength.

I glance over at Aunt Cassie. She's frowning and biting her lip—hard.

Mom says, "Cassie. No more drinking. Move back to the farm. Help Becca."

Aunt Cassie's hazel eyes grow huge with shock. Or is it fear? I can't tell.

"You can do it," Mom says. "I have some life insurance..." Mom's words slur together.

Aunt Cassie's eyes now look completely wild with panic, but she nods anyway.

Mom must still be out of it from surgery because otherwise, she'd realize Aunt Cassie can't handle those things. She's only ten years older than I am and can't even take care of herself. No way she'd be able to handle the farm or my career. Mom's dreaming. And she's cheating, too. Trying to pass off her responsibilities to her little sister.

I say, "Mom, you need to get better and come home."

"Probably not going to happen." Tears slide from the corners of her eyes and make gray spots on her white pillow.

I angrily drop her limp hand onto the thin cotton hospital blanket. "If you tried harder, you could beat this. It's just appendicitis, for Pete's sake." I'm crying too, the tears dripping onto my teal T-shirt. When I wear this shirt, Mom usually tells me the color compliments my red hair. Not today.

She whispers, "I feel so tired."

"Couldn't you try, Mom? For me?" I hate the whiny tone in my voice but I can't help it. I can't even *imagine* life without her.

She nods weakly. "But remember: You are strong."

I shake my head because I sure don't feel strong. Standing next to her hospital bed in that ICU room, I feel like a little girl very much in need of her mommy to take care of her.

She raps her finger sharply on the back of my wrist, the same gesture she'd used to teach me how to play staccato notes on the piano. "You *are* strong...you play concerts..." Her head drops back onto her pillow and she gasps for air.

I reach for the call button, but Mom weakly waves me off. "Not yet." Aunt Cassie pulls the oxygen mask up over Mom's nose and mouth again, and she lies still, just breathing for a full minute. Then, pushing the mask down past her chin again, she smiles tiredly. "I'm proud of you, Becca...you're a good person. You, too, Cassie. Take care of each other."

I collapse onto her chest. "Mom, please don't die. I'd miss you too much."

She strokes my hair as I listen to her heart pounding rapidly in her chest.

Dr. Baker reenters the room with a nurse. "We need to intubate your mother now to help her breathe. Why don't you both step out into the hall?"

Using one trembling finger, Mom turns my chin to face her and gives me a shaky smile. "It'll be okay," she whispers.

I hug her fiercely, wishing I could give her some of my physical strength.

She holds out her thin arms—needles, tubes, and all—squeezes me, and gently rocks me back and forth. Then she adds Aunt Cassie to the hug. Finally, she lets go of us and lies back, looking completely exhausted.

The nurse tugs our sleeves and tips her head toward the door.

Aunt Cassie kisses Mom's cheek and whispers, "I love you, sis."

"Love you, too."

I kiss Mom's burning forehead. "Mom, I love you."

"I love you with all my heart," she whispers clearly. "And I always will."

~~~

Everything happens much too quickly after that.

Mrs. Fox arrives ten minutes later, but before we can ask about her seeing Mom, an alarm sounds in Mom's room. Over the hospital's PA system, we hear, "Code blue, ICU." I've watched enough medical shows on TV to know what that means. But the voice sounds way too calm, like someone giving GPS driving directions instead of announcing that a patient's heart has stopped beating. A half-dozen nurses and doctors come running down the hall and rush through the glass door into Mom's room.

61

I hurry to the nurses' station and ask, "What's going on with my mom?" I desperately want them to tell me she's going to be okay.

One young nurse smiles gently. "We are doing everything possible for her. If you return to the waiting room, someone will come to update you on her condition as soon as possible."

Wrong answer.

Aunt Cassie, Mrs. Fox, and I sit together in the ugly orange chairs and hold hands.

"Dear God," Mrs. Fox prays, "please be with Margaret and give her strength to get through this medical crisis. We all love her so much."

I want to add a prayer of my own, but the right words won't come. When more medical personnel charge into Mom's room, pushing a variety of equipment carts, I just close my eyes and beg God, "Please send one of your miracles. I know you can heal her, so do it—please."

"Our Father, who art in heaven," Aunt Cassie begins, "hallowed be thy name. Thy kingdom come, thy will be done, on earth as it is in heaven."

Through the glass walls, I hear Dr. Baker barking out orders while different alarms blare discordant tones that make my ears hurt.

Mrs. Fox joins Aunt Cassie, praying, "Give us this day our daily bread, and forgive us our trespasses as we forgive those who trespass against us."

Someone closes the curtains at the perimeter of Mom's room so we can only see feet milling around her bed, rushing one way and then the other, dancing to the tones of the terrible alarms.

All three of us pray, "And lead us not into temptation, but deliver us from evil. For thine is the kingdom, and the power, and the glory, forever. Amen."

And then...nothing. Everything in Mom's room stops. No sounds. No movement. Just stillness. I know what that means, but I can't believe it, so I go numb—my body, my brain, everything. This can't be happening. Not to Mom. Not to Aunt Cassie and Mrs. Fox. Not to me. We sit in our little circle in the waiting room, still holding hands.

People emerge slowly from Mom's room, balling up their blue paper masks and gowns and tossing them into a red trash receptacle. They slowly trudge back up the hallway they dashed down just minutes earlier, shoving their heavy carts in front of them.

Dr. Baker appears before us and shakes his head. "I am so sorry," he says. "We did everything we could."

That isn't true. If they had done everything they could, this wouldn't have happened.

I stand up. "I want to see my mom," I say.

"Sure," he says. "You all may go in whenever you are ready."

I hesitate. Mrs. Fox is sobbing loudly and Aunt Cassie is hugging her and crying, too. They are too noisy. Mom wouldn't be able to hear what I need to say to her.

Dr. Baker asks me, "Would you like me to go in with you?"

I nod.

Leaving Aunt Cassie and Mrs. Fox in the waiting room, he leads me into Mom's glass cubicle and stops just inside the door.

Looking down at my snow boots, I approach the bed, afraid of what I will find there. When I do look at Mom, I find her body is draped with another white blanket, this one pulled up to her chin, covering all of the wires and tubes still attached to her, their outlines visible underneath the blanket. The only part of Mom I can see is her face, which is familiar and yet not. A plastic tube protrudes from her mouth. It looks so uncomfortable. Why don't they take it out? Her eyes are closed with her red lashes laying against her cheeks. Her skin is ashen white—gray, actually—with the dark purple bruises beneath her eyes fading away. Mom's nose freckles are lighter than usual but her eyebrows look darker. Someone has arranged her hair to be a shimmering red veil covering her pillow. She looks like a sleeping princess. Except Mom's *not* sleeping.

Last year as I stood in the reception line at Grandpa's wake, I heard several people say that he looked peaceful, "Like he's sleeping." At the time, I agreed with them, wishing he'd wake up.

But Mom doesn't look asleep. She looks *dead*. Her bright spark of life is gone. Mom isn't this soulless body lying in this hospital room, covered up with all these white blankets. This is just a shell. A container that once held Margaret Elizabeth O'Sullivan. She's not in there anymore. Mom's dead. Gone. And I don't know where she is.

Conscious of Dr. Baker watching me from the doorway, I bend and kiss the cold forehead. "Goodbye, Mom," I whisper. "I love you. And I always will." Then I turn and walk out of the cubicle.

In the waiting room, I curl up into a ball in one of the orange chairs and rock back and forth, waiting, while Aunt Cassie and Mrs. Fox go to say goodbye to Mom's body. When they return, they sit on either side of me, hugging me with their heads on my shoulders.

Mrs. Fox says, "Cassandra and I decided that you should come home with me tonight. We don't want you to be alone."

Aunt Cassie says, "Meanwhile, I'll go over to Jimmy's apartment and pack up my stuff so that I can move back to the farmhouse first thing in the morning."

"What time is it now?" I ask.

Mrs. Fox checks her watch. "It's eight-thirty, dear."

Eight-thirty? How had so much happened in such a short time? Today had all started out so *normal*, with farm chores and breakfast with Mom. She had said nice things about me growing up. And then she'd given me her Goat. What a surprise. And then Aunt Cassie made a beautiful cake because it's my birthday—I keep forgetting that. But then Mom got really sick and Mrs. Fox drove us here to the hospital. Mom had surgery. And then she *died*. Just like that. What had begun as a lame eighteenth birthday ended as the *worst* day ever.

I can't be here anymore, in this horrible hospital where Mom lies much too still. Mom has never been still before. Not ever. Whenever we watched a movie together, she was always knitting a pair of mittens or hemming one of my concert dresses or writing a letter to a friend at the same time. Eating meals, sitting in church, and even at my concerts, Mom always found some way to be in constant movement. Until now. Now she lies there, not moving. That isn't right.

I say, "I want to leave. Now."

"Yes, dear. You're coming home with me," Mrs. Fox says.

I shake my head. "I want to go to *my* home." I need to cuddle *my* cat and play *my* piano and sleep in *my* bed, surrounded by *my* things... and Mom's. I want to feel her near me. I need her.

Mrs. Fox pats my hand. "I'll take you home first thing in the morning. As soon as you wake up."

I shake my head harder. "I need to go to *my* home—*now*." I'm not yelling, but I'm not being hospital-quiet, either.

She hesitates and then nods. "All right, dear. Let me make a phone call to find someone to help me with Howard. And then we'll go home...to your home, I mean."

~

Back at the farmhouse, I throw my coat on the floor and dash up the stairs, my boots dropping a trail of snow and ice on each carpeted tread. In my room, I find BC asleep on my pillow. I scoop him up and hug him tightly, his purr vibrating against my breastbone. I rock him back and forth, back and forth, with my eyes closed, inhaling his familiar cat scent.

Sometime later, Mrs. Fox calls out, "Rebecca, would you please come down here? I'm afraid my knees aren't up to climbing the stairs anymore tonight."

I follow her voice down to the kitchen, carrying BC.

She pulls out one of the chairs for me. "Sit, please."

I do as I'm told, pressing BC into my lap.

Mrs. Fox sits next to me. She has laid out sandwiches for us, served on stoneware plates sitting on red calico placemats. They're Mom's sandwiches—the ones she'd made for my never-to-happen birthday party, Mom's plates, and Mom's placemats. In the middle of the table, Aunt Cassie's beautiful chocolate cake sits under a plastic cover, still waiting to be lit, cut, and eaten.

The legs of my chair screech on the wood floor as I stand abruptly, clutching BC to my chest. "I'm not hungry." I flee into the parlor and place BC in his bed atop our Yamaha grand. Mom had sewn the black-and-white fleece cat bed the day after we'd brought him home from the animal shelter. "So he can keep you company while you practice," she'd said. But I can't think about Mom sewing right now.

I beg BC, "Please help me find middle-C."

He does, and I give him an extra hug and kiss before returning him to his bed. I do my warm-up drills: scales in C, C sharp, D, D sharp, and so on, up and down the piano without pause. I begin by playing them carefully and evenly, the way Mom taught me, but then I grow louder and more violent until I'm slamming my fingers down on the keys. BC peers at me from his perch, crouched down, ears back, looking frightened. After the scales, I immediately launch into a prelude by Rachmaninoff, picturing two red-uniformed soldiers having a bloody swordfight. Then I attack an étude by Chopin while envisioning a raging wildfire sweeping through a bone-dry canyon, wiping out everything in its path. I'm pounding the keyboard, bruising the tips of my fingers, playing without any finesse at all. But it doesn't matter how—or what—I play, just as long as I keep playing *something*. Because the music *is Mom*. As long as I keep playing, she's not lying in that hospital bed, gray and motionless, with those thin white blankets covering her. As long as I keep playing, she is still alive and moving, and breathing with the music. As long as I keep playing, Mom—my mom—is *not dead*.

After some time—Twenty minutes? Two hours?—I become aware of Mrs. Fox standing next to the piano, wringing her hands. I stop Liszt's *Étude No. 8*—a pack of wild dogs frantically chasing a fox and ripping it to pieces—mid-phrase.

"I'm sorry to bother you, Rebecca," she says. "It's just that it's getting late and I was hoping to sleep here." She points to the sofa where Mom sat at night to read her classic novels.

The mantel clock reads one o'clock in the morning, five hours since Mom...

"Are you hungry?" Mrs. Fox asks.

I shake my head.

She places a soft palm on my cheek and nods toward BC. "Then why don't you take him upstairs with you and try to get some sleep?"

In my room, I curl around BC and pull up my favorite quilt—hand-sewn by Mom—not even bothering to undress or turn out the lights. "Hey, little man," I say. He purrs as I stroke the extra-soft fur on his belly. "What am I supposed to do now? How am I going to live without Mom?" I feel his warm breath on my neck as he rhythmically kneads my shoulder. "I guess Aunt Cassie's moving back in here tomorrow morning. She'll help me."

"Oh honey, I wouldn't count on that," a voice says very closely to my ear.

I fling back the quilt and look around frantically. "Who said that?" I whimper. The room appears empty, except for BC and me.

"It's just me, dear."

I scan the room once more and find only BC in the bed next to me.

"Yes. I'm talking to you." He sits up.

"B-but cats don't talk."

His large yellow eyes look up at me. "I'm sorry to have to contradict you, hon, especially with all you've been through today, but I'm afraid you're mistaken. Because, in case you hadn't noticed, I *am* talking to you right now." Although BC's mouth isn't moving, the voice does seem to be coming from him, and it sounds like the sort of voice he'd have if he could talk, soft and whispery. He sighs. "You poor thing. So unprepared for this, aren't you?"

"For what?"

"Being an orphan." He shakes his head and his ears make a flapping sound. "Don't worry, hon. We'll figure things out. Together."

Mrs. Fox appears in the doorway, out of breath and rubbing one knee. "Rebecca, are you okay? I heard your voice and thought you might be having a nightmare."

I point a shaking finger at BC. "He's talking to me."

Her eyebrows shoot up to her gray hairline. "The cat?"

"Yes, the cat. He says I'm an orphan."

BC sits, motionless and silent, staring at a corner of the ceiling.

Mrs. Fox clasps and unclasps her hands.

I look from her to BC and realize how crazy I must sound. "What I mean is... He had a funny look on his face and...well..." *God*, am I losing my mind?

Mrs. Fox totters over to sit next to me. "Dear, I can certainly understand that you're upset. That's only natural after all you've been through." She pats my hand. "What's most important now is that you get some sleep." She stands and scoops up BC with a grunt. "I'll take this boy downstairs with me so he doesn't...er...bother you anymore." She drapes him over her shoulder and gently brushes my hair away from my forehead. "You try to get some sleep now, all right?"

I nod.

As Mrs. Fox walks out of the room, BC winks at me over her shoulder.

The Return of Aunt Cassie

Sunday morning, I wake up smiling and eager to start my day: chores, breakfast with Mom, and then practicing with BC. Friday night's sonata concert went well, so I'm looking forward to finishing up the series with the last two concerts. Maybe later today Mom will take me up to Warwick to buy gowns for the shows.

It's not until I walk past Mrs. Fox's car on my way to the barn that I remember yesterday. That *terrible* day. I stand in the snow staring at her frosty car, desperately trying to think of another reason for it being here. In the barn, I rush through my chores in record time. I dash back through the kitchen door, praying that Mom will be there with breakfast waiting for me, her usual bright smile beaming from her beautiful, rosy face. But, instead, I find Mrs. Fox, looking sad and exhausted. She's made us scrambled eggs and weak coffee. No oatmeal. No toast with peanut butter and raisins. I sit at the table with Mrs. Fox and pick at the eggs, not bothering to comment on her menu choices since I can't eat anything anyway. BC wanders into the kitchen, sniffs at his kibble, and then lies down near my feet. Neither of us makes a move toward the piano parlor. What's the point?

At the hospital last night, Aunt Cassie had said she'd be here *first thing* this morning, but it's nine a.m. and there's still no sign of her. Mrs. Fox plays a few hands of cribbage with me to keep me company, but then she leaves to go home and take care of Mr. Fox.

I hate being alone. Everything's too quiet. Even BC. I am glad that he's not talking to me because hopefully, that means I just imagined it. But I wouldn't mind having someone else to speak with right now. Yesterday was so awful, and I don't know how to deal with it. Maybe if BC *did* speak, he could help me figure things out. But that's crazy, right? Because cats don't talk. I know that. I was just overwhelmed last night. *Understandably.*

I call and text Aunt Cassie's phone; both go unanswered. Still at the kitchen table, I sip my cold coffee with BC in my lap, warm and comforting. Outside, it's snowing again—sharp, grainy snowflakes, not fluffy, pretty ones.

What's it going to be like living with Aunt Cassie? Can we be a real family? Can she take care of all the stuff Mom asked her to do: the farm, my career, me? All my life, Aunt Cassie's been someone for me to have fun with, not someone to count on. Mom was the reliable one. Aunt Cassie has always been a kid—like me. No way she can handle grown-up responsibilities. And what about her drinking? It's a big part of her life. It's how she has fun. Can she give it up just like that? I doubt it. I love my aunt with my whole heart. There's enough of Mom in her to make her a wonderful person, even with her drinking. And she's always been there for me, at every one of my Christmases, birthdays, talent shows, and concerts. She's a good aunt and a great friend, but I don't think she can make the change to pseudo-mother. And I don't think she wants to, either. She's not done being a kid herself.

Several times I think I hear Aunt Cassie's truck coming up the driveway, but when I peer through the window, all I see are the ugly, granular snowflakes falling from a dead, gray sky. At noon, I dump some kibble and water into BC's bowls and nibble on one of Mom's sandwiches while staring at my still-untouched birthday cake on the table. Eating it feels wrong—like I'd be celebrating without Mom. But throwing it out feels wrong, too, after all the work Aunt Cassie put into making it. I wander around the house carrying a sleeping BC. We end up in the piano parlor where I call Aunt Cassie again. Still no answer.

I try to practice one of the new sonatas because I figure that's what Mom would want me to do. Within minutes, though, I realize I have no idea how to work on it. What phrases should I emphasize? When should I play faster or slower? What images should I have in my head while I'm playing? Nothing makes sense. I need Mom to explain these things to me. But she's dead. *Dead.*

BC and I must have dozed off on the parlor sofa, because the next thing I know, we wake up there to the sound of a car roaring up our driveway. I look out the window and see Aunt Cassie arrive in a black car driven by an unshaven guy dressed in a black jacket patched with silver duct tape. Jimmy. Aunt Cassie slumps out of the car and stands in the snow, shivering in a stretched-out URI sweatshirt. I stuff my arms into my winter jacket and hurry outside.

"Becca!" She gives me a tight hug and I notice she has earrings in only one ear, all of them silver skulls. Her breath smells like cigarettes and stale beer—the breakfast of champions. "My stupid truck wouldn't start so Jimmy helped me move my stuff. Isn't that sweet of him?" She sways and stumbles into the car door. "Jimmy," she slurs, "come over here and say hi to Becca."

He grabs a duffel bag and lumbers around the front of the car, whacking his knee into the bumper. "Shit!" He punches the hood with his fist and adds to a collection of similarly shaped dents. "What the fuck!" He glares at Aunt Cassie and me as if we had caused his bruise and car damage.

I hold out my hand toward the duffel. "Want me to get that for you?"

He backhands my arm away, knocking it into the rearview mirror.

With a gasp of surprise and pain, I look down at my hand and flex my fingers. I hope nothing's broken.

Jimmy stomps to the car's trunk, pulls out a pile of shabby clothing and a beat-up blender, and drops everything into the snow behind his car. "You two get over here and pick up this shit. I haven't got all fucking day."

Nice guy.

Aunt Cassie grabs an armful of her clothes and hurries into the house. I don't want to be alone with Jimmy, so I quickly pick up the blender and follow her. In the kitchen, I smile. "I'm so glad you're here. I was getting a little worried."

"Don't give me any shit, okay, Becca? I got here as soon as I could."

"What? I just meant I was glad to see you." I bite my cheek to keep from crying. I can't remember her ever talking to me like that before.

Her face suddenly looks green and pinched. Grasping her stomach, she says, "I'm not feeling so good. Would you go get the rest of my stuff out of the car?" She runs into the bathroom and slams the door. A moment later, I hear retching.

Great.

I go back outside in time to see Jimmy shove the contents of his backseat out the open door on the other side of the car. He sneers in my direction, slams the doors, climbs into the driver's seat, and takes off down the driveway, running over Aunt Cassie's rusty toaster oven in the process.

What a jerk.

While Aunt Cassie throws up in the bathroom, I haul in her belongings and carry them upstairs. I carefully fold her clothes and pile them on the bed, and then go back downstairs to find her standing unsteadily at the open refrigerator, drinking orange juice out of the carton.

"What did you do with my stuff?" she asks.

Pointing upward, I say, "I put it in your old bedroom."

"Fuck, no!" She throws the empty juice carton into the fridge and slams the door. "All my life I've wanted Maggie's room. Now she's dead, I'm taking it. And don't even try to stop me."

Her nasty words hit me hard, like a punch in the stomach. No amount of cheek-biting can stop the tears this time, so I cry quietly, wipe my eyes, and then follow her upstairs, where I see that she's thrown most of Mom's clothing and a bunch of her other things into the hallway. Aunt Cassie sits at Mom's vanity, pawing through Mom's jewelry box, holding earrings and necklaces up to herself, and then looking in the mirror. She's replaced her ugly skull earrings with some of Mom's pretty butterflies and flowers. Noticing me in the reflection, she says, "I've got to hand it to your mom; she had some nice stuff."

I pick up Mom's belongings from the hallway and carry them into Aunt Cassie's old room, one armful at a time, being careful of my sore hand that is already swollen and turning purple, thanks to Jimmy the Jerk. I can't ask Aunt Cassie to drive me to the walk-in clinic for an X-ray—she's too drunk. My hand will be fine. *Probably*.

I hold Mom's blouses and sweaters up to my nose and inhale lilac soap, Coach perfume, and ginger tea—Mom. Smelling these scents makes my heart ache. I carefully fold the shirts and place them in the dresser. I hang her dresses and pants in the closet, grouping them by type and color, as she would have done. When I finish with her clothes, I scoop up Mom's boxes and knickknacks that Aunt Cassie had dumped in the hall. I spend some time looking through a pile of photographs, mostly of me and Mom. A few of them show her when she was my age, touring Europe with the Juilliard Orchestra. She was so beautiful even back then. I tuck everything neatly into the spare bedroom closet and then wrap Mom's lap quilt—full of bright-colored floral fabrics—around my shoulders, lay down on the bed, and sob.

"There, there," someone says consolingly.

I lift my head to find BC sitting in the doorway, his yellow eyes looking at me.

Yesterday, my mother died. Today, I'm going crazy. *Great.*

Later, I do a search for "talking cat" on my laptop. After reading several postings about how cats don't have the same type of vocal cords or mouth structure as humans and so are incapable of actual speech, I come across an article from a psychiatric journal talking about "auditory hallucinations due to temporary, stress-induced psychosis." Maybe that's what's going on with me. I hope so. I especially like the word "temporary" because maybe that means if I can manage to come to grips with Mom dying—like after the funeral—I'll stop hearing BC talking to me. *Maybe.*

Funeral Preparations

Two days later, on Tuesday morning, I bang on Aunt Cassie's door to wake her up for our appointment at the funeral home. We're supposed to make the *final arrangements* for Mom. *Yuck.* I don't figure Aunt Cassie is going to be much help. She's been drunk and horrible ever since she showed up on Sunday, making me almost wish she hadn't moved back into the house. I didn't like being alone, but living with a nasty, drunken aunt isn't much better. I get that she's trying to cope with Mom's death, too, but I wish she'd sober up and be nicer, because there are *so many* things I need to talk to her about: Mom, BC (who's talking to me more every day), buying groceries—stuff like that. But Aunt Cassie just keeps on drinking. First, she finished off the few bottles of wine we had in the house, and then she went out and bought more booze—gross, cheap stuff that makes her breath smell terrible. She drinks *all* the time, morning to night. Good thing we get milk from Bessie and eggs from the chickens—otherwise, we'd be starving by now.

Yesterday, when Aunt Cassie was working her shift at the pub, I spent several hours going through Mom's office, looking for information about Dear Old Dad. I was hoping to find out for sure who he was, thinking maybe he could help us out somehow. Was he Mr. Zelinski? There seemed to be some suggestion of that at the restaurant last week. But then wouldn't Mom have said something? And wouldn't I have felt more of a connection with him when we had dinner together? I didn't like snooping through Mom's stuff, but she should have told me who my father was, or at least left me a letter explaining things. To be fair, I'm sure she didn't think she was going to die at the age of thirty-five. Who does? At one point yesterday I was excited to find a copy of my actual birth certificate—I'd never seen it before—only to be disappointed a second later when I noticed the line labeled "Father" was left blank. *Thanks*, Mom.

This morning, when I finally get Aunt Cassie out of bed, she grabs the keys to the GTO and stumbles through the snow to the barn, not bothering to change her clothes or comb her hair. She looks and smells like the homeless man who begs outside the hardware store in town. Driving across town to the funeral home, she weaves in and out of the lane as I clutch the dashboard with my self-bandaged hand, praying the whole time for God to keep us safe, even though I don't think He's listening. I mean, He sure didn't do anything when I asked Him to save Mom.

At the funeral home, the sickly-sweet smell of old flowers fills the air, making me feel nauseous. In the office, we meet with the funeral director, who is pale and gaunt and dressed in a dark, custom-tailored suit. He looks like a well-dressed vampire. Opening a black file folder, he asks us, "Have you made arrangements for the funeral at the church?"

Aunt Cassie and I look at each other and shake our heads. I never thought of calling the church. Why would I? The only funeral I'd ever been to had been Grandpa's, and Mom had taken care of all those arrangements.

"Would you like some assistance with that?" he asks. "We need to know where and when the funeral will take place to schedule the viewing and visitation around it."

"She went to St. Francis de Sales Church in North Kingstown," Aunt Cassie says. "Every Sunday, rain or shine."

Me, too. I had enjoyed sitting there with Mom, listening to stories from the Bible and well-played organ music—usually performed by one of Mom's old students. Who am I going to go to church with now? Aunt Cassie? Doubtful. I don't think she's set foot in a church for years.

"Ah, yes," the funeral director says. "Father Nick Smith is the pastor there. We know him well." He picks up the phone and calls the church, putting Father Nick on speakerphone. Together with Aunt Cassie, they make Mom's funeral arrangements. I don't say anything. It's just too much.

The funeral director hangs up the phone and jots some notes in his folder. Looking up, he says, "Now that we've taken care of that, there are some other matters to discuss. Such as, what type of wood do you want for the casket?"

I shoot Aunt Cassie a look of panic. I don't know how to make decisions like that. No way.

She stabs a badly manicured finger at one of the casket photos displayed on the man's desk. "That one looks good."

Whatever.

He makes a note of her choice and then asks, "What color lining would you like?"

She picks bright pink—a color Mom hated.

"What will the deceased be wearing? And how many people do you expect for the wake and the funeral?" The funeral director asks question after question. I wish I could squeeze my eyes closed and put my hands over my ears. *See no evil, hear no evil.* I want to make him and everything that's happened over the past few days disappear. Instead, I zone out by staring at his unnaturally white, pointy teeth and imagining myself playing Schumann's *Fantasie in C, Op.17.* When I perform it, I always envision a woman mourning the death of her husband. At the beginning of the piece, she's sad. Then she tries to convince herself he's not dead, followed by a section where she's mad at him for leaving her to deal with the mess of life alone. In the second movement, she begs God to bring her husband back to life, and when that doesn't work, she becomes depressed and thinks about killing herself. The piece ends with her accepting his death and being at peace—as if anyone can make sense of someone dying. Now, I realize this whole narrative is just another fairy tale I tell myself. A stupid, little-girl lie.

I don't say anything as Aunt Cassie answers all of the funeral director's questions. Her choices seem completely random to me, but I don't care. I just want to go home. I don't want to talk to the director or anybody else. Certainly not the dozens of people who have called or stopped by the farm over the past few days, offering their condolences. What is a *condolence*, anyway? What a stupid word. Like anyone can say anything that'll make me feel better about my mother being dead. *Dead.*

When Aunt Cassie and I finally get back to the farm, she goes to the refrigerator and I head for the stairs. "You want me to make us some lunch?" She twists off a cap of a beer and chugs down half the bottle.

"No, thanks," I say. "I'm not hungry."

"Suit yourself."

Up in my room, BC is snoozing on my pillow. I decide to let sleeping cats lie, mostly because I don't want to have a conversation with him right now. When he talks, he's kind and understanding—sounding a lot like Mom, actually—but his sudden ability to speak freaks me out big time, and I don't know what to do about it.

I flick on my laptop to zone out in front of an old movie, but an icon tells me that I've received an email at RebeccaOSullivan.com, my performance website. I click on it and read: "Dear Rebecca, Maja and I congratulate you again on your wonderful performance Friday night, and thank you and your mother for allowing us to join you for dinner after the show. We thoroughly enjoyed meeting you and spending the evening with you both. We hope that you will allow us to return the favor when one of your concerts brings you to our little corner of the globe. Sincerely yours, Krystian Zelinski."

He and his wife had left for Poland the morning after the concert, and since I hadn't posted anything about Mom's death, there was no way he could know what had happened to her. Which means I need to tell him. Clearly, he and Mom had shared some sort of past—maybe romantic. Why else would she have been so insistent about him coming to my show? If Mr. Zelinski is not my father, maybe he's somehow *connected* to him. I shake my head. Whatever. I need to let the Zelinskis know what's happened to Mom.

I hit *Reply* and type: "Hi Mr. Zelinski, I am sorry to tell you that my mother died of a burst appendix on Saturday, the day after the concert. Her wake and funeral will be held this Friday. Sincerely, Rebecca O'Sullivan." Although I know my email is pretty abrupt and probably rude, it's the best I can do right now. I press *Send*, shut my laptop, and curl up on the bed next to BC, no longer interested in a movie.

An hour later, my laptop wakes me up with a ping. Mr. Zelinski responds: "Dear Rebecca, I am so sorry to hear about your mother. Please accept my deepest condolences. With her passing, the world loses a talented teacher, a gifted musician, and a wonderful woman. Unfortunately, I will not be able to attend the services this Friday, since I have unavoidable engagements here in Poland. However, in light of your mom's passing, I do have an important matter I would like to discuss with you. Maja and I will be back in Rhode Island in mid-December, preparing for me to assume my post at the university, and so will plan on attending your last Beethoven sonata concert on December 21, with the hope that we might speak afterward. In the interim, please do not hesitate to contact me if I may be of any service to you. Sincerely yours, Krystian Zelinski."

What *important matter* is he talking about? Could it be something about my father, after all? Like, Mom died a few days ago, and now I'm finally going to find out who Dear Old Dad is? I can't deal with this. I drop my laptop onto the braided rug and hug BC to my chest.

Mom in Pink

The day of Mom's wake and funeral dawns cold and gray. It's Friday, one week after my seventh sonata concert. Hard to believe how messed up everything can get in just seven days.

At Grandpa's wake and funeral nearly a year ago, all I had to do was to put on a black dress, carry a lace hankie, and stand next to Mom. She took care of everything else: selecting the coffin, the flowers, the photos, the music, and the service—all tastefully done, of course. Typical Mom.

For Mom's wake, I wear one of my black concert dresses, with long sleeves and a high collar. Black tights, black ballet flats, and my hair in a poorly arranged bun to complete the outfit.

"You look very nice, dear," BC says. "Very appropriate."

"Thanks."

BC has been talking to me all week, so much so that I don't even think it's too weird anymore. Since Aunt Cassie's been completely MIA, I kind of appreciate that BC is talking. Otherwise, it's too quiet. Aunt Cassie went out drinking with Jimmy Tuesday night and hasn't been home since. So much for the two of us trying to become a real family. I never did believe it would work.

Mrs. Fox drives me to the funeral home. As soon as we arrive, I can tell everything's all wrong. For one thing, why did Aunt Cassie schedule Mom's wake from nine to noon on a weekday, when most people are at work or school? Probably nobody's going to come, which will be a lousy tribute to Mom. And the coffin Aunt Cassie picked out is shiny and cheap-looking, nothing like the rich, walnut-paneled one Grandpa had. I hate the flowers next to the coffin, too. They're smelly carnations arranged in an arch and look like they belong at the Kentucky Derby, not Mom's funeral. One mistake after another, all made by Aunt Cassie.

The vampiric funeral director takes our coats and then positions Mrs. Fox and me next to the casket in a *receiving line*. Can you have a line of only two? Aunt Cassie is still a no-show. Probably out getting sloshed somewhere, since that seems to be the way she deals with everything. But maybe she has the right idea. Maybe I should try getting drunk. Maybe that would make the pain go away. It's such an awful kind of pain. Not in my arms or legs or stomach. More like in my brain. Or my soul. But I don't have any booze—Aunt Cassie drank it all—so I just stand here with Mrs. Fox, next to the ugly box containing Mom's dead body, and feel like I'm going to throw up. Good thing I skipped breakfast.

I deliberately don't look inside the casket next to me. I don't want to see Mom's face caked with a ton of makeup. They did that to Grandpa—made him look like a drag queen, which, to be honest, he probably would have found hilarious—so they probably did it to Mom, too. She never wore makeup in real life. She was so naturally pretty, she didn't need it. But now she'll be wearing makeup for all eternity. So I don't look. I don't want to have that image in my mind when I remember Mom.

Instead, I want to picture her as healthy and smiling at me. Maybe tapping the side of her nose with her finger in our secret signal that meant "I know." As in, "I know what you're thinking right now," or, "I know how you're feeling." She loved me so completely, and I loved her just as much. How could she possibly be *dead*?

Dave Morales is the first person to arrive at her wake. He kneels in front of the casket and prays, which is a good thing. Over the past seven days, a lot of people have emailed and texted to tell me they were saying prayers for Mom. I hope God's listening to them because whenever I try to pray for her soul, I can't get the words to come out right. Instead, I keep asking God why she died, and so far He hasn't bothered to answer me.

Dave rises from the kneeler and walks over to Mrs. Fox and me. "Rebecca, I'm so sorry. Your mother was a wonderful woman. She was so kind to everyone."

I nod. What am I supposed to say?

"I can't even imagine how you're feeling. I want you to know that you can rely on me to help out in any way I can: during shows at the Courthouse Center, shoveling snow at the farmhouse—whatever you need."

I picture Mom kissing his cheek when he shoveled our driveway last week, right after she said, "Things are going to be different from now on." Turns out that was a *massive* understatement.

Dave smiles kindly at me and then moves over to talk to Mrs. Fox. My chest aches with the realization that he and Mom will never get to go out on a date together. What a stupid waste. They probably would have made each other very happy.

Music. Why isn't there any music playing? There was music at Grandpa's wake, and it certainly would have been a good idea for Mom's service today. She was a piano teacher, for Pete's sake. Why didn't Aunt Cassie think of it? There is a piano in the back of the room. I could go and play something for Mom, something beautiful—like her. I want to. But I can't, right? I'm supposed to stand in this stupid receiving line of two, greeting *condolence*-givers. That's what is expected of me. My hands twitch as I imagine myself playing Schumann's *Fantasie* for Mom.

A group of her piano students and their parents walk to the front of the viewing room. They all kneel at the coffin and then come over to Mrs. Fox and me, and mumble the same three phrases: "so sorry," "wonderful woman," and "kind to everyone." Is someone passing out scripts at the door to the funeral home, telling everyone what to say? And they all have the same horrible look of pity in their eyes. Don't they know their words and looks make me feel worse, not better?

Next, John Foster and Sally Johnson, the farmers that lease our cornfields, come into the room with their spouses. They look uncomfortable. When John stops to talk to us, I notice that even though he works with his hands all day, every day, his fingernails are clean and neatly trimmed. How does he manage that? Why does it matter to him?

I look down at my chipped nails and realize that I should have gotten a manicure for the funeral, or painted them myself. Mom was the one who always arranged my manicures, haircuts, and stuff like that. Not anymore. She's *dead*.

Another group of people comes into the room, unbuttoning their winter coats in the heat of the funeral home. And then a few minutes after that, more people arrive and the room grows even hotter and more crowded. Over the next three hours, more and more show up in an endless parade of Mom's students and friends. All of them cycle through the room: praying at the casket, shaking my hand, talking to Mrs. Fox, repeating the required phrases to both of us, and making the room even hotter yet. Mom was such a popular person in our community, someone folks counted on for a sympathetic ear or a helping hand. And now the people who had borrowed her ears and hands have come to offer their *condolences* to me. Why? What does this accomplish?

With less than a half-hour left of the viewing, Aunt Cassie finally shows up. I'm relieved she doesn't have Jimmy the Jerk with her. She's wearing a very wrinkled, very short, lacy black dress, accessorized with lots of Mom's beautiful jewelry, which just makes her dress look that much worse. For twenty minutes, Aunt Cassie stands between me and the casket and laughs too loudly at whatever anyone says, funny or not. Her laughter is shrill and harsh and bounces off the walls of the viewing room.

Noon finally arrives. Father Nick says a short prayer and then we all put on our coats, go out in the arctic weather, climb into our salt-covered cars, and drive to our church on the other side of town. I ride in the back of a stretch limo with Aunt Cassie, who keeps taking swigs from a Poland Springs water bottle she pulls from her purse. By the smell of her breath, I can tell the clear liquid in the bottle isn't water.

The funeral mass begins with a Bach fugue performed well by Julius Whitford, the church's organist, and one of Mom's former students. As the music fills the church, Aunt Cassie and I process in after Mom's casket. The funeral director has put it on a skirted, wheeled rack that reminds me of the carts I've seen waiters use to push around trays of food in fancy restaurants. As I walk slowly behind the coffin, I smile at the thought of Mom being an entrée. Maybe eggplant parmesan, her favorite? I lean over toward Aunt Cassie to share my stupid joke with her but then she stumbles and I remember how drunk she is, so I don't bother.

Aunt Cassie and I sit in the front pew, right there for everyone to stare at. After everyone else is seated, Mrs. Fox reads a psalm. I can't make myself pay attention to it. Then Aunt Cassie slurs and stumbles over a short Bible verse, loudly bumping her nose into the microphone—three times. The top button of her dress comes undone and I see that she's wearing a white lacy bra under her black dress. For some reason, I find that funny, too. I've never felt sadder in my life, and yet I'm giggling. Why? Maybe I *am* going crazy.

Father Nick steps to the pulpit. "We are gathered here today to say our goodbyes to a truly remarkable woman," he begins. Since Mom and I attended church here regularly, he's talking about someone he actually knew personally. But as he starts to list her many accomplishments and kindnesses, I realize that neither Father Nick nor anyone else in that church really *knew* Mom the way I did.

No one knew about the tea party Mom and I'd had when I was four, and she'd taken a sip and remarked that the tea was "jolly good."

In response, I'd loudly plunked my cup into my saucer and sulked.

"What's wrong?"

"Tea parties are for stupid babies."

"Who told you that?"

"Olivia."

"Are you stupid?"

"No."

"Are you a baby?"

"No."

"Are we having a jolly good tea party?"

"Yes."

"Then I guess Olivia is wrong."

No one in the church knew about the time when I was five and she'd pointed to the gold letters above our baby grand piano's keys. "Middle-C is right below the *Y* in Yamaha. Find the *Y* and you'll find middle-C."

"But what if we get another piano, Mommy? One with a different name?" I asked.

She brushed my hair away from my forehead. "This piano will always be here, honey. Just like me." She hadn't meant to lie.

No one else at Mom's funeral knew about the time when I was twelve and I'd found Mom sitting in our parlor, her metal knitting needles clinking like tiny wind chimes.

"What are you making?" I asked.

"A pair of mittens for you."

"Why?"

"Because those little piggies of yours work magic on a keyboard, and I want to protect them from the cold."

"What if I quit playing piano right now? Would you still knit me the mittens?"

"Of course."

"Why?"

"Because I love you."

And Father Nick didn't know about the time when I was fourteen and Mom had stared down an entire orchestra for me. I had been the guest soloist with the Boston Symphony Orchestra, and a few of the musicians had laughed about BC being with me during the performance, in his bed on top of the piano. Mom had mounted the conductor's platform, glared at the offending violinists, and said, "Rebecca feels more comfortable playing with her cat onstage with her. Does anyone have a problem with that?"

Mom had been my protector, teacher, manager, champion, and friend. Sitting at her funeral in that hard church pew, listening to Father Nick's eulogy with Aunt Cassie snoring softly beside me, I can't imagine how I'm going to live without her.

⁓

It's eight p.m. by the time the last of the guests finally leaves the reception at our house. Aunt Cassie and Mrs. Fox clean up the kitchen while I sit at the table and cuddle BC. He hasn't said a word since this morning, so I guess I'm done with my *auditory hallucinations* now that Mom is buried. I'm going to miss hearing BC talk—he always said kind things—but I'll be glad not to worry about going crazy. I've got enough to deal with.

After the dishes are done, the three of us gather around the fireplace in the parlor. I stab at a burning log with the poker while Mrs. Fox and I sip chrysanthemum tea from delicate china cups. Aunt Cassie is drinking something much stronger from her teacup. I look around and notice how plain the room looks. This morning before the funeral, I'd considered putting up some of Mom's Christmas decorations, but it had seemed pointless since she isn't here to enjoy them.

"Dear," Mrs. Fox says to me, "have you notified the Guinness World Records people that you won't be completing the B32 challenge this year?"

"What do you mean?" I ask.

"Well, the last concert is supposed to be in two weeks, isn't it?"

I nod. "Plus, there's another one scheduled for Mohegan Sun Casino next Friday, as a warm-up for the Courthouse show."

"That's much too soon after your mother's death for you to be performing again. No one would possibly expect that of you."

I feel completely lost. What am I going to do all day if I'm not practicing for my next concert?

"Wait a minute," Aunt Cassie says, sitting up abruptly. "Maggie would have."

"Margaret would have what, dear?" Mrs. Fox asks.

"She would have expected Becca to play those shows. And so would Dad—Becca's grandpa. That's the O'Sullivan way: 'Our word is our bond.'"

"Whatever are you talking about?"

Aunt Cassie juts her chin toward me. "You should tell the Gronk story."

Mrs. Fox frowns. "I have no idea what a Gronk story is, but if it will explain what you're talking about, please go ahead." She sits back on the sofa, places her swollen feet up on the ottoman, and takes a sip of her tea.

Aunt Cassie urges me on with another nod.

I'm wiped out and don't want to talk, but I can see Aunt Cassie is determined, so I sigh, take a deep breath, and begin. "Grandpa loved the New England Patriots football team. His favorite player was a tight end named Rob Gronkowski. Grandpa thought Gronk looked and acted like a good ol' farm boy, which was a major compliment coming from Grandpa, of course. Even after Grandpa got sick, he and I still spent most Sundays on the living room sofa, rooting for Gronk and the Pats. The time we watched the games together was special, something the two of us shared ever since I was big enough to know what a football was."

Mrs. Fox nods and takes another sip of her tea.

"But Grandpa had never seen the Patriots play live. So, last year, when one of Mom's students gave her two box seats to an upcoming game, she came running out to me in the barn, where I was feeding the animals. 'Look what Basma's father gave us!' she said, waving the pair of tickets.

"I said, 'That's great, Mom. You and Grandpa get to go to the game.' I must admit I felt pretty jealous.

"Mom smiled and said, 'No, silly. I'm driving you and Grandpa there.'

"I was very excited about going to a real live Patriots game with Grandpa, but when Mom and I showed him the tickets that night at dinner, he said he couldn't go. He'd promised George Wilson that he'd be on his team for the tractor pull at the Grange's fall festival on the same day as the game. Grandpa felt he had to give up the chance to see Gronk and the Pats live so that he could keep his word to his friend.

"Grandpa said, 'A man's word is his bond. I can't go running off on George just because I got a better offer somewhere else. I promised him I'd help him out at the Grange festival, and that's where I'll be.'

"So, three weeks later, Mom and I went to see the Patriots play the Dolphins. Down on the field after the game, Rob Gronkowski—who was *huge*—listened as we told him about Grandpa and how he was such a big fan. With a big, boyish grin, Gronk signed a jersey, 'To my pal, Patrick. From your fan, Gronk.'

"Grandpa loved that shirt and wore it to watch every Patriots game from then on. One Sunday, a few weeks later, he had it on in his room at the hospice center where he'd moved for the *end game*, as he called it. We were watching the Pats clobber the New York Jets and I said, 'So, Grandpa, tell me the truth. Are you sorry you didn't go see that game in Foxboro?'

"He winked, pointed to the small, plastic trophy next to his television, and said, 'And miss out on winning second place at the Grange's tractor-pull contest? *Never!*'"

As I finish telling the story, I pull a lace hankie from my pocket and wipe away tears I hadn't been aware were streaming down my face. I'm still so sad about Grandpa dying. How am I supposed to cope with Mom being dead now, too?

Aunt Cassie says, "So, that's the Gronk story, and that's why Dad and Maggie would have wanted Becca to play the Mohegan Sun gig next week, and the Courthouse gig after that. She signed contracts, giving her word that she'd be there, and her word is her bond."

Mrs. Fox shakes her head, looking very tired. "Well, if you both feel that way, I'll certainly do what I can to help you get ready for those shows, Rebecca, but I'm afraid I can't take any more time away from Howard. You'll have to come over to my house for lessons."

I ask Aunt Cassie, "Can you drive me?"

"When?"

"If the first show is in a week, we'd best get started right away," Mrs. Fox says. "How about tomorrow morning at ten?"

Aunt Cassie says, "Yeah, but Becca, you need to get your license. I'm not going to be your personal chauffeur forever."

"I'll start working on it," I promise. "But, Aunt Cassie, if we're going to do these two concerts, there are other things you'll need to do this week, too—as my manager, I mean."

"Like what?"

I hesitate, afraid she'll refuse. "Umm...like, call Mohegan Sun and get everything set up for the show next Friday. And then call Dave Morales at the Courthouse Center and fix things for that one, too, the following Saturday."

"Sure. Whatever." She answers her ringing phone. "Hey, Jimmy. Yes, it's all over. Come pick me up. I could use a drink." She chuckles and wanders out of the room, still talking to him, her short dress hiked up so high I can see her undies. *Yuck.*

Mrs. Fox nods toward Aunt Cassie's back with a frown puckering her already wrinkled face. "I'm not sure how much help she is going to be for you, Rebecca."

I paste on a smile. "Oh, she's just a bit overwhelmed tonight, with the funeral and everything. She'll be fine." Of course, Aunt Cassie has been *overwhelmed*—i.e., drunk—ever since the day Mom died, but I don't bother to mention that.

"I do hope so." Mrs. Fox looks at her wristwatch. "My word! Look how late it is."

She slowly climbs to her feet and I help her into her coat and out to her car.

"So, I'll see you tomorrow morning?" she asks.

"Ten o'clock," I say, and then watch as she carefully drives away just as Jimmy slides to a stop in front of the house.

Aunt Cassie brushes past me and hops into his car, calling out, "Don't wait up!" They peel out, fishtailing all the way down the snowy driveway.

Back inside the farmhouse, I say to BC, "If Aunt Cassie's going out drinking with Jimmy now, I doubt she's going to get up tomorrow morning, so I'll be walking the two miles to Mrs. Fox's house. Right?" I don't expect BC to answer me. I'm just whining.

But he does. "Did you actually believe she was going to help you?" he asks.

Clearly, BC *hasn't* stopped talking, which means I probably *am* going crazy. Good to know. I grab my gloves and head out to the barn for the evening feeding and milking, wondering what new *awfulness* tomorrow will bring.

Coping

Three days later, I crouch on my dining room floor with my back flattened against the front wall and my head ducked below the sill of the bay window. In my arms, BC squirms and hisses, his black-and-white fur standing on end like the bristles of a brush.

"Please, be quiet!" I beg him.

The doorbell rings again.

"Is anybody home?" a male voice calls out from the porch.

"Read the note," I mutter. I just can't handle making small talk with another person. So many have called or stopped by the farmhouse in the past few days to offer their *condolences* and their pitying looks, and I just can't stand it anymore. So, I taped a note to the door, asking the delivery person to leave the groceries in the empty coolers I put on the porch.

Since I hear nothing else, I roll to my knees, trapping the cat between me and the wall, and peek over the windowsill. At first, all I can see is the back of some guy's ski hat as he reads my note. But then, when he turns slightly, I recognize him by his curly hair and dark eyes and complexion: Dak Ronen, Mom's never-to-be future piano student. What's he doing here, freezing on my front porch?

I wish Aunt Cassie could answer the door. She'd probably like flirting with a cute guy like Dak, even if he is my age. She might even get a kick out of the whole older woman / younger man *cougar* thing. But Aunt Cassie isn't here. She hasn't been home at all since the night of Mom's funeral and hasn't even bothered to answer my calls or texts. I was *really* hoping that she'd stick around the house more because I would *really* love her company—provided she went back to being nice to me. She and I used to have a lot of fun together. And I could *really* use her help, too. For one thing, if she were home more, she could have gone to the grocery store and I wouldn't have had to arrange for this stupid delivery.

For a second, I consider ignoring Dak by ducking down again and waiting for him to leave, but in my head, I can hear Mom scolding me, saying, "I raised you better than that."

"Fine!" I say, releasing BC, who claws my arm as he jumps away. Pulling up the sleeve of my sweatshirt, I find inch-long scratches on my forearm, all four of them oozing a few drops of blood. Hoping they won't interfere with Friday night's concert, I hurry to the front door and yank it open, startling Dak, who jumps back, slips on some ice, and catches himself on the railing, barely avoiding falling off our porch.

He rights himself and laughs. "Hi, Rebecca. I'm not sure if you remember me, but I'm—"

"Dak Ronen—I know. What do you want?" Inwardly I wince, knowing Mom would have objected to my sassy tone. "That's no way to speak to a visitor," she would have said.

With a ski-gloved hand, he points behind him to the grocery store van. "I saw your order come in and volunteered to deliver it."

"You *volunteered*?"

"Well, I work at Frank's Market. I don't usually do deliveries, but I wanted to stop by to tell you how sorry I was to hear about your mom. She was a nice lady."

Great. More *condolences*. And he'd said two out of three of the funeral home phrases, too. Cute as he is, I didn't like him when he came to see me backstage after my last concert, and my opinion of him isn't improving much now.

We stare awkwardly at each other.

He gestures toward the van again. "Do you want me to bring in your food?"

What I *want* is to get back to practicing, so, I say, "Just leave the stuff here on the porch. I can take it in the house later."

"Technically, I'm supposed to bring it inside for you. It's part of the service."

"Fine. Whatever." Letting him bring in the food will probably take less time than arguing with him. I hold the door as he carries in four boxes of groceries from the van. I'm glad he doesn't comment about the burnt food and dirty dishes in the sink.

For the past three days, I've been trying to manage on my own, without Mom, and without Aunt Cassie, too. I'm eighteen years old, for Pete's sake. I should be able to deal with normal day-to-day tasks by myself. But nothing's going right. Not my attempts at cooking—everything keeps burning, and I can't find half the ingredients for any of the recipes I download. Or my piano practicing—even with Mrs. Fox's help, I still have *no idea* how to play the last four Beethoven sonatas, and my next concert is on Friday, just four days away. And then, of course, I have to deal with BC the Talking Cat. Since the funeral, his comments are no longer soothing and helpful but instead have become annoying questions that make me double-think everything. I don't know what to do about him. Or anything.

Dak helps me unload the food from the boxes and store it in the refrigerator and kitchen cabinets. When we're done, I realize I should tip him, but I don't have any cash.

"Do you want a cup of coffee?" I ask lamely. Coffee's the one thing I've figured out how to make.

Dak accepts with a nod and a crooked smile. While I brew the pot, he mops up the floor with some paper towels, cleaning up the snow and ice he's tracked in on his boots. Thoughtful of him.

We sit at the kitchen table, sipping from steaming mugs.

Dak asks, "Do you live here by yourself now?"

Just then, BC saunters into the kitchen and hisses at Dak. I pick him up, wondering why he's being unfriendly. Usually, he greets new people at the house with leg rubs and purrs. Come to think of it, he hasn't been purring much for me either these past few days. I hope he's not sick. I'll ask him later.

To Dak I say, "BC and I live here. And my Aunt Cassie, too. She just moved back in, but she works a lot, so she isn't home very much, which is why I had to have the food delivered." What is it about this guy that makes me say such *stupid* things? I mean, I don't usually babble like such a moron.

"So, you don't have a car? Me neither." He points to his grocery store uniform shirt. "I'm working this second job to make money to buy one."

"I guess technically I do have a car now—my mom's," I say quietly.

"Oh. What kind is it?"

"A 1967 Pontiac GTO convertible. She and my grandpa restored it together when she was in high school."

Dak's mouth drops open, like in the cartoons. "You have a '67 Goat Convertible?"

I point toward the back of the house. "Out there in the barn. But I don't know how to drive it."

"Standard transmission?"

"I have no idea. I don't know how to drive *any* car."

He frowns. "What do you mean?"

"I never got my driver's license." I feel my face turning splotchy red with embarrassment, expecting him to make fun of me.

But he doesn't. He's quiet for a moment and then he flashes another one of his lopsided smiles. "Can I see it?"

"The car?"

He nods.

"Sure, I guess." At least I won't have to sit awkwardly here in the kitchen with him anymore. I deposit BC on my chair and put on my boots and coat.

Out in the barn, I flick on the overhead lights, which are instantly reflected a hundred times in the acre of shiny blue steel and chrome that is Mom's Goat. She always took great care of it, waxing and polishing it so that there isn't a speck of rust anywhere on it.

Dak walks slowly around the Goat, checking out its four round headlights, split radiator grille, and eight rectangular taillights. "This is way cool. I've never seen one like this before."

"Mom told me there were only about 9,500 of this model ever made."

He points toward the driver's door. "Do you mind?"

I'm not happy about the idea of someone sitting in Mom's car and trespassing on her territory. At the same time, I'm pretty sure if she were here, she'd encourage his curiosity, so I shrug.

Dak slides into the black leather bucket seat. "Just look at this wood steering wheel and dashboard." He shakes his head of curly hair. "They certainly don't make cars like this anymore." Stepping out, he gently closes the door and walks around the Goat once more. "Your mom and grandpa did a great job restoring her."

I smile. Mom would have enjoyed Dak's compliment.

Back in the kitchen, Dak pulls off his coat and ski gloves. "So, you don't know how to drive?"

So, he *is* going to tease me, after all. I'm instantly angry. "I had other things to do, you know. Like winning piano competitions, performing with nationally known orchestras, and graduating from high school early." I cuddle BC on my lap, wishing Dak would leave.

But instead, he raises his palms. "I'm not criticizing you. I'm just thinking about an exchange of services." Now he sounds like a slick salesman.

"What do you mean?" I ask warily.

"Well, I was thinking I could teach you how to drive your mom's car since it might come in handy for you now. Especially with your aunt gone so much."

"Why would you do that?" Was he trying to trick me out of the car somehow?

"In exchange, you could teach me to play the piano—enough for me to pass my audition for entrance into URI's School of Music. A straight trade: driving lessons for piano lessons. One for one."

I frown. "I've never taught a piano lesson in my life."

He shrugs. "How hard can it be? I already know how to read music, so you won't have to worry about that part of it. Just the piano-playing part."

"And you'd teach me how to drive?"

He nods.

"Have you ever taught anyone to drive before?"

"I'm teaching my little sister right now."

"I thought you said you don't have a car."

"I said I don't *own* a car. I have to borrow my mom's or bum a ride from a friend whenever I want to go somewhere."

"Oh." I scratch BC under the chin, but he doesn't purr.

"So, do we have a deal?" Dak asks.

I do a quick assessment of his proposal. Plusses: I'll be able to get my license and won't have to rely on Aunt Cassie—or anyone else—to drive me places or deliver my groceries. And being able to drive a car may help me feel more in control of my life, which would be a good thing because everything feels so out of control right now. Minuses: I'm not sure if I can handle driving. What if I run into something and wreck the Goat? That would be *awful*. And I'd have to spend more time with Dak, who is annoying...but kind of cute. So, how bad would his deal be? I mean, I can always cancel out of it, right?

"I guess we could give it a try," I say.

"Great." He smiles as he shrugs on his coat. "How about starting Wednesday? I'll stop by here on my way home from school. Around two-thirty?"

I nod and we exchange phone numbers.

At the door, he looks at me with his dark eyes. "Becca, I know you don't know me very well yet but I'm a really good listener. If you ever want to talk about your mom, or whatever, you can give me a call. Okay?"

I nod again. As I watch the van drive away, I wonder if Dak's just being nice to me so I'll teach him piano or if he might actually like me. I've never had a guy interested in me before—not really. It all seems so complicated. And I probably shouldn't even be *thinking* about going out with someone. Not with Mom just dying. I shouldn't even want to.

BC sneezes violently five times and then slowly walks away.

"Are you getting sick?" I ask him, but he doesn't answer. I sure hope he's okay. I couldn't handle anything happening to him right now.

I'm still in the kitchen a few minutes later when I see Aunt Cassie's beat-up pickup truck lumber up our frozen driveway. She clomps into the house, looking hungover but more or less sober for the first time since Mom's death. What's the occasion? I wonder.

Dropping her coat on one of the ladder-back chairs, she looks around the messy kitchen and huffs, "You know, Becca, it wouldn't kill you to clean up a bit."

I quickly pick up my coffee mug and carry it over to the sink. "I've been trying to work on those sonatas for the Mohegan Sun concert Friday. Mom always told me that my job was to practice for the concerts and that she'd take care of everything else."

"Yeah well, your mom's not here, and I don't have time to clean up your shit." Maybe she's not drunk, but she's still being mean. She turns on the water, squirts some dish soap into the sink, and sighs tiredly. "You say you've been practicing for the show...How's that going?"

"Not great, actually. Mrs. Fox teaches me differently than Mom did. I don't know what I'm supposed to be doing with the sonatas. They just feel like a group of notes with no soul. I just wish..." I stop talking when I realize she isn't listening to me at all.

After a few moments of silence, she looks up from the sink and mutters, "I'm sure you'll do fine. You always do."

"Okay. But, how about those things you were going to take care of for the show?"

"Oh yeah. I forgot. What do I have to do, again?" She dumps some of the crusty dishes into the soapy water.

I pull a sheet of paper from my jeans pocket and lay it on the counter next to her. "I found this contract with a checklist in Mom's office. I think it covers everything."

Aunt Cassie swipes her hair from her eyes, leaving a trail of soap bubbles on her forehead. Looking at the list, she says, "Twenty-five things? Shit. By Friday?"

"Actually, you should probably take care of them before that, like maybe today."

She grunts and goes back to washing the dishes.

"And I have another piano lesson with Mrs. Fox on Wednesday at one o'clock. Do you think you could give me a ride?" I've walked the two miles to and from both of my lessons so far.

"One p.m. Wednesday. Sure thing."

"And John Foster called. He and Sally Johnson want to get together with you this week to discuss their contracts for leasing our cornfields next year. That's his number." I point to a pad of paper by the house phone.

She shakes her head slowly. "Anything else?"

"I ordered some groceries for us," I offer. "They were just delivered."

"You did something useful," she mutters. "Good for you." She looks up at the wall clock. "Shit. I've got to change and get back to the pub. I'm on for lunch *and* dinner today." She drops the sponge into the still-full sink.

"But you're going to take care of all those things—for the concert and the farm—right?"

She waves a hand over her shoulder as she runs up the stairs. "Yup. Sure thing."

A half-hour later, Aunt Cassie leaves for the pub, dressed in her all-black waitress uniform, wearing a ton of makeup and silver jewelry. I deposit BC in his piano bed and stare at the sheet music for the last four Beethoven sonatas. At my lessons so far, rather than telling me how to play the pieces, like Mom would have done, Mrs. Fox keeps saying I should *feel* the music. I have no idea what that means. And every time I try to practice here at home, I think about Mom, lose my concentration, and cry.

Now, I do my warm-up scales fine but don't even get halfway through the first sonata before I find myself staring out of the parlor window at the leafless, snow-covered trees and empty cornfields, missing Mom *terribly*. I miss her smile. The sound of her voice. How she tucked her hair behind her ears. The way she snorted when she laughed. And she did laugh—*a lot*—with me, because we found the same things funny, things that other people didn't understand. Will I ever laugh again, without her? Tears fill my eyes as I smack my hands on the keys, shaking the piano and waking BC.

He stands up in his bed and slowly stretches, first his front legs and then his back. Settling on his haunches, he focuses his yellow eyes on me. "Are you quite sure you must do these last performances? They seem to be too much for you to handle."

"Mom would have wanted me to do them."

"I'm sure she'd have understood if you postponed them a month or two."

"I can't postpone them. To get the world's record, I have to perform all thirty-two Beethoven sonatas before the end of the year."

He clacks his tongue twice. "There's always next year."

"I gave my word that I'd do these two shows. And my word—"

"—is your bond. Yes, I know. O'Sullivan code of conduct, and all that bullshit."

BC is certainly not being as nice as he was last week.

He yawns. "It sure would be easier for you—and me—if you didn't do the shows. No one would blame you...poor little orphan girl, and all that. They'd understand." He hops from his bed to the bench to the floor and strolls out to the kitchen, holding his black tail straight up in the air.

The idea of canceling the shows and taking off from piano for a few weeks—or months—seems very appealing right now. I could curl up in bed with BC and watch old movies on my laptop, twenty-four/seven. Just until things settle down, until I feel better. I would miss playing the piano—I really do love it—but maybe some time away from the keyboard would help me reassess my priorities now that

Mom's...*gone*. I mean, I don't know what I really want to do, and I don't know who to ask for advice, either. Aunt Cassie is so wound up in her own life—working at the pub, dating Jimmy, drinking beer, and partying. Plus, she's supposed to be taking care of the farm and managing my career, so I shouldn't ask her to deal with my emotional issues, too, right? Mrs. Fox is so old and has her hands full already, taking care of Mr. Fox, who seems to be slipping more and more every day, so I shouldn't burden her, either. I completely dumped Olivia, Hayley, and Chelsea last year, so I can't go crying to them now. Dave Morales was Mom's friend, so talking to him would be *weird*. I hardly know Dak Ronan so that wouldn't work, either. BC—well, he's a *cat*. And there's no one else. Bottom line: My life is completely screwed up, and I've got *nobody* to help me.

I can't practice and I don't want to eat, so I climb the stairs to my bedroom with BC trailing behind me.

Lessons Gone Wrong

Wednesday afternoon, I sit alone at Mrs. Fox's piano. This lesson is not going well either. Aunt Cassie didn't show up to drive me—no surprise there—so I had to trudge the two miles through the snow to Mrs. Fox's house again, arriving out of breath and sweaty despite the cold weather. And then, almost as soon as I got here, Mr. Fox called out from the bedroom, saying he needed Mrs. Fox's help to stop a cyberattack on London. As she left the room, squeaking down the hall in her velour jogging suit and orthopedic sneakers, she said, "Start playing the first piece, Rebecca. I'll be listening," which is not much help for me with a concert just two days away.

I spread out the ten sheets of music for Beethoven's *Sonata No. 29* because I still don't have it completely memorized. It's one of the most difficult pieces of classical music there is and I have no idea how I'm going to manage to play it well—or even halfway decently—for the show. I position my hands over the keys and correctly strike the opening chords. But by the time I reach the twenty-fourth measure, halfway down the second sheet of music, I've lost my concentration.

BC, who I left sleeping back at the farmhouse, has been talking to me even more over the past two days, urging me to cancel my upcoming concerts. I know he probably isn't *actually* speaking, but it sure seems real. I wish he'd talk when Aunt Cassie is around, so I could get a reality check on the situation. But Aunt Cassie hasn't been around much anyway. She stops by to shower and change her clothes once in a while and then heads right back out the door. I don't know if she's taken care of the managerial tasks for my concerts, either. I've so much to worry about with trying to learn the sonatas, I don't feel like I can handle the business stuff, too. But whenever I ask Aunt Cassie about it, she ignores me, which makes me nervous.

And it makes me *mad* at Mom. I am really, really pissed off at her because *all* of this is her fault: the cat talking, the messy kitchen, the empty refrigerator, me not being ready for this concert Friday—everything. If she hadn't ignored her appendicitis symptoms, given up, and died, none of this would be happening to me now. How did she expect me to deal with all of this without her? I know I shouldn't feel this way about Mom—she certainly didn't *plan* to die—but I do.

Mrs. Fox totters back into her piano parlor and sits down heavily on her teacher's chair. "Oh, my goodness. Howard's back to being James Bond today, which makes him happy, but makes my life a bit more difficult. He just insisted that I find him the phone number for the prime minister of England. So, I gave him the number for Filippo's Pizza. He's chatting about cybersecurity with Nikko, the owner, right now." She chuckles. "Never a dull moment." Pointing to my sheet music, she asks, "Why did you stop playing?"

"I can't seem to concentrate." I don't want to tell Mrs. Fox about being mad at Mom. She'd think I was a terrible person.

"It's no wonder, dear," she says. "Are you sure there's no way I can convince you to cancel or at least postpone these concerts?" Both she and BC, with their similar round faces and fuzzy hair, are trying to talk me out of performing. Maybe I should listen to them.

I sigh, feeling exhausted. "Mom worked so hard to set up these shows and to work out the deal with Guinness for the national tour. If I don't go through with them now, I'll feel like I'm letting her down. Big time."

Mrs. Fox presses her lipsticked lips together and pats my hand. "Okay, dear, let's see what we can do."

I play the first movement badly and then stop. "So, what should I be thinking about while I perform this? What images should I have in my mind?" I haven't been able to come up with stories to go along with any of the last four sonatas.

"I don't know, dear. Can't you just play the piece the way Beethoven wrote it?"

"Mom always suggested stories—she called them *soundtrack images*—that match the music. They help me remember the pieces and remind me to play them in a certain way."

"Oh, well, that's not something I ever taught Margaret. She must have come up with that technique on her own. I'm afraid I won't be able to help you with that."

I feel even more lost and confused.

"Why don't you just play them and we'll see how they go," she says.

An hour later, we've only made it through two of the four sonatas—*poorly*—and are working on the second movement of *No. 31* when Mr. Fox calls out loudly, "For God's sake, send ballistic reinforcements—now!"

Mrs. Fox nods toward the mantel clock. "We might as well call it a day, anyway. Your aunt is due to pick you up any minute."

"But what about the rest of this piece...and all of *No. 32*?"

"You seem to be on track, now. You'll be fine."

"In two days?" I've never felt so unprepared for a concert in my life. I don't even have the pieces fully memorized yet, for Pete's sake.

From down the hall, Mr. Fox yells, "Lay down some sniper fire, you imbeciles!"

"I'd better go," Mrs. Fox says, slowly rising from her chair. "I'll try to come to your show on Friday. It depends on how Howard is doing." She shuffles away.

⁓

Aunt Cassie doesn't show up to pick me up after my lesson—*big surprise*—and won't answer my calls or texts, so I speed-walk the two miles home from Mrs. Fox's, trying to get there before my scheduled lessons with Dak. I almost make it, too. He catches up to me just as I pass our empty farmstand at the entrance to our driveway. "Need a ride?" His smiling face leans out the driver's window of a small silver car.

I'm cold, tired, worried, mad, and a dozen other emotions, so I wordlessly hop in, wondering if I made a mistake by agreeing to these lessons.

As we roll to a stop in the snow in front of my house, he says, "Since we're already here in the car, do you want to start with your driving lesson?"

I frown. "I thought you were going to teach me to drive my *mom's* car."

"I will. But this car's an automatic, so it's easier to drive. I thought we might start with it and then graduate to the Goat after a few lessons."

"I don't have time right now to learn how to drive *one* car, let alone *two*. The deal was you were going to teach me to drive *Mom's* car. Let's stick to the deal."

He does a palms-up. "If that's what you want. Do you have the keys to the Goat?"

I hold up my mittened hand, showing him the keyring Mom gave me on my birthday less than two weeks ago. I remember her smiling eyes when she handed it to me.

"Okay, let's go," he says.

My heart hurts from missing Mom so much, and I feel so tired. But it seems like too much of an effort to cancel our plans, so I follow Dak to the barn.

He slides open the huge doors. "Do you want to try backing it out of the barn?" he asks.

Looking at all of the Goat's gauges and levers, the idea of driving it seems completely overwhelming to me. What if I scratch or dent it? I shake my head.

"Okay." He takes the keys from me. "Just wait here."

The car rumbles to life, emitting a small puff of blue smoke from its chrome tailpipe. Dak slowly backs it out, turns it around, and leaves it running with its long nose pointed toward the house. "Wow. This baby's got a lot of power. This is going to be fun. Come on. Hop in." He holds the driver's door open for me.

The car looks huge and frightening and complicated—not my idea of *fun*.

Dak smiles encouragingly. "Hey, compared to those Beethoven pieces I heard you play at the Courthouse Center a few weeks ago, this is going to be a piece of cake."

I smile at his use of one of Mom's favorite sayings: *a piece of cake*. That's how she'd describe a new song I needed to learn so I wouldn't be afraid of it. She probably would have used that phrase, too, if she had been the one giving me this driving lesson instead of Dak.

I get into the driver's seat and he slides in on the other side. "Seat belts, everybody," he says. We click ours into place. Then he explains about a car's pedals, gears, brakes, blinkers, and a million other parts— way more than I can keep track of. By the time he finishes talking, I feel like my head's going to explode.

Dak smiles. "I can see from the look on your face that I've over-explained things again. My sister said I did that to her during her first lesson, too. Don't worry about it. Let's just get her rolling. Okay?"

I nod but wonder if I should bail out. Do I really *need* to learn to drive?

"Okay. With your right foot on the brake—that's the middle pedal—use your left foot to push the clutch to the floor. The one on the left."

I do as he says.

"Now, shift the car into first gear."

I consult the diagram on the wooden shifter knob and push it into first.

"You're doing great. Now, ease up on the clutch while you gently push down on the gas pedal with your right foot."

I shoot him a panicked look.

"You can do this. Just pretend they're the pedals on your piano."

I slowly lift my left foot while pushing the gas with my right. The car revs loudly, violently bucks forward three times while making terrible choking noises, and then comes to an abrupt stop with two tires buried in a snowdrift next to the driveway.

I cover my face with my mittened hands. "I *ruined* my mom's car."

"No, you didn't."

"Yes, I did. I killed it."

"Becca, you just stalled the engine. It's no big deal."

I slide down my hands and peek at him. "Are you sure?"

He nods. "Everyone does that when they're learning to drive stick shift."

"Stick shift?"

"Stick shift—standard transmission—same thing. Everyone stalls the engine at first."

"And it doesn't ruin the car?"

"I'll show you. Put it in neutral."

I shake my head.

He points his chin to the gearshift. "Come on. Just do it."

Reluctantly, I push down on the clutch and pull the shifter out of first.

Dak reaches over, twists the key, and the Goat roars to life immediately. "See? No harm done."

I exhale dramatically. "Good. Let's keep it that way. Would you please put the car back into the barn?"

"Don't you want to continue your lesson?"

"I've had enough fun for today. Please, just put the car away and meet me in the piano parlor." I hop out and hurry through the snow to the kitchen door.

A few minutes later, Dak joins me in the parlor, where I sit in Mom's teacher's chair, briskly stroking a purring BC. Being here with BC feels safe and comfortable to me. Way better than trying to learn to drive. Maybe I should just stick to the piano.

"The Goat's okay?" I ask.

"Just fine. Tucked away in the barn."

"Good." I point toward the piano. "Show me what you got."

He shrugs. "Like I told you, I don't know anything about a piano."

"But you know where middle-C is, right?" Even BC knows that.

"Nope."

"Nothing?"

He shakes his head.

"Oh." I have *no idea* what to do next.

"Did your mom have books that she used with beginner students?" Dak suggests.

"I'm sure she did, but I don't know where they are." Why didn't I plan out his lesson? Duh. How *embarrassing*. We look on the piano and in the nearby bookshelves but only find books for intermediate and advanced students. Inside the piano bench, however, we discover two books that claim to be "ideal for the beginning piano student."

Pointing to the date on the cover of the top book—1995—he chuckles. "I guess you've had these books around for a while."

113

When we open it, we find writing declaring it to be the "Property of Margaret O'Sullivan."

"Mom's first piano book," I say, with tears in my eyes.

We open the identical second book and discover that it's the "Property of Cassandra O'Sullivan."

"*Aunt Cassie?*" I say. "I didn't know she ever played the piano."

"Do you think she'd mind if I borrowed her book for a little while so I can learn the basics?"

"Do you have a piano at home to practice on?"

"Not yet. But my band buddy, Jonathan, is going to lend me one of his electronic keyboards starting this weekend. He's got a bunch of different ones, so he says he won't miss it."

"Okay. But first, I owe you an apology." I flash him a small smile.

"I don't know about the apology, but I do like to see you smile."

His kindness makes me blush. "Thanks. I know I was a bad driving student earlier, and now I've been a bad piano teacher. I'm worried about these two concerts I have coming up, and other stuff that's going on..." For a second, I think about telling him about my drunk aunt and my talking cat, but I can't. I don't want him to think I'm a pathetic nut case. "Anyhow, I'm sorry. I'll make it up to you."

"I forgot you had more concerts to perform. I guess I figured that you'd postpone them, with your mom and all. When are they?"

I sigh. "I'm performing at the Mohegan Sun Casino Ballroom in two days and at the Courthouse Center next Saturday."

"No wonder you're freaking out."

"And I'm having a lot of trouble getting ready for the concerts."

"I'm not surprised."

"Anyhow, if you'll wait until after the Mohegan Sun show, we can reschedule our lessons. I think I'll do a much better job the second time around."

"Sure. But if you want to wait until after the second concert, too, that would be fine with me."

I shake my head. "Let's plan to get together on Saturday morning at ten. That way, I'll have something to look forward to if I bomb at Mohegan Sun on Friday."

"Do you really think you're going to bomb?"

"It's a *definite* possibility."

"What time's the show?"

"Six. Why? Are you thinking about coming to it?" It might be good to have someone I know there for support, but at the same time, I don't want him to witness what is probably going to be a disaster.

"Six on Friday?" He frowns. "Unfortunately, I'm scheduled to coach a basketball game at the Boys and Girls Club that night. I might be able to find someone to cover for me, but I doubt it. Most folks don't like to work on Friday nights."

"You work at the Boys and Girls Club, too?"

"For five years, now. It's great helping out kids."

"Dave Morales, the stage manager at the Courthouse Center, works there, too. Do you know him?"

Dak nods. "He's my uncle."

"What? I didn't know that." But now that he mentions it, I can see the resemblance.

"He's my mom's brother, and he's the one who got me interested in working at the B and G in the first place."

"Is that what you want to do after college—work with kids?"

"In one way or the other, yes. I've applied to URI to double-major in music and education. I think it might be fun to teach music to kids in school, or at the B and G, or somewhere. I love all three—teaching, music, and kids—so picking that for a profession seems like a no-brainer." He stands. "Hey, if you've got a concert Friday night, I'm sure you want to get in some more practicing today. Right?"

I nod. Not that it will do me much good.

"Okay. Then I'll get going. And I'll plan on seeing you Saturday morning for a redo of our lessons. Good luck with the show."

"Thanks. I'm going to need it."

"I bet you'll do fine." With one last crooked smile, he slips on his coat and strolls out the door.

I smile as I lay out the sheets for *Sonata No. 31* on the piano's music stand. Contrary to my first impression of Dak, he *might* be a nice guy.

"You should watch out for that one, Rebecca," a raspy voice says from the sofa.

I turn to find a pair of yellow eyes staring my way. "What do you mean?"

"Boys like that use girls like you and then kick them to the curb like yesterday's garbage." BC struts from the room, swishing his black-and-white bottom.

The Night Before the Show

I practice the final four Beethoven sonatas until midnight on Wednesday and all day on Thursday, memorizing them, applying Mrs. Fox's meager advice, and then adding in what I think Mom would have suggested. But it doesn't help much. The songs sound *terrible*—like an amateur is playing them.

Late afternoon on Thursday, I take a break to grab some food, hoping some nutrition might help me to concentrate better. BC follows me into the kitchen and bats the cabinet with his paw, requesting an early dinner. He crunches his kibble and makes ugly faces at me as I slice an apple and slather on some peanut butter. BC certainly hasn't been much help to me in preparing for this show, with his repeated warnings for me to cancel it and steer clear of Dak Ronen, neither of which I want to hear. When BC first started talking right after Mom died, he was nice and comforting, but he's getting more and more critical of me, and I definitely don't need that. I'm really hoping once I finish my two concerts, I'll stop hearing him talk because the idea of having him ragging on me for the rest of my life makes me feel hopeless.

As I eat my apple, I ask him, "Why the eye-rolling?" I know I'm inviting more criticism, but it's way too quiet in the farmhouse.

"Because you won't listen to reason," he says. "I suppose you intend to go back to practicing after you finish your *dinner*?" He sneers at my apple-and-peanut-butter meal.

"If I keep working hard on the pieces until we leave for the show tomorrow afternoon, I might be able to play them well enough to get by."

"Whatever," he mumbles while licking a paw.

Our conversation is interrupted by a loud knock on the front door.

Farmers John Foster and Sally Johnson stand in the cold twilight on our porch. "Hi, Rebecca," Mr. Foster says, his red plaid, rabbit fur, earflap hat in his hands. "Is Cassandra here?"

I pick up BC and tuck him under my chin. "Not at the moment. Would you like me to give her a message?"

He frowns. "She told us to meet her here at five o'clock, to go over the leases for the fields for next year."

I pull out my phone. "It's after that time now." My call goes straight to Aunt Cassie's voicemail. "I'll...umm...tell her you were here."

"Thanks," he says. "That would be great."

"Told you this was going to be a waste of time," Mrs. Johnson mutters to Mr. Foster as the two of them tromp back down the snowy porch stairs to their pickup trucks.

I close the door, still cuddling BC.

"I sure hope Aunt Cassie manages your career better than she's managing the farm," BC says, hooking his claws into my sweater.

"She'll be fine. She just needs to figure out a few things."

"Hmmph."

I detach BC's claws from me, deposit him back in his piano bed, and return to practicing the first movement of *Sonata No. 32*, the last of the final four pieces. I swear it doesn't sound any better than it did two weeks ago. I've memorized it, but just barely. I often lose my place and have to look at the written music—something I can't do during the Courthouse show next week, not if I want to join the B32 Club. The soundtrack image I came up with—a puppy flouncing through a field of wildflowers—is lame, and doesn't help me play the sonata with any real feeling, but I can't think of a better narrative. Without Mom, nothing works. God, I *miss* her. I find myself sobbing—again. Will this terrible pain ever go away?

A few minutes later, I hear Aunt Cassie slam through the front door and then rummage in the refrigerator. She appears in the parlor with two bottles of beer. Shucking off her coat and slumping down on the couch in her work clothes, splattered with some sort of white sauce, she zaps on the TV next to the piano—the only TV in the house—and noisily chugs one of the beers. A raunchy movie about a drunken Santa Claus blares across the room, drowning out my pitiful attempts at playing Beethoven.

I drop my hands into my lap. I want to yell at Aunt Cassie. To tell her that she should stop drinking and be a whole lot nicer to me. Because she promised Mom that she would get sober and help me, and I could *really* use some of that help right now. But if I tell her how I feel, she might leave me altogether. And then where would I be? All alone in this big farmhouse with a failing concert career and a talking cat. Not a very good situation. So, instead, I say, "Mr. Foster and Mrs. Johnson were here a few minutes ago. They were supposed to meet with you to discuss farm business?"

She smacks her forehead. "Completely forgot. Oh well. I'll call them back and reschedule. It's not like the fields are going anywhere, right?" She chuckles at her own bad joke and returns her attention to the movie.

"Umm...any chance you could hold off on watching that movie for a little while?" I ask. "Or maybe watch it on your laptop somewhere else?"

"You like movies, right? Why don't you watch it with me? Get you in the mood for the season. Christmas is less than two weeks away, you know."

Mom *was* my Christmas. It was her enthusiasm that made the holiday special. Come to think of it, it was her attitude that made so many things worth doing, like playing piano, having a birthday party, or going for a ride in the car while singing along to the radio. Without her, nothing matters much. I sigh. "I have to get ready for my show at Mohegan Sun tomorrow. Which reminds me...Did you get the chance to call them and set up everything for the show?"

BC laughs—or coughs. I can't tell which.

"Yeah, whatever," Aunt Cassie says.

I glance at the clock and see that it's too late to call the casino tonight to verify the concert arrangements. Its business office is closed by now, so in the morning, I'll have to remember to ask Aunt Cassie to call them. Unless she already did, which is doubtful.

She holds out the other beer to me. "You want it?"

"I don't drink."

"Your loss." She chugs it down and then heads back to the kitchen, leaving the television blasting.

"You know," BC says, "your aunt might have the right idea."

"What, drinking? Beer isn't going to help me get ready for the concert."

He shakes his head so hard his ears flap. "It's not like you're going to get any better in the next few hours anyhow. If you haven't learned those pieces by now, you aren't going to know them by tomorrow night."

"That's not true. If I keep working on them—"

Aunt Cassie returns carrying two more beers and looks around. "Who are you talking to?"

"Oh...umm...just myself."

120

"Huh." She slides down on the sofa and clicks up the TV's volume a couple more notches.

BC leans toward me and whispers, "You know, your mom drank wine with dinner sometimes." His whiskers tickle my cheek. "And your grandpa had several beers every Friday night when he went to the dances at the Grange."

"You're not helping."

"I'm just saying, a drink might do you some good, relax you a bit, and help you get ready for the show. You should consider it."

Aunt Cassie hits the mute button. "Did you say something?"

I shake my head.

She holds up another beer. "You really should try one of these. Our liquor distributor at the bar gave them to me for free. They're from Ireland and they're not half bad."

BC stares fixedly at me.

"Oh, why not?" I reach out my hand.

Aunt Cassie's eyebrows shoot up as she gives me a bottle.

I say, "I'll watch the rest of this movie with you, but then I have to practice."

"Cool." She scoots over to make room for me on the couch.

Taking a sip of the beer, I find it has a nice, nutty flavor, kind of like drinking multigrain bread. I finish the bottle quickly, taking bigger and bigger sips, and then drink another one. It must be weak beer because the alcohol doesn't seem to have any effect on me at all. When the stupid Santa movie ends, *It's a Wonderful Life* comes on—one of my all-time favorites—so, we watch that one together, too, and I drink another beer. Hanging out with Aunt Cassie makes me feel a little less lonely.

The last thing I remember doing that evening is vomiting into the toilet while she holds my hair. *Yuck.*

The Mohegan Sun Casino Concert

On Friday morning, I notice there are two things wrong with the sun. First, it's much brighter than usual. And second, it's coming into my bedroom window at a much higher angle than normal for early morning. I roll over and the whole room rotates with me. My stomach gurgles, my head pounds, and my eyeballs feel like they're going to explode. Groaning, I sit up and find myself wearing the jeans and sweater I had on last night.

BC is perched on one corner of my bed, noisily gnawing on his claws and snickering at me. "Good morning, Mary Sunshine. Or I should say, good afternoon."

"What?" I grope for my phone. "One o'clock!" I scramble to my feet. "We're supposed to be at the casino at three for the sound check, and I still have to practice and iron my dress, and it's a one-hour drive. The show's at six and I'm nowhere near ready!" I can hear my heartbeat in my ears.

123

"Chill out, girl," BC says with a wide yawn. "It's not like anyone at Mohegan Sun cares about hearing some girl playing classical piano music. It's a gambling casino, for Pete's sake, not a symphonic hall."

I run down the hall and bang on Aunt Cassie's door.

"Get up! We have to leave for Connecticut in an hour."

I hear a prolonged groan.

"And don't forget to pack a bag, too," I call out. "They're giving us a room for the night."

Her door springs open. "Wait. We get to stay at the casino hotel? For free?"

"It's in the contract."

"Why didn't you tell me that before?" She grabs her phone and punches a speed dial number. "Hey," she says into the phone. "Pack a bag. We're going to Mohegan Sun!"

I wave her off, whispering, "We don't have time to pick up Jimmy." I don't want to be late—Mom would have considered that to be very unprofessional—and I *really* don't want Jimmy at my show.

"Relax. His place is on the way there." She closes the door but I can hear her continuing to make plans on the phone.

It takes me much more than an hour to feed the animals, grab a shower, press my dress (poorly), and shove my hair into an unattractive bun. Even though I know it will make us even later, I still try to run through the four sonatas one last time. But within minutes of sitting down at the piano, I'm staring at the keys with tears dripping from my chin, feeling *completely* overwhelmed.

BC huffs. "As I said, this isn't a real concert. No need to get yourself so worked up over it."

Mom and Grandpa would not have agreed.

I pack BC into his carrier, shove my arms into my dress coat, and lug him and his piano bed out to Aunt Cassie's truck in the snowy driveway.

"We're *not* bringing that cat with us," she says flatly. She's smoking a cigarette, leaning against the rusty tailgate.

"I've *never* performed without him, and this is my first concert without Mom. I *have* to have BC with me."

"I've always thought it childish for you to bring your pet with you to performances. Like a little girl with her dolly. Besides, we're staying at the casino hotel tonight. No way they're going to let you have a cat with you."

Why is she being so mean to me? Doesn't she see that I'm struggling? I plead with her, "I'm sure Mom made arrangements for him. Check the contract."

"Come on, Becca. We'll be back tomorrow morning. Just throw some extra cat food in his bowl and he'll be fine." She tosses her cigarette into the snow and checks her phone. "We'd better hit the road—we still have to pick up Jimmy."

We leave BC at the farmhouse.

~

At 4:45, I burst through the doors of the casino lobby with a garment bag slung over my shoulder, and my snow-covered boots squeaking on the stone tile floor. Aunt Cassie and Jimmy lag far behind me, strolling at a leisurely pace, carrying their own duffel bags and laughing. They're both dressed in ratty coats, torn jeans, and combat boots, and look more like homeless people than a couple about to attend a classical music concert. And Aunt Cassie is supposed to be my manager. *Hah.*

I rush up to the casino's front desk and then turn around, expecting Aunt Cassie to check us in. But instead, she and Jimmy disappear into the mouth of the gambling hall. My panic ratchets up another notch.

"May I help you?" The attractive woman behind the desk smiles pleasantly.

My garment bag slips off my shoulder and splats on the floor. "Umm...yes...I'm Rebecca O'Sullivan and I'm supposed to...I mean, I'm scheduled to perform a piano concert here...I mean, in the ballroom, tonight...at six." I pick up my bag, wishing I could be *anywhere* but here.

"Welcome, Ms. O'Sullivan." She hands me an envelope. "That's your hotel room information and keys, room 811. I'll let the stage director know you're here." She picks up the phone and punches a button with a long, dark red fingernail.

I look down at my chipped nail polish and cringe. It's still the same polish I had on for my last concert, two weeks ago. Mom always made sure I got a manicure before every performance. But of course, she wasn't here to schedule one for me this time. And I didn't think of it. Neither did Aunt Cassie. Just one more thing in my life that's messed up.

A tall man in a tailored blue suit approaches the desk. "Good afternoon, Ms. O'Sullivan. I'm Rahul Patel, the stage director for the casino's ballroom." He takes my garment bag and strides quickly past the waterfall and pool in the center of the lobby, making me jog to keep up with him. He says over his shoulder, "I'm glad you're here. When we hadn't heard from you and you weren't here for the sound check at three, I was afraid you might not be coming."

"Didn't my aunt...er...manager call you earlier this week to finalize arrangements?"

"I'm afraid not. So, we've prepared the stage using our best estimation of your requirements." He checks his watch. "With the show beginning in about an hour, there's not much time to make adjustments, though, so I hope you'll find everything to be satisfactory."

After a nearly ten-minute rush through multiple lobbies and down long, carpeted hallways, we finally arrive at the ballroom, where I find that everything is certainly *not* satisfactory. Far from it. The piano is white—not black, a no-name brand, absolutely enormous, and has the worst key action I've ever felt. There's no way I'll be able to play well on such an inferior instrument but Mr. Patel informs me that there is not enough time to get a different one. *Great.* Microphones are mounted inside the piano for amplification but they make the pieces sound like electronic exercise music rather than the melodies of Ludwig van Beethoven. And the stage spotlights are poorly positioned, causing a terrible glare off the white piano. When Mr. Patel asks me how he should adjust the microphones and lights to fix the problems, I have *no idea* what to tell him. Mom always handled those details.

I stare out at the rows of plush red velvet seats, imagining the faces of the audience members staring back at me. I look at the seat dead-center in the front row. For the first time in my life, Mom's smiling face won't be there when the curtain opens because she—the only person who ever really understood me—is dead. *Why?*

A few audience members walk into the ballroom to take their seats, so I grab my garment bag and escape to find my dressing room. I run into Aunt Cassie and Jimmy lurking outside the stage door, already unsteady on their feet and reeking of alcohol.

"There you are!" Aunt Cassie says. "I've been looking everywhere for you."

"I was onstage, trying to get ready for the performance. Mr. Patel told me that you didn't call ahead of time to set things up?"

"Whatever," she says. She waves a hand as if shooing away a fly.

Is that all I am to her—a pesky nuisance?

She asks, "Do you have a key to our hotel room? Jimmy and I want to get dressed for your show."

Glad to hear that at least she's not planning on wearing combat boots to my concert, I slap one of the key cards into her hand and then hurry backstage to change into my black gown, the same one I wore to the seventh concert at the Courthouse Center because Aunt Cassie didn't buy me a new one for tonight's show. She never even asked me what size I wear.

Five minutes before the show is scheduled to start, I'm sitting on the hard, white piano bench behind the closed curtain in the casino ballroom. I can't see another living soul. No Mom to encourage me. No BC to find middle-C for me. Not even a stage manager to smile at me and give me a thumbs-up. *No one.* I have never felt so alone in my whole life. My hands shake, my stomach is roiling, and my badly arranged hair sticks to my neck in ugly red curls. Too late, I realize I've forgotten to put on stage makeup. *Great.* I'll look even paler than usual. My dress is wrinkled and bunched up under me but I don't bother to do my smoothing ritual. What's the point? I feel sick. Why didn't I just cancel this concert like BC and Mrs. Fox suggested? *Stupid me.*

A pre-recorded woman's voice informs the audience of the nearest exits and asks them to turn off their cell phones, and then Mr. Patel does a poor job of introducing me, getting everything wrong, including announcing me as *Rebecca Sullivan*—no "O." Grandpa would have given him hell for that. With all my heart, I wish he and Mom were here. I hear a smattering of applause, the curtain goes up, and I find myself sitting at the ugly white piano on the bare black stage in front of fewer than fifty people in the Mohegan Sun Casino Ballroom. *Rebecca O'Sullivan: World-Class Flop.*

My eyes are automatically drawn to the center seat of the front row. I know Mom won't be there, but I look anyway—and I see Aunt Cassie, dressed in Mom's gown, the one she wore to my last concert. But it looks *terrible* on Aunt Cassie—like a silk drape on a skeleton, especially since she's wearing every piece of pearl jewelry Mom owned. They look like strings of teeth against her pale skin. I picture Mom in that gown: beautiful, smiling, and laughing with me. That night, before the seventh sonata show, Mom had told me I was gorgeous, amazingly talented, and played beautifully, but she didn't have to say any of those things. Just one look from her in her front-row seat was enough to give me the confidence I needed to perform. Tonight, no one is going to give me one of those looks—*especially* not Aunt Cassie—because she is slumped in her seat with her chin resting on Mom's pearl necklaces, completely passed out, with Jimmy snoring loudly next to her. Thanks, Aunt Cassie.

I play the four Beethoven pieces, *Sonata No. 29* through *No. 32*, one after the other, without an intermission, just to get them over with quickly. And I play them *terribly*. I stumble over some of the more difficult passages, completely forget to play others, use poor inflection and no emotion, giving—without a doubt—the *worst* performance of my life. During the entire hour-and-a-half show, tears drip slowly down my cheeks, mixing with my sweat. Some of them are tears of embarrassment since I have never been so badly prepared or played so poorly in my professional career. Some are tears of sadness because I miss Mom with every cell in my body. Some are tears of frustration as I keep wondering why no one is helping me. But, if I'm honest with myself, I know that most of the tears are tears of anger: Because why did Mom have to die and leave me in this mess? How did she expect me to be able to deal with everything? I'm only eighteen years old, for Pete's sake, and have *no idea* what I'm supposed to be doing. It's just not fair. I know I'm thinking like a spoiled rotten brat, and I hate it. Right now, I hate myself and my life, too.

I strike the final chord of the fourth sonata, stand up and bow, and am appropriately rewarded with lackluster applause that isn't even loud enough to wake up Aunt Cassie and Jimmy. Before the clapping dies away, I rush to my dressing room where I fall into an uncomfortable, non-swiveling, black chair, aching to cuddle BC in my arms and feel his soothing purr against my sweaty chest. Looking at my face in the mirror, I catch a glimpse of Mom. "I'm so sorry," I say to her as a flood of tears splashes into my empty lap.

A knock sounds on the dressing room door, making me jump. I quickly wipe my eyes with a lace hankie. Mom always carried a white hankie with her, wherever she went, and insisted that I do the same. Before, I'd always considered it a stupid, old-fashioned habit, but I am glad I remembered to bring one tonight—a little bit of Mom here with me in this awfulness. I hide the crumpled hankie in my fist. "Y-yes? Come in."

Mrs. Fox, dressed in a full-length fake fur coat and an azure evening gown, shuffles in wearing her tan orthopedic shoes and sits heavily in the chair next to mine. Patting my knee, she smiles kindly. "I know you tried your best out there, Rebecca O'Sullivan, and I want you to know that I am very proud of you."

I throw my arms around her and sob while she gently rubs circles on my back and says, "There, there," over and over again. Her kindness helps, but all I really want is Mom.

I finally calm down, and Mrs. Fox makes me wash my face and then sit knee-to-knee with her as she rests her soft hands atop mine. "I'm sorry I played so badly," I say. "I tried to do what you'd told me, but I just couldn't."

"Oh honey, *I'm* the one who should be apologizing to you. I've been so busy with Howard these days that I didn't give you the help you needed to prepare for this concert. And then you had to contend with that terrible piano and those glaring stage lights. My goodness!"

"Aunt Cassie is supposed to be handling those things now, but I guess she needs more time to learn the routine." I don't want Mrs. Fox to be disappointed in Aunt Cassie, too.

"I hope so, dear." She pats my hands gently. "But for now, I think you ought to consider canceling that last concert at the Courthouse Center next week. I know it's for the world's record, but it's putting too much pressure on you too soon after your mother's death." She boosts herself to her feet. "Let's not talk about that now. What you need, more than anything, is a good night's sleep. Are you planning to stay here at the hotel tonight?"

I nod.

"Would you like me to drive you home, instead? You could sleep in your own bed."

That sounds *wonderful*, but I don't want Aunt Cassie to think I abandoned her. Because I have to believe that somewhere underneath all of the booze and meanness is the sweet aunt I've known and loved all my life. The one who loves me, too. I say, "No, thanks. Aunt Cassie and her boyfriend are here and are probably wondering where I am."

"Will you be back at the farmhouse tomorrow morning?" Mrs. Fox asks.

"We're supposed to check out of here by nine a.m."

"Good. I'll stop by your place once I get Howard settled for the day and then we can talk about the Courthouse concert. Okay?" She pats my cheek. "I've got to go now."

I don't have the energy to change my clothes, so I just pick up my garment bag and follow her out to the lobby.

In front of the casino's towering glass doors, Mrs. Fox hugs me warmly. "Don't be hard on yourself for your performance tonight, dear. It was just too much for you to handle too soon. You were very brave to even try."

I kiss her pillow-soft cheek and watch her shuffle out into the cold night.

I wish BC was here with me. I could use some cuddles.

⟡

As I step off the elevator on the eighth floor of the casino hotel, I hear the thump-thump-thump of loud music pounding from a room halfway down the hall. Room 811—*of course*. With a swipe of my keycard, I open the room door to reveal two dozen strangers, laughing, drinking, sitting, and standing around the room. Rap music blares, all the lights are on, half-filled cups and bottles litter the room, and it smells like beer and sweat. It takes me a full minute to find Aunt Cassie splayed on Jimmy's lap on a sofa near the window, still wearing Mom's gown and pearls. The shoulder straps have slipped down her arms to reveal her pale, bony chest.

"Becca! There you are!" Aunt Cassie stands up unsteadily on a pair of Mom's dress heels and then holds up her arms and throws back her head in an exaggerated model's pose. "What do you think of my dress? I borrowed it from Maggie." She giggles. "I didn't think she'd mind, now that I'm your *manager*."

A large woman in an ugly silver gown twinkles her fingers at me from the other end of the sofa.

Aunt Cassie says, "We all came to see your show, Becca, and we thought you were *great!*" The people around her cheer, making me wonder how many of them slept through the concert, too.

I lean toward Aunt Cassie's ear and whisper, "Please could we go home now?"

Her face falls into an exaggerated pout and she collapses back onto Jimmy's lap, who gasps like a deflating balloon. "I don't want to go home. Me and my friends are having such a good time." Cupping her hands on either side of her mouth, she bellows, "Is everyone having a good time?"

The room erupts into hoots and shouts.

Aunt Cassie points her red plastic cup toward the suite's mini-bar. "Go get yourself a drink and chill out, girl. I've got some business to take care of." She wetly kisses Jimmy on the lips as the others on the couch cheer them on.

I go in search of my bedroom and find it occupied by a drunken couple sprawled out across a bed full of winter coats. "Umm, this is my room," I say, feeling very awkward. I stare at a woman's red handbag to avoid looking at the couple.

"We were here first," the woman says, and they go back to rolling around together.

All I want to do is go to sleep and forget everything. Maybe the casino would give me another room.

The guy looks up at me. "Are you still here? *Piss off!*"

Still lugging my garment bag, I bolt through the suite and into the hallway—where I come face-to-face with Dak Ronen, wearing a jacket embroidered with "Boys and Girls Club of Rhode Island."

"Well, hello there," he says with a chuckle. "You look very nice."

I grimace a fake smile.

"I went backstage looking for you after your show, but a guy told me you'd already left. It took me some time to find your room." He looks over my shoulder into the suite. "Looks like you've got company."

"My aunt and her boyfriend and some of their *friends*."

He nods toward the bag on my shoulder. "Going somewhere?"

I shrug.

"Hungry?"

I shake my head.

"Want a ride home?"

I nod and a tear slips down my cheek.

He takes my garment bag. "Why don't you go tell your aunt you're leaving?"

⌒‿⌒

As he drives us north through Connecticut on Interstate 95, I ask, "So, what did you think of my concert?" I figure this will be a good way to find out how honest he is.

"I'm afraid I missed it. I couldn't get anyone to cover the B and G basketball game for me, so I didn't arrive until after you'd finished playing."

"You missed the show? Then why'd you bother coming all the way down to Mohegan Sun?"

"The other day, you seemed worried about your performance and I thought you might need some support."

"Wait...You drove all the way to Connecticut because you thought I might need a *friend*? You hardly even know me."

He shrugs. "How'd it go?"

"*Terribly.*"

"I'm sure it wasn't that bad."

"Yes, it was, actually. Mrs. Fox—my mom's old piano teacher, who tried to help me get ready for tonight's concert—came to my dressing room after the show and said I was brave to perform, but that I'd done a lousy job."

"She said *that*?"

"Basically. She's coming to the farmhouse tomorrow morning to help me cancel next week's performance at the Courthouse Center. She said it was creating too much pressure on me too soon after Mom's..." I can't finish the sentence.

"What do *you* think?" he asks.

"About what?"

"Performing next week."

I shake my head. "No idea."

"That's important, you know—figuring out how *you* feel about things and what *you* want to do about them."

"*Obviously.*" Feeling vaguely irritated, I stare out into the darkness, deliberately *not* looking at Dak.

He says, "Hey, I've got an idea. My band and I have another gig at the Pump House tonight. Why don't you come with me? It might do you some good to see how fun music can be."

I'm instantly pissed off. "Why do you and everyone else think that playing classical music isn't fun?"

He pauses a second and then says, "I was reacting to the look on your face and the tears in your eyes. Not the type of music you play."

"Oh." I feel like an idiot.

"Although you have to admit that rockabilly music is bound to be more fun to perform than Beethoven. Right?"

"No. *Not* right." I'm back to being angry.

He says, "With classical music, you've got all those rules and traditions to live up to. With rockabilly, we get to have fun and play around a lot more."

"Those rules and traditions are what make classical music challenging—and fun—for *serious* musicians."

"Hey, just because we're not playing Mozart and Chopin doesn't mean we're not serious musicians." Now *he* sounds pissed off. "We practice all the time, and work hard to make our songs tight."

"That's not the same as playing complicated classical pieces with difficult key signatures and intricate melodies."

"Yes, but we play together, as a band. That's bound to be more fun than practicing and playing all by yourself."

I roll my eyes even though he can't see me inside the dark car. "Hello? Have you ever heard of an *orchestra*? Most of the time I perform, I'm accompanied by thirty or forty other musicians, all working together in perfect harmony. It's pretty amazing—and *a lot* of fun."

He's quiet for a minute, and then he says, "Let's make a deal. You come with me to the show tonight and, after watching us perform, if you still think classical music is as much fun to play as rockabilly, I promise I'll never say another bad word about it in my life."

I can't help but laugh. "In your whole life?"

"Yup. As long as I live."

"I'm so tired, all I want to do is go to bed, but I don't see how I can pass up this opportunity to gain a lifelong fan for classical music."

"Pretty sweet deal, right?"

I shake my head. "It's not like I have anything to go home to anyway. No one's there but BC and he's—" I stop myself just in time.

"He's what?"

"Nothing." I'm not ready to discuss my talking cat with Dak yet. To change the subject, I lift the hem of my black gown. "I'm not exactly dressed right for a rockabilly concert. My street clothes are all crumpled up in my garment bag."

"So, wear your dress. You'll class up the place a bit. No worries."

"What time's the show?" I ask.

"We're the headliners tonight, so we go on at ten."

According to his car's clock, it's nearly nine now. I sit quietly for a minute, and then say, "Okay. Why not?"

I can see his smile by the light from the dashboard. "Great! And we have enough time to pick up something for dinner."

"Come to think of it, I am feeling a bit hungry."

"That's a good sign."

An hour later, Dak and I arrive at the Pump House after grabbing some sandwiches at Subway and eating them in the car. He's pulling his guitar and amp out of the trunk when a guy hurries up to us. I recognize him from high school. "Hey, Dak," he says.

"Hey, Mike. This is Becca."

"Hey, Becca," Mike says with a smile. "I think we had gym together sophomore year."

I nod awkwardly.

Turning back to Dak, he says, "We've got a big problem, man. Jonathan's sick."

"*Sick* like he can't sing very well, or *sick* like he's not coming?" Dak asks.

"*Sick* like he's home in bed. He called me about an hour ago and said he'd been puking his guts up all day. He was hoping he'd get over whatever it is by now, but that didn't happen. He sounded awful." Mike shrugs. "So, we're down one vocalist slash keyboard player tonight. Think we should cancel?"

Dak checks his phone. "Nine-thirty." He frowns. "We can't ditch on them now. It's way too late for them to find another headliner. We'll just have to deal without Jonathan. You can fill in for his vocals, and we'll have to go with just guitar, bass, and drums. Unless..." He looks at me and smiles. "You play the keyboard, don't you?"

"No. I play the piano...the *classical* piano. An entirely different animal."

Dak shrugs. "Yeah, but if you can play Schubert, you can play the Stray Cats, right? By comparison, our melodies would probably seem elementary to you." His smile feels like a dare.

I shake my head. "I don't know any of the songs your band plays."

"Yeah, but you know music fundamentals. Most of our tunes are in C, G, and F—easy keys to play in—and they have relatively simple chord progressions."

I laugh. "Why in the world would I want to get up on stage with you guys and play songs I don't know on an *electronic* keyboard? That sounds like a recipe for disaster, and—as you might recall—I already had one disastrous show tonight. I certainly don't need another one."

Dak squints, presumably thinking, and then holds up an index finger, like a teacher making a point. "I'll tell you why."

I cross my arms over my dress coat and wait. This should be good.

"You should play with us tonight because that's the only way you and I will ever be able to truly compare playing classical music with playing rockabilly."

I frown. "How do you figure?"

"Unless one of us performs both genres of music, neither of us will know what each of them truly feels like. Since I can't play or perform classical music *yet*, you are the logical person to do this experiment. And"—he raises his index finger again—"you will be performing both types of music on the same night, putting you in the optimal position to evaluate the relative merits of both."

"Fancy language," I say with a smile.

"Thank you." He bows. "So, what do you think? Are you willing to provide this valuable information for our debate?"

I picture BC's furry face when he told me I should stop performing for a while to keep from embarrassing myself. Apparently, he had a valid point, as proven by my Mohegan Sun show earlier this evening. But then I remember Mom's encouraging smile when she repeatedly coaxed me to try new things. And I see Dak's eager, raised-eyebrows expression right in front of me now, daring me to take this chance. What do I have to lose? I've already played the most *pitiful* concert of my life tonight, so how much worse can it get? And it might be fun to perform with Dak and the Hep Cats—something different. Just thinking about it makes me feel excited and alive for the first time in weeks. My mouth opens and I'm shocked to hear myself say, "Yes. Okay. I'll do it."

Dak and Mike say, "What?!" at the same time, their eyes wide with surprise.

"You do have a keyboard here, right?" I ask.

Dak points into his open trunk. "Jonathan lent me this one for me to practice on. What do you think?"

It's a full-sized, high-quality keyboard, so it should be a decent substitute for an actual piano. I like that it's the same brand as my baby grand at home, with both of them having middle-C positioned under the "Y" of "Yamaha." I nod my approval.

Dak flashes me a huge smile. "Okay. Let's do this thing!"

Thirty minutes later, I'm standing in front of an audience of fifty or sixty people on the Pump House's stage with three members of the Hep Cats. Mike introduced me to their drummer, Pedro, who looked more than a little surprised to find out I was filling in for Jonathan. A copy of the band's playlist—with the key and tempo noted for each song—is perched on a music stand in front of me, difficult to see because of the hot stage lights beaming down on our heads. The emcee introduces us, the audience claps, Dak bobs his head, the four of us jump into the first song, and I become a temporary member of a rockabilly band. How *crazy* is this? For some reason, I'm not afraid, though. I guess it's all happened so fast, I haven't had time to think about it.

The first song we play is "Jump, Jive an' Wail" by the Brian Setzer Orchestra. I've heard it a few times before, so I kind of know how it goes. I have to admit that Dak does a decent job with lead vocals and the guitar breaks, and he looks pretty good in his maroon and black bowling shirt. All three of the guys are wearing bowling shirts, which makes me feel ridiculous in my full-length gown, but there's nothing I can do about it, so I try to put it out of my head and concentrate on playing the song as well as I can. I hang back and play only chords and arpeggios, filling in the empty spaces in the music. With the stage lights, I can't see the audience very well, which is probably a good thing. At the end of the song, Dak catches my eye and gives me a wink and a smile. I guess he thinks I'm doing okay. Am I having fun? *Maybe.*

For the second song, we do the oldie, "Mystery Train." I know this song well because Mom liked to play Elvis tunes on the GTO's radio when we'd go out for drives. "Old songs in an old car," she'd say. Remembering her now makes my chest hurt, but I keep playing the song, hoping she'd approve. I hang back again for the first verse and chorus, but then pick up the melody and even take an instrumental break, playing the lead part after the second verse. I see Mike and Pedro exchange a look of surprise, but Dak gives me a thumbs-up, and I realize that I *am* having fun, especially when I hear a smattering of applause after my break. *Cool.* I'm not even nervous.

For the rest of the show, I play each song a little better than the last, and with each of them, I relax a little more, enjoying the music and the performance. At first, I'm very aware of the difference between the electronic keyboard and a wood-and-wire piano, but by the end of the show, I forget all about it, my fingers finding the keys without effort. We play nonstop for over an hour, and then return to the stage for two encore songs, finishing up with the Stray Cats' "Rock This Town." I love playing it, with its great melody and syncopated beat. I even take two instrumental breaks. Then I join Dak, Mike, and Pedro at the front of the stage for a group bow while the audience hoots and whistles, certainly a different reaction than I'm used to.

Afterward, the guys and I hustle into the small backstage room, laughing and slapping each other on the backs. We flop down on dusty restaurant chairs, tired but hyped up.

Mike raises his hands in front of my face. "Put it there, girl. You did an awesome job!" I give him a double high-five, which I repeat with the other guys, ending with Dak.

He says, "You did a super job, Becca. If I didn't know for a fact that you'd never played this stuff before, I wouldn't have believed it. And those breaks you came up with for the encore were *incredible!*"

I feel truly happy. "Thanks for letting me play with you guys. I had a *blast*. If Jonathan is ever out sick again, give me a call."

"*Definitely*," Pedro says with a smile while the other guys nod.

"Hey, we usually go over to the Muse for a late dinner after the show," Mike says. "Want to join us?"

I grimace. "I'm sorry, guys, but now that the show's over, I am crashing, *big time*. Don't forget, this is my second show of the night."

They look genuinely disappointed.

"But please go ahead and have fun." I look at Dak. "Would you mind dropping me off at home on your way there? I know it's out of the way..." I wish I had my driver's license already.

He says, "No problem. I have an early shift at the grocery store tomorrow morning, six to nine, so I've got to get home anyhow."

"You sure?" I ask. I'm afraid I'm keeping him from having fun with his friends.

"Yup." He hops to his feet. "Come on, guys. Let's go pack up the equipment."

In the car on the way home, Dak glances over at me and smiles. "So?"

"So...what?" I know what he means, but I feel like playing with him.

"So, what's your decision? How does playing rockabilly compare to playing classical music? I think you're as close as we're ever going to get to an expert on the topic."

"An expert, huh?" I laugh. "Grandpa always said an expert was a guy from out of town with a briefcase." I wonder how Grandpa would feel about me playing rockabilly. Somehow, I think he'd like it.

Dak chuckles. "I wish I'd met your grandfather. He sounds like a smart guy. Funny, too."

"He was all that and more." I can see the beautiful crinkles Grandpa had around his eyes whenever he smiled at me—which was often.

"Ahem," Dak says. "I'm still waiting to hear your judgment. Which show was more fun to play tonight?"

I frown. "That's not a fair question. My performance at the casino was *terrible*. I was totally unprepared and I've never played worse in my life. It was certainly *not* fun."

"You weren't prepared for our concert either, but you had a good time, right?"

"Yes, but that was different."

"How?"

Good question. "Maybe because no one was expecting anything from me. Including myself."

"What do you mean?" he asks.

"I've been performing classical piano concerts for seven years now. And, with my mom's help, I've been getting better and better. Everyone expects me to improve with every show. And that's the way it was going. Until tonight."

He shrugs. "Don't you think you're being hard on yourself? Every performer makes mistakes once in a while."

"Making mistakes is one thing. But not being prepared—not knowing my pieces well enough—that's *not cool*. I'm supposed to perform my pieces at a high level. People expect it, and rightly so. And tonight, at Mohegan Sun, I let them down."

"Who did you let down? Who's expecting so much of you?"

More good questions. "The audience, for sure."

"But most of those folks there tonight probably have never heard you play before. I'll bet they thought you did just fine."

I shake my head. "Even if there was just *one* person in the seats who was disappointed in my performance, that means I didn't do my job."

He nods. "So, you're playing for the audience?"

"Not just them. I'm also playing for people who know me, like Aunt Cassie—"

"I thought you said she slept through the whole show?"

"Yes, but maybe somewhere in her brain she realized that I played terribly. And Mrs. Fox. She was there and she *knew* my performance was terrible. She said so." I look down at my mittened hands in my lap. "And then, of course, there's Mom...and Grandpa. I don't know how this whole afterlife thing works, but I have to believe they were both around somewhere, heard me play, and were very disappointed."

"Don't you think they realized how tough that show was for you to do?"

"Maybe. But Grandpa always encouraged me to do my best, and Mom trained me to play so much better than I did tonight. I feel like I let them down. *Big time.*"

At a stoplight, he squints in my direction. "You know, there's one person you haven't mentioned—the only person who matters, the only one you *should* be playing for. *You.*"

His words hit me like a slap. Why hadn't I mentioned myself? More importantly, why hadn't I even *thought* about me?

Before Mom died, we were a team. Whatever she thought was best was what I did. No questions asked. She knew all about being a concert pianist, having been one herself, so it naturally made sense for me to listen to her advice.

~

At the age of seven, Mom started lessons with Mrs. Fox. Right away she practiced more than the average student, first a half-hour a day, then an hour, and then two hours or more, even while she was still in elementary school. I did the same thing but started even earlier—at the age of five.

Like me, Mom began performing at annual recitals but quickly progressed to being a top contestant in local, regional, and then national piano competitions, winning her first one when she was fourteen. Under Mrs. Fox's tutelage, and with the help of frequent master classes she took in Providence and Boston—at the same places I take my master classes—Mom kept getting better and better. By the time she was a senior in high school, she had most of the top music schools in the country recruiting her, many of the same ones who are now calling me to offer me scholarships, too. Mom chose Juilliard in NYC and did *great* there, even winning a spot in their touring orchestra as a freshman, which was almost unheard of. But then, after just one year, she became pregnant with me, quit school, and moved back to the farm. Mom always told me that she had no regrets, but I can't see how that could be true. To go from touring Europe with an orchestra to being a piano teacher and raising a baby in the backwoods of Rhode Island? That *had* to hurt.

Anyhow, with all of her training and experience, she knew what she was talking about when she taught me to play. Even more importantly, I knew she had my best interests at heart, which was why I listened to her advice without question, never considering what I thought or what I wanted. I truly believed Mother knew best. Sometimes I got the feeling that she wanted me to succeed in her place, to go on to play with an internationally known orchestra and tour the world because she hadn't been able to. She never said anything like that, but I felt like I needed to do the best I could to make her proud of me, partially due to what she gave up to raise me. I still feel that way.

Which makes my terrible performance at the casino even more awful. Tonight, I'd let Mom down, plain and simple.

"Hey, Becca," Dak says.

I look up and find we are parked in front of my house. How did we get here? I must have completely zoned out, thinking about Mom. The dashboard clock says it's just after midnight.

"Are we still on for driving and piano lessons tomorrow morning?" he asks.

"Tomorrow? Lessons? Oh, sure. If you still want to. I mean, it's so late now, and you have to get up for work at dawn."

He smiles. "No problem. Unless you have something else you need to do, like practice for your show next week?"

"We agreed to lessons tomorrow, so that's what we should do," I say.

"You're big on keeping your word about things, aren't you?"

"It's an O'Sullivan thing." I imagine Grandpa's eye crinkles again as he looks down and smiles approvingly at me.

"Okay then, see you at ten."

He waits while I unlock the house door and turn on the light in the foyer. I wave through the window as he drives away.

"How did your show go?" BC asks from the top landing, sarcasm oozing from his every word.

"Don't ask." Would I have played any better if BC had been there? Probably not, especially with the way he's been acting lately.

He chuckles meanly. "I know I shouldn't say this, but I can't help it: *I told you so!* Maybe now you're ready to listen to me and cancel that other show. Or do you feel the need to humiliate yourself further?"

BC looks sharply out the window at the disappearing taillights. "Hey, wait a minute… Who drove you home? You weren't supposed to be back until tomorrow morning. Why are you here now?"

I lock the front door and lean my back against it. "That was Dak. He came to Mohegan Sun tonight."

"That loser? What did he think of your performance?"

"He had to work so he didn't see the show. He came afterward, just to be there for me."

"Isn't that special." More sarcasm.

"Yes, it was, actually. Aunt Cassie and Jimmy were drunk and partying it up in the hotel room, so Dak was nice enough to drive me home. Except he also invited me to go to his band's show tonight. I filled in for their keyboard player who was sick." I sling my garment bag over my shoulder and trudge up the stairs, passing him.

"Wait. Are you saying you played with the Hep Cats? Onstage?" He pads after me to my room.

I nod. "It was *different*, but a lot of fun."

"My, how the mighty have fallen."

"What do you mean?"

"You do a crappy job playing your sonatas at the casino and then you lower yourself even further by playing hippity-hoppity music at some dive bar, probably on some plastic electronic keyboard." He shakes his head. "You know Dakky Boy is just using you, right?"

"What? How?"

"To try to make his crappy band sound better. And ruining your reputation as a classical pianist, in the process. Tsk, tsk, tsk...Your mother certainly would have been disappointed in you."

"I don't think so. She always encouraged me to try new things."

"New things *within your field*, like accompanying an award-winning string quartet or touring with a different orchestra. Not playing hillbilly ballads with a bunch of stoners from your high school." He squinches his fuzzy nose. "How *revolting*."

"It was fun," I say lamely. I change into my pajamas and crawl under my quilts. I wish with all my might that I could turn back the clock two weeks. Back to the time before everything in my life became so *difficult*.

The Morning After

On Saturday, I drag myself out of bed, throw on jeans and a sweatshirt, and do my usual chores of taking care of BC, Bessie, Snowy, and the chickens. As I store the fresh milk and eggs in the barn's refrigerator, I wonder how many of the other farm chores are *not* being done by Aunt Cassie. All of them, probably. I hope we're not late on mortgage payments—Do we have a mortgage?—or buying fertilizer for the fields or anything else that's important. Grandpa always worked hard on something every day, so there must be a lot of things Aunt Cassie should be doing that she's not, things I suppose I should take over. But I just *can't*. I've got all I can handle just trying to get ready for my last show. That's what Mom would want me to do, right? She asked Aunt Cassie to take care of all of the other stuff.

I eat a breakfast of cold cereal, which uses up the last of the granola. This means I'll have to get Aunt Cassie to go to the store—not likely—or put in another grocery order at Frank's Market. Will Dak volunteer to deliver it to me again? I smile.

Dak. I liked spending time with him last night. And, if I'm being honest with myself, I have to admit that playing with his band was the most fun I've had onstage in a long while. I loved the back-and-forth with the other band members, each of us stretching the music into different shapes before allowing it to snap back to its normal composition. All of my recent piano concerts have been solo shows, and the Beethoven sonatas are ridiculously hard to play. Especially without Mom.

After breakfast, I shower, dress, and sit at the piano. *Alone.* BC refuses to stay with me and won't tell me why. I'm kind of glad he's not speaking to me today since he was so nasty last night. I guess he was pissed off because I didn't take him to either of the shows but he sure did make me feel lousy about playing with the Hep Cats. Was that such a bad idea, like he said? Would Mom really have been disappointed in me for doing it? At the time, it had seemed harmless, but maybe BC is right. Maybe I did damage my reputation as a classical pianist by playing rockabilly at a bar. I don't know. And I've got no one to ask for advice.

I do my normal warm-ups and then practice the four final Beethoven pieces, the same ones I played at Mohegan Sun last night. But, like last night, I feel no joy, no flight of the soul. I'm just playing uninspired combinations of notes, and I'm not even playing them well. I try coming up with new scenes to imagine while I'm playing each movement, but nothing fits. The third movement of *No. 29*, the Adagio Sostenuto, is so slow and mournful, all I can think of is Mom lying dead in her pink-lined casket. Tears drip onto the backs of my hands. Why would Beethoven think anyone would want to hear something so sad?

When I grab the sheet music and toss it on the floor, I see Aunt Cassie's beginner piano book. I open it and look at a few of the yellowed pages. Mrs. Fox pasted gold stars and wrote comments like "Good job!" and "Well done!" next to nearly all of the exercises. I guess

Aunt Cassie was an excellent student. I'll have to ask her about it the next time she's sober. *As if.* I spend several minutes reviewing the first few exercises in the book to have them ready for Dak's lesson later this morning. I owe him that much, even if I don't know how I feel about him. When I first met him, I didn't like him at all. He seemed so casual about everything—as if nothing really mattered. But since then, he's acted like he cares about me. *Maybe.* I'm not sure. It was nice of him to come down to Mohegan Sun for me last night and to let me play with his band. BC says Dak's a loser and he's taking advantage of me. I don't feel like that's true, but maybe I'm wrong. I don't know how good I am at reading other people. I wish I could talk to Mom about Dak. She'd know what I should do.

A half-hour later, I'm making myself a cup of coffee when Aunt Cassie's truck rumbles up the snowy driveway and rolls to a stop at the side of the house. She stumbles through the kitchen door and flops into a chair, looking tired in her dirty farm coat and ripped jeans. I open my mouth to ask her what she's done with Mom's beautiful gown but then don't. She's probably ruined it by rolling it into a ball and stuffing it into her duffel bag.

Pointing to my coffee, she asks, "You got any more of that?" She gulps down half a cup and then drops her head onto her forearms, making her stubby ponytail stick straight up like a bunch of dead cornstalks in a field. "Freaking casino people threw us out of the hotel at five-thirty in the morning," she mumbles. "*Five-thirty.* Can you believe that shit? Said we destroyed hotel property and disturbed the other guests."

"Did you?"

She lifts her head, slurps some more coffee, and shrugs. "We might have been a little rowdy, but I swear the table was already broken when we got there. Charging us three hundred dollars for it was totally bogus." She holds up a hand. "Don't worry. Jimmy paid for it, so you won't be getting a bill the next time you play there."

After my terrible performance last night and now Aunt Cassie's eviction from the hotel, I'm pretty sure there isn't going to be a *next time* for me at Mohegan Sun.

Mrs. Fox arrives a few minutes later, decked out in a tinselly red and green sweater, a sad reminder to me of Christmas less than two weeks away. I pour her a cup of coffee and we sit in a cluster at one end of the kitchen table, with BC on the floor in a patch of warm sunlight, preening himself with wet smacky sounds. *Gross.* He still hasn't said a word to me this morning, although he keeps shooting me nasty looks.

"Well, Cassandra," Mrs. Fox says, "I told Rebecca last night that I think it would be best if she cancels next week's Courthouse show. It's too soon after her mother's passing for her to be able to perform at that level."

Aunt Cassie sits up and shakes her head as if trying to clear away some mental fog. "Cancel the show? Why? She did all right at Mohegan Sun."

Mrs. Fox pats one of my hands and smiles at me. "Rebecca certainly did her best, but her performance wasn't...well... She would benefit from some time off. Don't you think?"

Why is Mrs. Fox talking to Aunt Cassie instead of me? I feel invisible.

Aunt Cassie refills her mug and leans back against the kitchen counter, crossing her scuffed-up combat boots at her ankles. Frowning, she says, "Look. I know I didn't do such a hot job of helping Becca last night. I forgot to call the stage manager before we got there and then I ditched her and went to the casino with Jimmy. I admit it. I fucked up."

I see Mrs. Fox wince at Aunt Cassie's choice of words.

"But this next concert... Well, that's another thing. It's right here in our backyard, at the Courthouse Center, with that nice guy, Dave, as the stage manager. It's Becca playing in front of a bunch of people we all know. It's for the world's record and that touring contract. And

I promised Maggie I'd do this shit." Aunt Cassie swipes her tears away with the back of her hand. "So, I don't think we should cancel the concert." She slumps back into her chair, looking even more exhausted.

I'm surprised by what she says, especially considering the way she acted at the casino—like she didn't care about me at all. Which version is the real Aunt Cassie: last night's or this morning's? This is all so confusing.

Mrs. Fox uses a paper napkin to dab her own eyes and blow her nose. "I had no idea you felt so strongly about this next concert, Cassandra. I suppose we can try even harder to help Rebecca make this one a success." She envelops Aunt Cassie in a hug, and, after a few moments, they include me in their embrace. BC rolls his eyes and saunters out of the room.

The three of us are still hugging when a knock sounds at the side door, followed by Dak and Dave Morales walking into the kitchen. Dak says, "I hope you don't mind that my uncle came, too. He was hoping to get a chance to talk to Cassie about something."

Why would Dave want to talk to Aunt Cassie? They hardly know each other. I shoot a questioning look at Dak but he just smiles in return. He's all casual today, in a flannel shirt and jeans. He looks *good*.

Mrs. Fox says, "Actually, David, we were just discussing Rebecca's concert at the Courthouse Center next week, and would appreciate your advice about preparing for the show. As you know, Cassandra is new to being a manager—but she's learning fast."

Dak looks at me. "So, you're going ahead with the concert?"

Aunt Cassie answers for me. "Yes, we are."

I sigh. If she wants to play manager now, I suppose I should let her. She'll take care of the business stuff and I'll concentrate on playing. Right?

Dave smiles. "The show is a two o'clock matinee, so just have Becca there by noon for the sound check. After doing all the other concerts of the series, we have the rest of the details pretty well worked out."

"That's good news," Mrs. Fox says. She climbs to her feet. "Cassandra, if you could have Rebecca at my home at ten on Monday morning, and then again at the same time every morning next week, we'll try to have those sonatas ready for Saturday's show."

Aunt Cassie nods without consulting me, making me feel invisible again.

"Good," Mrs. Fox says. "Now, if one of you gentlemen would be so kind as to escort me through the snow to my car, I'd best be getting home. Heaven only knows what stories Howard is telling Roberta today."

"We'd both be honored," Dave says, as he and Dak each offer Mrs. Fox an elbow to grasp.

"Well, look at this," she says with a giggle. "Not one, but *two* handsome men to assist me. My, my." The three of them slowly make their way out to the driveway.

When the guys return to the kitchen, they join Aunt Cassie and me at the table, each of us cradling a mug of coffee. It's *way* too quiet in here. I take a sip and look at Dave. "Dak said you wanted to talk to Aunt Cassie?"

He says, "I was wondering if either of you knew how I came to be working at the Courthouse Center for the Arts."

We shake our heads.

He chuckles. "I had a feeling Maggie never told you."

"Mom?" I ask.

"Yup. Want to hear?"

Aunt Cassie leans back in her chair and crosses her arms like she's expecting him to say something she doesn't want to hear. "Sure. We *love* stories. Right, Becca?" She sounds sarcastic, but I nod anyway.

Dave says, "Well, I was born and raised just up the road in Warwick, but I always wanted to get out of Rhode Island. I thought I was too good for this tiny little state. So, I studied hard and managed to get myself a scholarship to Harvard. I was the first person in my family to go to college—and an Ivy League school, no less. I thought I had it made. In four years, I earned a degree in finance and headed straight to Wall Street."

"*Really?*" I ask. The background he's describing doesn't match my idea of him as a stage manager at all. And why is he telling us this?

He nods. "But I couldn't take the pressure, so I started drinking. Big time. That January I was making five thousand bucks a week, but by October I'd lost my job and my apartment and was sleeping in my car."

Aunt Cassie grins wryly as if she understands.

Me, I don't get how someone could want alcohol so much that he'd let it ruin his life like that. Why wouldn't he just stop drinking?

"Then a guy in a bar told me I could make some beer money working backstage at Carnegie Hall, building props and scenery, so I applied and got the job. I told the manager some bullshit story about how I wanted to use my experience at the Hall and my Ivy League education to go into theater finance. He bought it. So, I worked there for a while, making enough to afford my booze and an apartment I shared with a couple of other drunks. Then—lucky for me—I met your mother."

Aunt Cassie shakes her head. "I don't see what Maggie could have to do with you working in New York. Unless... *Wait.* She went on tour with the Juilliard Orchestra her first year in college, and their first concert was at—"

"Carnegie Hall," Dave says. "*Bingo.* Before her show, she and I were talking and found out we were both Rhode Islanders, and then she slapped me upside the head—just metaphorically, of course—and got me to see how stupid I was being. She said I needed to do better than being a drunk stagehand, told me about a management job opening at Kingston's Courthouse Center for the Arts, and made me realize I'd be dumb not to apply for it. So I did, got the job, moved back to Rhode Island, and stopped drinking. Now I work at the Courthouse

Center and the Boys and Girls Club in Wakefield, and I'm happier than I've ever been."

"You don't miss Wall Street?" I ask.

"Not one bit," Dave says. "The salary was great but the job focused on all the wrong things. I *love* working with the kids at the B and G and the artists at the Courthouse. It's so much more rewarding."

"Well, Dave, thank you for telling us your life story," Aunt Cassie says. "It certainly is inspirational." She sounds defensive—as if she feels like Dave is somehow criticizing her.

He says, "To get off the booze, I joined Alcoholics Anonymous and I've been going to meetings ever since. They help keep me focused on what matters in my life. Cassie, I was wondering if I could convince you to go with me to an AA meeting this morning."

Aunt Cassie laughs and shakes her head. "I don't think so. I've heard about all the Bible-thumping that goes on in those meetings and it doesn't sound like something that would work for me. The Twelve-Step Program, and all that? No thanks."

Dak stands up abruptly and turns to me. "You know what, Becca? I just remembered I'm supposed to be giving you another driving lesson right now. Why don't we go see if we can get the Goat all the way down the driveway this time?"

Glad to escape the awkward conversation, I avoid Aunt Cassie's squinty-eyed look, grab my coat and keys, and follow Dak outside into the lightly falling snow.

Driving Lesson Number Two

We walk past Dave and Dak's snow-dusted cars to our barn where Dak slides open the heavy, red doors. "So, do you think there's any chance your aunt will go to an AA meeting with Uncle Dave?"

"I doubt it. As we walked out the door, she looked at me like I was a rat abandoning a sinking ship. She probably thought the three of us had planned that whole scene—like an intervention."

"Hopefully it won't come to that. But it sure would be good if she could get her drinking under control."

I try to imagine Aunt Cassie not drinking...and can't. Every memory I have of her involves her drinking, drunk, or hungover. That's so *sad*.

Dak turns the car around and I get in behind the cold steering wheel.

"Do you remember how shifting works or do you want me to tell you again?" he asks.

"*No!*" I say quickly and then laugh. "You scared me to death the last time, with your long explanation. I think I've got the clutch and gas pedals figured out. Maybe you can just tell me whatever else I need to know as we go along?"

"Sounds good. Whenever you're ready." He fastens his seat belt, sits back, and waits.

I close my eyes, take a deep breath, and think, "Mom, please help me do this." *Weird.* This is the first time I've prayed to her...as if she's an angel now, watching over me.

Checking that my seat belt is clicked, I shift the car into first, ease up on the clutch, and press gently on the gas pedal. As the car begins rolling slowly down the driveway, I grab the wooden steering wheel with both hands and stare intently through the slightly powdered windshield. "What do I do about the snow?" I ask.

He studies the dashboard and then flicks on the windshield wipers. "I'll show you where that knob is later."

"Sounds good." I flash a huge smile. "Hey, I'm driving a car!"

"Doing great."

Traveling just a few miles an hour, we creep past the house and down the long driveway. I oversteer on the first curve, narrowly missing a stone wall, but correct in time.

"Doing great," he repeats, sounding much calmer than I feel.

After the second curve, a large tree looms ahead of us, *way* too close to the driveway. I veer sharply to the right, run off the driveway into the snow, and stall the car at the edge of one of the empty cornfields.

It takes a minute for me to relax my white-knuckled grip on the steering wheel. A small brown and white wren perches on a nearby cornstalk and twitters happily, apparently unconcerned about our near disaster.

"We might need to practice your steering a little more," Dak says with a chuckle.

"Yeah, that didn't exactly go the way I'd planned."

"Everyone oversteers and stalls the car when they're first learning. No big deal."

"Really?" That makes me feel a little better.

He nods. "But I can't believe you've never tried to drive a car before. Didn't your grandpa offer to teach you?"

"Mom was against me driving. She said I should just concentrate on my music, but I think she might have been afraid I'd get hurt and jeopardize my career. I'm not very coordinated—as you can see." I point back toward the dead cornstalks I mowed over with the car.

"You did fine." He leans his back against the passenger door, seeming to be in no hurry to go anywhere. "So tell me, is your whole life about playing the piano?"

"I wouldn't exactly put it that way." That makes me sound like such a *geek.*

"How would you put it?" he asks.

I slouch against my door. "Well, I started playing when I was five, but I did other things, too. I went to school and played with friends. I was even on a soccer team for a year when I was ten."

"But lately?"

"Ever since I won a big orchestra competition when I was eleven, it *has* been a lot about practicing and performing." I quickly add, "But I don't mind," because I don't want him to think I'm whining about my life.

"Do you miss hanging out with friends, going to movies, and stuff like that?"

I shrug.

"Don't you get lonely?"

"Sure. Sometimes."

"I heard you had to drop out of school."

"Some kids were giving me a hard time about being a piano nerd, so I asked Mom to homeschool me for my last year and a half of high school. I needed to concentrate on practicing for the sonata series."

"How was that—the homeschooling?"

"It was *fun*. Mom tutored me in history and math and science. And then, when I was playing a concert somewhere, we'd check out the local museums and go to some of the famous places we read about, like the Vietnam Wall in DC or the Grand Ole Opry in Nashville."

"Sounds like you and your mom got along well." He smiles.

"She was *cool*."

"I'm so sorry she died," he says sounding as if he truly means it.

I nod. "I miss her every day."

We sit in silence, staring through the snowy windshield. A red-tailed hawk keens while flying in huge circles overhead.

I realize I know practically nothing about Dak. "What about you?" I ask. "What's your story?"

"I've lived in Exeter my whole life."

"Really? Do you go to public school?"

He zips up his coat and nods. "You and I had freshman English together."

Despite the cold seeping into the stalled car, I can feel my cheeks grow warm. "I'm sorry I didn't remember you." With the way he looks, I can't understand why. Maybe he's right—I *am* all about the piano.

"No big deal," he says.

"How about the Hep Cats? How long have you guys been playing together?"

"Jonathan, Mike, Pedro, and I started the band sophomore year and we've been at it ever since. The Four Amigos."

"Is your music important to you?" I ask.

He laughs. "Do I hear a little classical musician's snobbery?"

I shrug. "I'm just trying to figure out if you feel the same way about your music as I do about mine."

"How do you feel about yours?" he asks.

I close my eyes and take a deep breath, connecting to my feelings. "My music is as much a part of me as my red hair or my nose freckles."

"That's intense."

I laugh. "And true. At first, I thought I only liked classical music because Mom did. It was something we shared, something we did together. But then one day, a few years ago, our piano was being tuned so I couldn't do my usual morning practicing and I realized I genuinely missed it. I missed the feel of the smooth keys on my fingers. I missed pressing them down, one after the other, shaping the notes and phrases to create exactly the sounds I wanted. I missed that rush I get when I reach the end of a song and realize I've played it well. But most of all, I missed that feeling I get from playing something that thousands—maybe millions—of other pianists have played, all trying to bring out something new in the piece while playing exactly the same notes. It always makes me feel like I'm part of something bigger, a historical community of people who love the music the same way I do."

"Wow. That's cool." He nods several times. "I'm not sure I feel the same way about my music. I mean, I enjoy playing it. And I think about the guys who have played it before me. But we're only talking forty years of history, not two hundred. And with the stuff I play, it's all about improvising and adding my own notes and sounds. No one plays a song the same way twice." He's quiet for a moment. "But I do love the music. I love the way it makes me feel and, even more, I love the way it can pick up an audience and make them fly. I feel like I've done a good job when I see people in the crowd smiling and dancing and having a good time, all because of me and the music I'm playing. To me, that's what it's all about."

I smile. "It sounds like you really do care about your music—maybe a little differently than me but just as much."

"I love it. And it's also a great way to kick back, and make a little extra money."

I laugh. "Along with your two *other* jobs?"

He shrugs. "Just trying to help out my mom and save for a car and college."

"No dad?"

"Nope. He took off right after my sister, Gracie, was born. It seems he didn't like being a family man."

"Do you ever see him?"

He shakes his head. "He lives out west with his new wife now. Arizona, I think. Doesn't even bother with birthday cards anymore." He does a palms-up. "How about you? Where's your dad?"

I mimic his palms-up. "No idea. Mom never told anyone who he was. I looked through her stuff last week, but couldn't find anything."

"Any guesses?"

I shake my head. "She was on a concert tour in Europe when she got pregnant, so Dear Old Dad might be one of the musicians she was touring with or he could be someone she met there—in France or Switzerland or Poland. Sometimes when I'm playing a concert, I imagine he's one of the men in the audience. I look at all the faces and try to find one that looks like me." I laugh. "When we went out to eat with the Zelinskis after my last Courthouse show, there was a moment I *thought* that he and Mom might be talking about my father—or even that Mr. Zelinski might *be* my father—but then *nothing*. Now I guess I'll never know." Saying that out loud makes it feel so final. *Wow.*

"What about Ancestry.com or a website like that?" he asks. "Could you find your father that way?"

I shrug. "Maybe. But that would probably take years."

"I guess Gracie and I should be glad that at least we know who our dad is."

"How old is Gracie?"

"Sixteen."

"That's right. You said you're teaching her how to drive. Just the two of you, then?"

He nods. "And Mom. She's a shrink—a psychologist. She's just starting her own practice down in Wakefield, near the B and G."

160

"Where do you live?"

"South County Trail, near where Schartner Farms used to be."

Huh. That's only about five minutes away from here.

The circling hawk suddenly swoops down into the snowy field, snatches up a squirrel with its razor-sharp talons, and flies off toward the trees.

"Whoa!" Dak says. "That was cool."

"Not for the squirrel." While he watches the hawk fly away with its breakfast, I study his smooth skin, dark eyes, and curly hair some more, and decide he's majorly cute. Without thinking, I ask, "Do you have a girlfriend?"

He chuckles. "Why do you want to know?"

"No reason. Just curious." I can feel my face blushing bright red.

"No girlfriend. I was seeing someone, but we broke it off a couple of months ago when she left for college. What about you? Do you have a boyfriend? Just curious." He grins.

"No time."

Dave Morales's SUV pulls up on the snowy driveway next to the Goat. The passenger window slides down and Dave leans over Aunt Cassie to call out, "Hey, guys!"

I crank down my window. Some snowflakes float in and tickle my face.

"We're headed into town for an AA meeting," Dave says.

Aunt Cassie does a half-shrug. I notice that she's now wearing one of Mom's pretty sweaters and some of her basic jewelry. She looks *a lot* better.

Dave asks us, "Are you stuck? Do you need help getting the car out of the snow?"

Dak says, "No, we're fine. Just talking."

"We'll be gone for about two hours," Dave says.

"No problem," Dak says. "See you later."

I roll up the window and we watch the SUV crunch down the driveway toward the street. "Guess your uncle talked Aunt Cassie into going to a meeting, after all."

"Looks that way."

Will it make a difference? It would be so cool if she stopped drinking. She'll never be another Mom, but maybe she and I could be...*good friends*?

Dak sits up in his seat and jerks his thumb back toward the house. "So, what do you say? Want to give driving another try?"

I laugh. "You sure you're willing to risk it?"

"I'm a brave guy."

I adjust my shoulder strap. "Ready if you are." I crank the key and the GTO's engine starts with a roar. Dak shows me the knob that makes the windshield wipers noisily scrape away the thin coating of snow. "Where's reverse?" I ask.

"All the way over to the right and down."

"Here we go." I carefully shift and ease the car backward, onto the driveway.

"Pretty impressive," he says.

He smiles at me and I realize that I feel happy. And then I immediately feel guilty, like I'm not missing Mom enough. But wouldn't she *want* me to be happy?

Dak says, "Okay, clutch, shift, gas, steer."

I follow his directions, one at a time, and nose the car along the driveway while slowly accelerating.

After a few seconds, he prompts, "Try second gear: clutch and then shift straight down."

I manage to put the car into second with just a slight wobble in the steering, but by the time we pass the house, we are *barreling* toward the barn, so I slam on the brakes, throwing us against our shoulder straps and stalling the car *again*.

Dak laughs. A nice sound, low and throaty.

I laugh, too. "If you don't mind, I'll let you drive the car into the barn. I think we've cheated death enough for one day."

With a grin and a nod, we trade places.

Inside the barn, he cuts the engine and smiles at me. "Pretty cool, Becca. I mean, you...this...today. Pretty cool."

I roll my eyes. "I managed to run off the driveway and stall the car—not once, but twice. *Pretty amazing.*"

"Don't pretend this was nothing because we both know it wasn't. Okay?"

He looks so sincere, I don't argue. "Okay."

"Come on," he says, climbing out of the car. "You owe me a piano lesson."

Piano Lesson Number Two... and Lunch

B ack inside the farmhouse, I join Dak in the piano parlor, grinning. Because he's right: Driving the Goat is scary for me. But I did it anyway, which *is* brave. And he recognizes that. Pretty cool.

For the piano lesson, BC glares at Dak from his bed and then struts out of the room with his fur all spiked up like he's mad or afraid. I'm embarrassed. Why is BC being such a jerk to Dak? Luckily, Dak doesn't seem to notice.

I sit in the teacher's chair and open Aunt Cassie's beginner piano book, reminding myself to ask her why she stopped playing. I launch into my lesson for Dak, lecturing him about the fundamentals of piano playing. After fifteen minutes, he holds up his hands in surrender. "Now I know how you felt when I overdid my explanation at the beginning of your first driving lesson." He shakes his head. "I have no idea what you're talking about, so just show me, okay?" He slides over and nods for me to join him on the bench.

I show him the proper hand position for the basic C major scale. "Okay. I get it." He gives me a small shove with his hip.

Smiling, I slide over and let him have the center of the bench again.

For the next hour, we go back and forth that way, with me demonstrating something on the piano and then him imitating me. Finally, I ask, "Do you still have that piano keyboard from Jonathan?"

"It's all set up in my bedroom."

"All right. For your next lesson, practice the exercises we went over today, up to page ten."

He salutes. "Yes, ma'am."

"Don't you dare *ma'am* me, young man," I say, using Mom's words with a smile. I think she would like Dak. But would she approve of him as a potential boyfriend for me? *Whoa!* Why am I thinking about that?

I stand up abruptly and point toward the kitchen. "Want some lunch?"

Dak raises his dark eyebrows. "Are you offering to cook?"

"That depends on what groceries we have left. The delivery boy hasn't been here for a while." Did I just *flirt* with him?

He chuckles. "Let's go see what we can find." He follows me into the kitchen where BC scowls at us from one of the wooden chairs. Dak scratches him behind the ears, but BC doesn't purr. What is his problem? Does he sense something about Dak that I'm not seeing?

I find a can of soup in the cabinet and hold it up for approval.

"Looks good," Dak says. "Should we make grilled cheese sandwiches to go with it?"

"Sure. How do we do that?"

"Wait... You don't know how to make grilled cheese?"

I shake my head and wait for him to make fun of me.

Instead, he smiles. "Would you like me to show you how?"

"Sure." It's about time I learn to feed myself.

He asks, "Do you have bread?"

166

I locate a partial loaf of multigrain. "Will this do?"

"Sure. How about cheese?"

I check the fridge. "Cheddar okay?"

"Definitely. Butter?"

I pull a tub from a compartment in the refrigerator door. "Homemade."

"Great," he says. "Now grab a frying pan and a saucepan and let's get cooking."

Ten minutes later, we sit down for our lunch of grilled cheese sandwiches and tomato rotini soup, made by me with step-by-step instructions from Dak. *Not bad.* Sitting next to him feels so comfortable and so *right*. Considering I hardly know the guy, this is kind of strange.

As we eat, BC alternates his time between glaring at Dak and making disgusting smacking sounds while cleaning himself. *Lovely.*

"You think you'll be ready for your concert Saturday?" Dak takes a huge bite of his sandwich.

"Mrs. Fox and Aunt Cassie seem to think so, based on what they were saying here this morning." I still feel a little irritated about the way they excluded me from the conversation about my concert.

"But what about *you*? Do *you* want to do the show?" When I don't answer the question right away, he says, "Becca, sometimes I wonder if you spend too much time doing what you *think* you should do or what other people *tell* you to do, rather than what you *want* to do."

"What difference does it make?" I ask, confused. "I never bother to think about stuff like that. Before, I figured Mom knew what was best for me so I didn't need to worry about it. Now, supposedly Aunt Cassie is going to take care of that stuff for me. Why should I waste time thinking about what I *want* to do?"

"So you can make your own choices, guide your own destiny. Like William Ernest Henley said, 'Be the master of your fate, the captain of your soul.'"

Dak's career advice sounds like criticism to me—like he thinks I'm doing everything wrong. "I don't know your Mr. Henley," I say, "but I do know I am expected to perform next Saturday at the Courthouse Center and do a whole lot better than I did at that Mohegan Sun concert last night. *Period.* End of story. If I work my butt off for the next week, maybe, just *maybe*, I'll be able to pull that off and not embarrass myself again."

Dak frowns.

I worry that I've said the wrong thing so I change the subject. "What about you? Are you planning on coming to the show and actually seeing me play this time?" I'm trying to be flirty again but feel like I'm failing miserably. I wish I was better at this social stuff.

"Yup. I already bought my ticket," he says.

I grin with happiness but hide it by wiping my mouth with my napkin.

Dak points to BC, who is still licking himself disgustingly. "Will he be there?"

I nod.

"Tell me again why you bring your cat to all your concerts."

I hope he's not going to tease me about BC. I shrug. "We grew up together. Mom and I got him from an animal shelter when I was five. He's kind of like a furry little brother. And when he's with me, I'm usually calmer. So, I pretty much take him everywhere I go."

"In that case, I'm surprised you don't bring him along for our driving lessons," Dak says.

"He throws up in the car."

"Got you."

"But I still bring him to all my shows—every one of them except Mohegan Sun, and you know how badly that turned out. So, I'm *definitely* taking him with me to the Courthouse show next Saturday. I'll bring his carrier too, though, just in case he causes trouble and I have to lock him up in the dressing room."

"Are you expecting him to cause trouble?"

BC sneers at me and then resumes his preening.

"No. Not really," I say. Unless he talks...

We do the dishes together and then Dak slips on his coat. "My sister Gracie is in a ballet company," he says. "Right before every performance, all the dancers say *Merde!* to each other, which is French for—"

"Shit?" I ask, remembering one of the curse words that I picked up in my middle school French class.

"Supposedly that brings them good luck."

"Really?" I laugh. "That seems rather random, doesn't it?"

He shrugs. "Anyhow, in case I forget to say it to you on Saturday—*Merde*, Becca."

"Thanks. And thanks for the driving and cooking lessons...and for everything else today, too." I think we *are* becoming friends. Maybe more. Does he feel that way, too? Or is BC right, and Dak is just trying to see what he can get from me?

"No problem," Dak says. "Hey, when do you want to have our next driving and piano lessons?"

"After the concert. Next Sunday? I'm going to be pretty busy till then."

"Sunday sounds good. In the meantime, give me a call or text me if you get lonely or bored or...whatever. Otherwise, I'll see you Saturday at the show."

As I watch him drive away in his mom's car, I smile. "I like Dak Ronen," I say aloud.

BC coughs up a hairball and *a lot* of slime.

Another Lesson with Mrs. Fox

Ten o'clock Monday morning finds me seated at the upright piano in Mrs. Fox's parlor, driven here—*on time*—by Aunt Cassie. And Aunt Cassie didn't even give me trouble about bringing BC with me, so he's here too, snoozing high up in his bed on top of the piano. For some reason, I feel like Mom's here, as well, helping me prepare for the show. It's a sad but comforting feeling.

Mrs. Fox shuffles her fluffy bedroom slippers into the piano parlor and drops into her teacher's chair. "Howard's just fallen asleep, so we should have at least an hour to work on these sonatas. Let's start with *No. 32* today and work our way backward, shall we?"

For sixty minutes, Mrs. Fox and I diligently review the last sonata, breaking down the difficult passages into manageable sections and practicing the phrasing over and over again until I can feel the music in my soul. Together, we even come up with interesting soundtrack images for the piece's two movements based on scenes from *The Three Musketeers*, a novel both of us love. By the time Aunt Cassie texts me to say that she's waiting for me in the driveway, I'm enjoying playing classical music again. Thank you, God. And thank you, Mom, because I know you're helping, too, somehow.

"Same time tomorrow to work on *No. 31*?" Mrs. Fox asks.

I nod and give her a huge hug.

"If your rehearsals continue this way, you should do just fine on Saturday," she says, patting my shoulder.

"I think you're right."

BC yawns.

Back at the farmhouse, I carry BC into the kitchen and give him some kibble for lunch. Aunt Cassie grabs salad ingredients from the fridge—she went to the grocery store on Sunday—and pulls out two cans of seltzer, not beer. Actually, she hasn't had a drink since her party in the casino hotel room three days ago, the longest time I can remember her ever being sober. And she's attended an AA meeting every day with Dave. She's also quit her job at the pub and has dumped Jimmy—thank God. I never liked him. But I worry about so many big changes in Aunt Cassie's life, all at once. They're *good* changes, but I can tell she's hurting because of them. Her hands shake all the time, she can't keep down much food, and her face, which has always been pasty-white—like mine—now looks practically ghost-like, almost green. And I'm not sure how happy she is, either. She's always fidgeting with her rings and earrings and looking out the windows as if she wants to go somewhere...anywhere.

Ever since Aunt Cassie returned from that first AA meeting Saturday, I've been doing the dishes and keeping my stuff cleaned up. I even made us a Sunday dinner of soup and grilled cheese sandwiches. It wasn't much, but I hoped it helped her out a little bit. I want to do whatever I can to help her stay sober.

After today's session with Mrs. Fox, I fork up my lunch salad while Aunt Cassie barely nibbles at hers and then pushes it away. She looks tired and colorless, despite wearing one of Mom's prettiest red sweaters. "Just to let you know," she says, "everything's set for the concert Saturday. Dave and I went over all the details a few times so there shouldn't be any mix-ups like at the Mohegan Sun show."

"That's great. Thanks so much."

"And I called John Foster and Sally Johnson about the cornfield leases. They're going to be here Friday afternoon to sign the papers."

"Good job."

BC noisily throws up into his water bowl. Is he trying to say something or is he just being a cat? I wash the bowl and set out some fresh water for him, but he ignores it and stares at me. Maybe this would be a good time for a reality check... I casually ask Aunt Cassie, "Have you noticed anything different about BC lately?"

"How do you mean?"

"Since Mom died, have you seen or heard him do anything *strange*?"

"Are you saying BC needs kitty therapy? Please." She rolls her eyes. "I have enough shit to deal with right now. I'm not going to worry about whether or not the dumb cat is depressed."

So much for a reality check. "No big deal." I clear away our lunch plates as BC snorts several times. He *might* be just clearing his sinuses, but it sure sounds like he's laughing at me.

Aunt Cassie picks at her chipped blue fingernail polish. "It's only been a few days since I quit working, but I really miss the guys from the pub. Most of them are big into booze, which I know wouldn't be so good for me right now, but they were really fun to hang out with."

I'm afraid to say anything, afraid that she'll take whatever I say as an encouragement to go back to drinking with her buddies.

"And Jimmy," she says. "I know he's an asshole when he's drunk, but he sure knows how to make me laugh."

I look down at the yellowed bruise he caused on the back of my hand.

"I don't know how you stand it," she says, "being cooped up here in the house, playing the piano day and night, never going out. Don't you get bored? Or lonely?"

I scoop up BC. "I have this guy." I nuzzle his chin with my nose. "And you. And Dak..."

BC sneezes violently three times.

"Yeah? What's the deal with Dak?" Aunt Cassie asks with a grin. "Are you two going out or something?"

"No!"

She laughs. "It'd be all right, you know, if you did go out with him. He seems like a nice enough guy."

"He's teaching me to drive, and I'm teaching him to play the piano. That's *all*."

She shrugs. "Suit yourself. But he is kind of cute. And a date or two wouldn't be the worst thing that ever happened to you." She looks out the window at the snow falling in fat, wet flakes, and shakes her head, the grin sliding from her face. "This weather sucks. We've had snow on the ground ever since the week before Thanksgiving. It sure would be nice to get a break from all this cold, even if it's just for a day or two." She sounds a little desperate.

Checking her phone, she pushes herself to her feet. "I'm supposed to meet Dave at an AA meeting at the church in a half-hour—fun, fun—so, I'd best be going." She scratches BC's tummy. "I hope you and your pal here have a good afternoon." She trudges up the stairs to her room and then, moments later, slumps out the front door, slamming it behind her.

Nope. I don't think she's very happy right now. Maybe she'll feel better after the alcohol gets completely out of her system. How long does that take? I'll have to google it. Or maybe if she makes some new friends at the AA meetings? What if she and Dave hit it off? Not too long ago, I thought he and Mom might have a thing, so it would make some sense if he and Aunt Cassie end up getting together.

That night, after a successful day of practicing *Sonata No. 32*, BC and I curl up together on the sofa, munching microwave popcorn while watching *Stella Dallas*, another favorite movie of mine. It's all about a mother who gives up everything so that her daughter can have the good things in life. Is that what Mom did for me? Did she resent me for it? That would be *awful*—if Mom was unhappy because of me.

Aunt Cassie comes home, grabs a handful of popcorn, and slumps off to bed, saying, "This sobriety shit is wearing me out."

After she leaves, BC says, "That woman's going to crash and burn. It's only a matter of time."

This is the first time he's spoken in two days and I'm surprised. I'd almost convinced myself that I'd been imagining him talking. But wait... I *am* imagining him talking, right? This is so confusing. I place him on the cushion next to me and stare at him.

"Hello? Anyone home?" he asks.

"What?"

"I was talking to you about your loser aunt and how she's going to start drinking again any day now."

"Aunt Cassie? No. You're wrong. She's sober, going to meetings, managing my last concert, and working on farm stuff. She's doing *great*."

"Keep telling yourself that if it makes you feel better." He licks the fur on his stomach.

My phone chimes to announce the arrival of a text.

"Is that from your *boyfriend*?" BC asks mockingly.

"Oh, shut up." I type a response to Dak telling him about my good practice session and asking him what he's been up to, hit *Send*, and put my phone facedown on the arm of the couch. "Dak is *not* my boyfriend."

"Could have fooled me with the way you're constantly daydreaming about him."

"What are you talking about? I worked hard all day. And that last sonata is sounding pretty good, if you hadn't noticed."

"I don't know why you're bothering to practice. I mean, who cares if you play the concert on Saturday?"

"A lot of people: Dak, Mrs. Fox, Aunt Cassie. They all want me to do well. And, if he were still here, Grandpa would have wanted me to play so that I'd—"

"—keep your word? Yeah, I've heard that stupid Gronk story a million times." He yawns. "Well, your grandpa's *dead*, sweetheart. So, there's no need to worry about him, is there?"

"And of course there's Mom—I can't disappoint her."

BC sighs. "Becca, my dear, if you haven't noticed yet, your mother's *dead*, too. You can't disappoint dead people."

"But she spent her life helping me to be a concert pianist. Don't you think I should do this concert in her memory?"

"Memory, schmemory. She's *dead*. She doesn't care."

"I wish you'd stop saying that!"

"What? That your mom's *dead*? Umm... I think someone around here might need a reality check."

A talking cat is telling me I need a reality check? That's a *good* one. "I know Mom's dead, but you don't have to say it over and over again. It makes it feel so...final."

BC snickers. "Honey, death is about as final as it gets."

My phone pings again and I reply to Dak, texting him about my practice plans for the rest of the week. I hit *Send* and give BC some popcorn as a peace offering. "Could we please just watch the rest of this movie? I want to chill out before bedtime."

"Whatever floats your boat, honey," he says, chewing his popcorn noisily.

The Day Before the Show

Tuesday, Wednesday, and Thursday go pretty much the same as Monday did. Every morning, I get up, do my farm chores, eat breakfast, and take a shower. Aunt Cassie drives me to Mrs. Fox's house, where we work hard on one of the final Beethoven sonatas. Afterward, Aunt Cassie and I return home and have lunch together. And then I practice that day's sonata late into the evening while being assaulted by nasty cat comments from BC. By Friday, I'm exhausted but feel ready for the Courthouse show scheduled for two o'clock the following afternoon. All is going well.

And Aunt Cassie has gotten her wish, too: the prolonged cold snap has finally broken, with a gradual warm-up all week. By lunchtime on Friday, the outdoor temperature is somewhere in the mid-fifties and the snow has melted from all but the shadiest areas of the farm.

After lunch, a loud knock on the door makes BC startle.

"That'll be John Foster and Sally Johnson, here to sign the field lease papers," Aunt Cassie says. She's wearing a flannel shirt and bib overalls. Is she trying to look like a farmer, too?

I pick up BC. "I'll go up to my room and get out of the way."

"No, *don't!*" Aunt Cassie says, sounding a bit frantic. "Stay and help, please. I don't know anything about this farming shit. Dad and Maggie always took care of it."

"I know even less than you do."

"Then just keep me company."

I reluctantly sit back down while BC chuckles meanly.

Aunt Cassie leads the two farmers into the kitchen and places steaming cups of coffee in front of all four of us. Opening a manila file folder, she says, "I found the lease agreements from last year, made copies of them, and changed the dates. If nothing's different, we can just sign them." She drops a packet of papers in front of Mr. Foster and Mrs. Johnson.

Mrs. Johnson says, "Actually, your sister was talking to us about switching things up this year, going from cash rent to crop share agreements."

"Crop share?" Aunt Cassie chews on her lower lip.

"Yes," Mr. Foster says. "But we were still going back and forth on the percentages, whether we were going to do thirty/seventy or forty/sixty splits."

"Hmmm...thirty/seventy or forty/sixty?" Aunt Cassie darts a panicked glance at me and then takes a big swig of her coffee while tugging at one of her earrings.

In my lap, BC's chest spasms with what feels like silent laughter.

Mrs. Johnson says, "And, of course, we need to decide who's going to purchase the seed, fertilizer, and chemicals."

Aunt Cassie says, "Of course."

By this point, BC is laughing so hard, I'm afraid he's going to fall off the chair. No one seems to notice but me.

Aunt Cassie jots some notes on her manila folder and then lays down her pen. "Sally and John, I'm not going to bullshit you. I have no idea what you're talking about with cash rent versus crop share and a thirty/seventy or a forty/sixty split. I might have lived on a farm most of my life, but my dad and sister were always the ones who handled the business stuff."

"It's not all that complicated," Mr. Foster says. "Cash rent means—"

Aunt Cassie holds up a palm. "John, I appreciate that you're willing to explain everything to me, but I think I need to do a little research first so I can wrap my head around it. If you'll both give me a few days to figure things out, I'd like to meet with you again next week, right after Christmas, to discuss all the particulars and sign the agreements."

"We've already come over here twice to take care of this," Mrs. Johnson says, a hint of irritation in her rough voice.

"I know, and I'm sorry," Aunt Cassie says. "If you'd like, for the next meeting I'll come out to one of your farms, or somewhere else that would be more convenient for you."

Mr. Foster smiles kindly. "Cassie, we understand that with Maggie's passing—and Patrick's passing only a year ago—you've had to take on a lot. Probably more than your fair share."

Mrs. Johnson slowly nods her agreement.

"So, you go ahead and do what you need to do to figure out all of this leasing mumbo jumbo. We'll be happy to make another trip back here to conclude our business once you're ready. What do you think, same time next week?"

Aunt Cassie smiles and nods.

"Fine." He rises to his feet. "We'll see you then."

"Thank you both," Aunt Cassie says. "I appreciate your understanding." She shows them to the door, refills her coffee cup, and drops heavily back into her chair.

"That went well," she deadpans.

"You were honest with them," I say, trying to at least offer some encouragement. "That's good."

"Except now they know they're dealing with a complete idiot. They're probably going to try to take me for a ride next week, figuring they can get away with it."

"They don't seem like that type of people."

"Becca, my girl, people aren't always what they seem to be. The sooner you learn that, the better off you'll be." She sips her coffee, looking through the window, down the driveway. "Hey, I've been meaning to ask you... What do you want to do for Christmas this year? It's less than a week away, you know."

BC slides to the floor and noisily laps water from his dish.

Just the word *Christmas* makes me feel sad. I still haven't been able to make myself put up any of the house decorations. "Without Mom and Grandpa, it seems almost pointless, doesn't it?"

She squeezes my shoulder. "Hey, we've still got each other, right? How about if we just cut down a small pine tree, decorate it together, make a nice breakfast, and exchange presents, just the two of us?"

I don't want to discourage her sudden family-oriented impulse so I say nothing and just stare at BC, who is now batting the water dish with a white paw.

"What?" Aunt Cassie asks.

I shrug. "Mom always said cutting down a Christmas tree was murder—killing a perfectly good baby pine tree."

She chuckles. "I forgot about the two of you being tree-hugging vegetarians. So, what did you do for a Christmas tree? I'm not digging up a live one and carting it in here, if that's what you've got in mind. *Way* too much work."

I point out the window to a small white fir Mom planted several years ago. "She always put strings of lights on that tree—said it made the farmhouse look festive—and then she decorated every square inch of the house downstairs. We put our gifts for each other under the piano and opened them up on Christmas Eve."

"Yeah. I remember that from last year."

Aunt Cassie had shown up so drunk, I'm surprised she remembers anything at all about the holiday.

She puts her empty mug in the sink. "I suppose you're planning on practicing all day today, again?"

"Most of it. It's my last chance before the concert tomorrow."

"How's it going? The pieces sound pretty good to me."

I smile. "Really well. Mrs. Fox and I finally figured out how to communicate with each other, and all four sonatas are just about ready."

Aunt Cassie nods, and I can tell she's actually listening to me. I really like this non-drunk version of her.

She says, "Okay. I'll go find some lights—they're probably out in the barn—and throw them on that tree outside. At least that'll be something, right?"

"Want me to help?"

"Nah. You practice and I'll decorate. It'll give me something to do until my AA meeting this afternoon." She sounds unhappy, but I don't know what I can do to make her feel better.

When our big John Deere tractor starts up a half-hour later, I figure Aunt Cassie is hauling hay bales into the barn for Bessie and Snowy, so I keep practicing *Sonata No. 29*. But then when I hear the tractor idling for a while near the farmhouse's front porch, my hands go still.

"What is that crazy woman up to, now?" BC asks. "Probably drinking."

I grab my coat and dash out the front door.

Aunt Cassie is crouched in the slushy snow behind the idling green tractor, wrapping a chain around the trunk of Mom's white fir tree.

"What are you doing?" I yell to be heard above the noise of the engine.

Aunt Cassie fastens the other end of the chain to the hook on the back of the tractor and climbs up into the glass-enclosed cab. The engine revs and the massive rear tires tear muddy, brown gashes into our gravel driveway as the ten-foot-tall tree slowly bends over and then, with a loud crack, is ripped from the ground, the huge root ball throwing up clots of mud and chunks of frozen dirt. Aunt Cassie continues to drag the tree away from the house until I sprint in front of the tractor and stop her. She shuts off the engine, climbs down, and glares at the fir, which now lies dead in the driveway.

"Why did you do that?" I ask tearfully. "Mom planted that tree and now you've killed it. *Why?*"

"Because she fucking planted it for me!" She has tears in her eyes, too.

"What are you talking about?" I ask.

"When she planted it, she told me that this white fir tree was like me: soft and delicate-looking but strong and tough enough to last through our shitty New England winters. She said she planted it to remind me that I was strong too, even stronger than I knew."

"Wasn't that a *nice* thing for her to do?"

"Yeah. Really *nice*. So *nice* that she probably fucked me up for the rest of my life."

I shake my head. "I don't know what you mean."

She wipes away her tears with a work-gloved hand. "I was going to show her and Dad that I could turn my life around. That I could quit drinking, get a real job, and make something of my life."

I nod. "Sounds like a good plan."

"Yeah. But then Dad died last year. Fucking cancer."

I *certainly* agree with her there.

"And now Maggie's dead, too. Appendicitis. What kind of bull-shit is that? When you get appendicitis, you go to the hospital, get your appendix taken out, and you're better in a few days. You don't fucking *die* from it!"

Good point. One I've thought about many times over the past three weeks.

She says, "So now, I'm working my ass off, trying to get my shit together, but there's no one here to see me do it, except for Dave—who I hardly know—and you. But you're just a kid." She cracks off a branch of the fir tree and swats it against her jeans. "Why bother? I might as well go back to being fucked up. It beats reality, any day of the week."

"You could do it for yourself," I offer.

"Do what?"

"Get your act together. You don't have to do it for anyone else. Not Grandpa. Or Mom. Or Dave. Or me. You could just do it for *you*." This sounds a lot like the advice that Dak's been giving me lately.

She kicks the tree trunk with her boot, causing dirt to rain down on the gravel. "Easy for you to say. You've only been drunk once in your life, right? You have no idea how hard it is to dry out. Because trust me, it *ain't easy*."

I hate seeing her this upset. "Don't the AA meetings help, the ones you've been going to with Dave? Isn't he your sponsor? He's a nice guy, right?"

"Yeah, Dave's nice and all. But that's one hour a day—when we're in a meeting together. What am I supposed to do for the other twenty-three hours? Take up knitting?" She snorts a laugh. "Trust me, I'm not the knitting type."

I brush the dirt off a porch step and sit down.

"Whatever," she says. "Even with Dave's help, I probably won't be able to stay sober anyway. I've been drinking for fourteen years now. Even *I* don't believe I can kick it." She sits down on the step with me.

"Mom did," I say quietly.

"Did what?"

"She believed you could stop drinking."

Aunt Cassie frowns.

"Remember, that last time she talked to us, in the hospital? She said that quitting drinking, running the farm, and taking care of me sounded like a lot for you to handle, but she *knew* you could do it. All of it."

"Yeah, well, for a smart woman, your mom was dumb that way—believing in people when she shouldn't." She throws her branch at the prone tree. "And now she's fucking dead, so what difference does it make?"

We sit side by side in silence. Finally, she bumps my arm with her elbow. "Hey, Becca, I owe you an apology. Probably more than one."

"For what?"

"For being such a bitch to you since your mom died."

I shrug.

"I mean it. I've been all fucked up, trying to deal with my sister dying, so I got stupid drunk and stayed that way. I've always liked drinking way more than I should, ever since I was a kid, but after Maggie died, I took it to the next level. Really dumb. And I was a jerk to you, big time. I'm sorry."

"It's okay."

She nudges me again. "Am I forgiven?"

I laugh. "Yeah. Sure." It feels so good to be talking to Aunt Cassie about real stuff. I'd love to talk to her about other things, too. Like my *possible boyfriend*. I'd sure like to get her honest opinion of Dak because I think he's a good guy, but BC says he's a jerk. And then there's my *talking cat* who's probably not actually talking. I really need to speak to Aunt Cassie—or someone—about BC, but it doesn't feel right to dump these things on her now. She's missing her sister, her boyfriend, and her friends, and she's going through alcohol withdrawal, too. She must feel terrible, for Pete's sake. I'll just have to deal with Dak and BC by myself, at least for a little bit longer.

Aunt Cassie checks her phone. "AA meeting in a half-hour."

"You going?"

"Yeah. Why not? Dave's supposed to meet me there."

I grin. "Dave—he's a good guy."

She narrows her eyes and smirks a little. "What's your point?"

"Oh, nothing. Just an observation."

"Huh." She points at the tractor. "I'll take care of this when I get back. Oh by the way, I'm going to stop in at the pub on the way home, to say hi to everyone. I kind of miss the gang."

"Is that a good idea—going to the pub?" I'm afraid she'll slip up and start drinking again.

"Don't worry. I won't stay long." She studies her boots for a moment and then looks at me. "Hey. Fun fact. When your mom and I were kids, Mrs. Fox said that I had more natural talent as a pianist than she did."

"Really? I've been meaning to ask you about a beginner book with your name written in it that Dak and I found in the piano bench. I didn't even know you took lessons. So, you were better than Mom, hunh?"

"Yup. But then when our mom died—your grandma—I started running around with boys and drinking, so I stopped practicing."

I had forgotten that Grandma died when Mom and Aunt Cassie were teenagers, too. I guess we have that in common. *Yay.*

Aunt Cassie wags her index finger like a stern librarian. "Words of wisdom from your auntie: watch out for boys and booze." She kisses me on the cheek and then, stepping over the chain that stretches from the tractor to the fir tree, she walks toward her beat-up pickup truck.

"Aunt Cassie," I call out, "I love you."

She turns and smiles. "Yeah. I love you too, Becca." She climbs into the truck and slowly drives away.

I practice the Beethoven sonatas all afternoon, eat leftovers for dinner, and then practice some more. By ten o'clock, I feel thoroughly ready for the show and a little bit more optimistic about life. Maybe, just *maybe*, things are going to turn out okay, even without Mom.

"So, stop playing those songs over and over again, will you? You're giving me such a headache," BC grumbles while chewing his claws.

I sigh. "I wish you would be a little more encouraging."

"Oh Rebecca!" he says in a high falsetto. "You are *soooo good!* Just *amazing!* Please give me your autograph!" He slashes the air, claws extended, and narrowly misses my nose.

"Stop that!" I'm surprised—and a little frightened—because he's never tried to scratch me before. I glance at the mantel clock. "I wonder where Aunt Cassie is. I thought she'd be home by now."

"She probably hooked up with her skanky ex-boyfriend Jimmy and they're out boozing it up."

"Or, she met some friends at the pub and just lost track of time."

"Why don't you call her and see where she is?" he asks. "Or call Dave and ask him if he knows?"

"I don't want to bother them. Besides, I'm sure she'll be home any minute." I wrap myself in Mom's lap quilt and curl up on the sofa. "I'll rest here until then so we can talk about what time we're leaving for the hall tomorrow." I close my eyes, just for a minute . . .

The Eighth Beethoven Sonata Concert

I wake up with my left ear buzzing loudly. I sit up in a panic. How am I going to perform like this?

"It's your phone, *genius*," BC sneers from the other end of the couch.

I toss aside Mom's quilt and find that he's right. I fell asleep with my head resting on my cell phone, which is now vibrating with an incoming call. I punch the green button on my phone. "H-hello?"

"Hi, Becca. It's me, Dak. I'm sorry... Did I wake you up?"

"No. I mean, yes. What time is it?"

"Nine o'clock. I was wondering if you'd like to go out for breakfast somewhere. I figure this is a big day for you, and you know what they say about breakfast being the most important meal of the day."

"No. I mean, no thank you. I mean... Would you please hold on for a second?" I run to look out the kitchen window where I see a gray overcast sky with tiny snowflakes falling and already accumulating on the ground. What I *don't* see is Aunt Cassie's truck because it's not in the driveway. Just the big tractor still attached to the dead fir tree. Dashing upstairs, I find no one. "Umm...Dak," I say. "We might have a problem here."

"What's wrong?"

"Aunt Cassie went to an AA meeting with your Uncle Dave yesterday afternoon, but apparently she never came home."

"Apparently?"

"Last night, I was practicing and then I was waiting up for her but I fell asleep. Anyhow, she's not here."

"Oh."

"She said that she was going to go over to Richard's Pub—where she used to work—on her way home from the meeting and I'm afraid...well..."

"I'll give Uncle Dave a call to see if he knows anything. I'll call you right back."

My call to Aunt Cassie's phone goes straight to voicemail. I think about calling Jimmy, but then realize I don't know his number or even his last name.

On the couch, BC yawns and stretches theatrically. "If you recall, I predicted this."

"Predicted what?"

"On Monday I said your aunt was going to crash and burn. And—I have to say it—*I told you so!*"

"You don't *have* to say anything," I snap. "Because you're not really talking. I'm just having—What are they called?—*stress-induced auditory hallucinations.*"

"Honey, you just keep telling yourself that."

Clutching my phone, I pace back and forth from the kitchen to the parlor, darting glances out the front window every few seconds. Five minutes go by. Then ten. Then fifteen. The snow keeps accumulating on the empty driveway, falling in ugly, gritty flakes. "Why hasn't Dak called me back yet?" I wonder aloud.

"I'm sure he's forgotten all about you, dearie. He doesn't give a shit about you or Aunt Cassie. Since you didn't jump at his breakfast invitation, I'll bet he just called another girl. You're probably just one of many numbers in his little black cell phone."

"Shut up!"

Dave Morales's SUV races up to the farmhouse with snow billowing in its wake. Dak jumps out of the passenger seat as I open our front door. "What's going on?" I ask, my voice quavering with fear.

He takes a deep breath and then says, "Your aunt's been in a car accident. She's at the hospital. Uncle Dave and I will drive you there. What do you need to do to get ready?"

"An accident! How bad? Is she all right?" I *can't* lose Aunt Cassie, too!

He shakes his head, scattering snowflakes from his hair. "We don't know. When we called the hospital, all they would say was that she was brought in by ambulance a short time ago. We should get over there."

"I need to change my clothes." I dash up to my bedroom and tear off my sweatpants.

BC watches me from the center of my bed while I throw on a pair of jeans and a sweater. "This is all your fault, you know," he says.

"What? Why?"

"You forced your poor aunt to do way more than she could handle: taking care of you, the farm, and your precious career. And then last night, when she needed you most, what do you do? Fall asleep! Nighty-night! Great way to pay her back."

Is he right? Should I have done something? "I didn't want to bother her."

He snorts. "Well, you might not have to worry about bothering her ever again."

"What do you mean? She's not going to die, is she? Not her, too!"

BC just stares at me with his yellow eyes.

I tear down the stairs. "I still need to take care of the animals," I say to Dak. He helps me so that within a few minutes we're in Dave's SUV, racing toward the hospital.

⌒

The nurse at the front desk confirms that Aunt Cassie was brought into the emergency room but says she's been transferred upstairs to surgery.

"Surgery? For what?" I ask.

"Are you her next of kin?" she asks.

"I'm her *only* kin," I say, feeling the horrible truth of the statement.

"Then I'm going to need you to give us some information about her."

"Can't that wait until we get up to the surgical floor and find out how she's doing?" Dave asks.

"I'm afraid not," she says. "I'm sorry. It'll only take a few minutes."

I quickly tell her what I know: Aunt Cassie's name, address, phone number, and primary care doctor—the same one I've had all my life—but when it comes to her insurance info, I shake my head.

"But she does have health insurance, right?" the nurse asks me.

"She quit her job last week, so I'm not sure."

The nurse frowns worriedly. "I'll get in touch with her doctor to see if she has any insurance information."

"Can we go up to see her now?" Dak asks.

The nurse points down the hall. "Through those doors and then take the elevator to surgery on the fifth floor. I'll be praying for your aunt," she adds with a kind smile.

By the time we rush off the elevator on the fifth floor, I'm crying hysterically with Dave and Dak holding my arms, one on each side. "I can't lose Aunt Cassie, too," I sob. "I just *can't.*"

We hurry to the nurses' station. "Would you please give us an update on the condition of a patient: Cassandra O'Sullivan?" Dave asks one of the nurses.

"Are you related to her?" she asks.

"I am," I say.

"Her daughter?"

"No, her niece. But I'm the only living relative she has now."

"Okay. Just a minute, please." The nurse consults her computer. "She's still in surgery."

"For *what*?" I ask. "What's wrong with her?"

"Didn't you speak with her surgeon before they took her in?"

"No. We just got here. Please tell me—is my aunt going to be all right?"

The nurse hits a few computer keys and frowns, then hits a few more and smiles. "Says here that she has a broken right tibia."

"Tibia? That's her leg, right?" I ask. "She has a broken leg?"

She nods. "The doctor will explain everything to you when he's done with the surgery."

"But she's *okay*? Except for a broken leg?"

"She was unconscious when the ambulance brought her in, so they'll probably want to monitor her overnight to rule out a concussion."

"But she's *okay*?" I ask again.

The nurse smiles reassuringly. "Yes, she's okay. The surgeon should be finishing up with her in the next few minutes. If you sit in the waiting area over there, I'll make sure he gives you a full report."

"Thank you very much," Dave says. He and Dak lead me over to a chair.

"So she's really okay?" I ask them.

"Yup," Dak says.

I burst into a fresh bout of tears and Dak holds me as I cry. Finally, I sit slumped against him with my head on his shoulder, exhausted.

Dave kneels on the floor in front of us. "I hate to bring this up right now, Becca, but I'm guessing you want to cancel your show for this afternoon, right?"

"*Oh!*" I spring to my feet, bumping my head into Dak's chin and knocking over Dave. "I forgot all about the concert! What time is it? I don't have my music or my dress or BC..." I take a few steps toward the elevator and then back to the waiting area. Why won't my head work?

Dave gently guides me back to my chair. "Becca, there is *no way* you can perform that concert today. It's not humanly possible. I'll make some phone calls now and take care of canceling it."

"Canceling it?"

"Just for today. Once Cassie gets out of surgery and we find out what's going to happen next, we can talk about rescheduling the concert, or whatever you want to do. Okay?"

I nod and slump back to Dak's shoulder, suspecting that even Grandpa would understand about me not being able to keep my word this time.

An hour later, Aunt Cassie's doctor comes to the waiting room and reports a very successful surgery. "She should be jogging in a few months," he says. As far as I know, Aunt Cassie has never jogged in her life—not once—but I don't bother to mention that to him. An hour after that, the desk nurse informs Dak, Dave, and me that Aunt Cassie is in a recovery room, awake, and ready to receive visitors. "Yes!" I say and sprint down the hall. But when I reach her room, I slowly push open the door and peek in, afraid of what I might find.

Thank God Aunt Cassie doesn't look anything like Mom did. Actually, except for a large bruise on her forehead and a bright pink cast on her right leg from her ankle to her knee, Aunt Cassie looks fine: smiling and full of life. I burst into the room and hug her hard.

"I guess this means you're glad to see me," she says, laughing.

Dak and Dave push through the door. "Hi, Cassie," Dave says. "How're you feeling?"

"Not too bad, considering," she says, sitting up a little and smoothing down her hair. "I do have a monster headache. What time is it, anyway?"

Dak checks his phone. "Almost two."

She frowns. "I must have been in that ditch for a while. What time did they bring me into the hospital?"

Dave says, "A little after eight this morning."

"What happened?" I ask. "If you don't mind telling us..."

"First of all," she says, "I want you all to know that I didn't have *anything* to drink. You can have them do a breathalyzer test or a blood test or whatever you want. You won't find any alcohol in my system."

Dave says, "I believe you."

I believe her too. I can't wait to tell BC he was wrong.

She says, "Last night, after the meeting, I stopped by the pub and then we went over to April's house to play Cards Against Humanity. Have you ever played that game?" she asks me.

"I've never heard of it."

"It's really fun. Kind of like Apples to Apples for misfits. Anyhow, it got late, so I decided to just stay over at April's. I figured I'd just come home early this morning. No big deal. But of course this morning it was snowing, and my stupid truck gets terrible traction with its rear-wheel drive. I came around that corner on Victory Highway, over near the fire station, and just skidded right off the road into that ditch—the big one by Queen River."

"I'll bet that was scary," Dak says.

"*No shit.* And I must have hit my head on the steering wheel, because I don't remember anything else until I woke up in here, with this." She points toward her cast and then grins. "Doc tells me I'm bionic now, with a titanium plate and screws in my leg."

"I'm just glad you're okay," I say. "When Dak told me that you'd been in an accident and brought here by ambulance, BC said that it was all my fault and that you might be dead."

Everyone goes silent.

"The *cat* told you that?" Aunt Cassie asks.

I can't believe I said that out loud. "No, of course not!" I sputter. "What I *meant* is that I was holding him and I was worried about you and I was afraid that you'd been working too hard, trying to take care of everything..." I know I'm babbling so I just stop and hug her tightly again. "You're the only family I have left, Aunt Cassie. I can't lose you, too."

"I'm not going anywhere, kiddo." She gives me a one-eyebrow-raised look, squeezes me, and kisses the top of my head. "However, when I tell you the next bit of news, you might wish I were."

"That's not possible."

"Well, it turns out that I don't have health insurance right now." She shrugs her shoulders. "I fucked up. I was supposed to sign up for a private plan after I quit my job at the pub last week, but I haven't gotten around to it yet. So, I'm afraid we're on the hook for the cost of the ambulance, the surgery, and these luxurious accommodations." She waves a hand in a big arc, indicating her hospital room. "I tried to get the doc to let me check out tonight, to avoid more charges, but he says I might have a concussion, so I have to stick around until morning."

"Any idea how much it's going to cost?" Dave asks.

Aunt Cassie drops her face into her hands, one of which has an IV hooked up to it. "My patient's advocate—a nice gal named Jan—said that the bill will be somewhere around $30,000."

Dak whistles. "That's a lot of money."

"No shit," Aunt Cassie says. "And the last time I looked, I had something like $500 in my checking account. So, I have no idea where I'm going to find the extra $29,500." She grins but her eyes look pinched and worried.

"Mom said that we'd be getting some life insurance money," I offer.

"We already got it," she says, "but it isn't very much. Just enough to pay for groceries and utilities and stuff like that. Nowhere near enough for this kind of bill."

Dave smiles at her. "Don't worry about the money right now. We'll figure that out later—*together*." He pulls a Sharpie marker from his coat pocket. "Right now, *you* need to decide where you want me to sign your cast."

She laughs. "Anywhere you want." Halfway through his signature, she gasps, "Your concert, Becca! I forgot all about it!"

"Dave made some calls and canceled it."

"Canceled it? Or postponed it?"

"We'll talk about that later, too," Dave says. He finishes by drawing a big smiley face and holds out the marker toward Dak and me. "Who's next?"

I take the Sharpie just as Mrs. Fox bustles into the room. "Oh, Cassandra!" she says. "Are you all right? I went to the Courthouse Center and there was a sign that said the concert was canceled but gave no explanation. I couldn't reach anyone by phone and no one was at your house. Then, I called my nephew, the fire chief, and he told me that you'd been brought here this morning by ambulance, so I found someone to stay with Howard and I rushed right over. What's happened?" The poor woman looks ready to collapse.

Dak helps her into a chair and Dave gets her a cup of water while Aunt Cassie retells the story of her accident and surgery.

Mrs. Fox sits back and sighs. "I am so glad that you're going to be fine, Cassandra. It's too bad Rebecca's concert had to be canceled, though. Did you talk to the Guinness people? Will they let her try again next year?"

Good question. I draw a cat on Aunt Cassie's cast.

Dave slowly shakes his head. "Unfortunately, that won't work. This morning when I called the Guinness rep, he told me there's a young pianist in Germany who's also trying for the Beethoven sonata record right now. He'll be eighteen and a half if he completes all thirty-two by December 31. So, if Becca starts over next year and completes the challenge then, she'll get to join the B32 Club, but she won't win the record for being the youngest member."

"And that means the Guinness folks won't sponsor a concert tour for her, will they?" Aunt Cassie asks.

"I don't believe so," Dave says. He looks at me. "Sorry."

So, all of Mom's hard work of setting up the eight concerts and then helping me get ready for them—more than a year's worth of effort—was for nothing? She and Grandpa *definitely* must be disappointed in me now. My chest feels so heavy I can't breathe right. I stand up and ask, "Is anyone else thirsty or hungry? I just realized that I haven't had anything to eat or drink today, so I'm going down to the cafeteria. Does anyone want anything?"

"I'm feeling a bit peckish too," Dak says in a fake British accent. "I'll come with you."

I nod.

Mrs. Fox pats my arm. "Right now, I'd like to visit with Cassandra, but I'd love a cup of coffee if you wouldn't mind bringing me one."

"Sure."

Dave asks Mrs. Fox, "Would it be all right if I keep you and Cassandra company?"

Mrs. Fox smiles and nods.

"Then, please bring me a cup of coffee, too, and maybe a sandwich. Any kind is fine," Dave says to me.

"No problem."

Dak and I ride the elevator together in silence and then follow the signs to the hospital cafeteria. A few minutes later, as we wait in line to pay for the food, he asks, "So, how do you feel about canceling your show today?"

"To tell you the truth, I don't know. Everything's been happening so fast the past few weeks." I shake my head. "It's hard to believe that it's only been that long since the seventh Beethoven concert and Mom d-dying and Mohegan Sun and...everything." Saying the "d" word out loud physically hurts.

"So much in such a short time," he agrees quietly.

"And now with Aunt Cassie's accident and the fact that she's going to be laid up for a while, there's no way she's going to be able to reschedule the concert before the end of the year, so I guess I'll just have to forget about the B32 Club and the concert tour and every-thing. No big deal." But if I'm being honest with myself, it *does* feel like a big deal. I'm not mad at Aunt Cassie for having her accident, or anything like that—I know it wasn't her fault—but at the same time, I can't stop myself from being very disappointed. I mean, I worked so hard for so long to take this next step in my career, and then *poof!* It all goes away just like that. How is that fair?

As we slide our purchases closer to the register, Dak says, "Becca, you do know you could do it yourself, right?"

"Do what?"

"Anything you want. Like rescheduling the concert. You could call the Guinness folks. And I know a guy you could talk to about rebooking the Courthouse Center." He grins.

"Your Uncle Dave." I frown. "But I don't know how to manage my career. That was Mom's job. And now it's Aunt Cassie's."

He shrugs. "You could handle it."

I give the cafeteria cashier my bank card, smile at her, and then turn back to Dak, irritated. "That's easy for you to say. You've always *handled* everything yourself: working two jobs, playing in a band, helping to take care of your sister and your mom. Me, I've spent my time practicing the piano and learning how to perform difficult classical pieces. I don't know *a thing* about business or promotions or any of that stuff."

He says, "You're smart. You'd figure it out." He pays for his purchases and follows me to the elevator.

Back in Aunt Cassie's room, we distribute the food and coffee and then I excuse myself and take my lunch out to the waiting room, saying I needed a few minutes alone. I unwrap my hummus sandwich and flop into one of the waiting room chairs. I wish BC were here so I could talk things over with him. Even before he could answer me—well, maybe not *really* answer me, but whatever—I've *always* talked to him. Hearing myself say things out loud makes them clearer to me. I just wish BC would stop being so snarky and would go back to being my best furry friend cat. Come to think of it, I'd like *a lot* of things to go back to being the way they were before.

My phone vibrates with an incoming call identified as coming from England. "Hello?" I say tentatively. "This is Rebecca O'Sullivan."

"Hello, Rebecca. This is Nigel Thompson from Guinness World Records. I hope you don't mind me calling you. I would have tried to reach your business manager but I understand from Dave Morales that she's had a bit of an accident. How is she?"

"She's fine. Thanks for asking."

"Wonderful to hear. Please give her my wishes for a speedy recovery."

"Okay..."

"Let me get right to the point. When I spoke to Dave this morning, he said that you might consider trying to reschedule your performance in the next few days, so that you could still get the record for being the youngest B32 player. Is that correct?"

"Umm...I don't know. We haven't had the chance to talk about it. We're still at the hospital."

"I do apologize for disturbing you there. It's just that I wanted to let you know that I've decided to stay here in Rhode Island for a few days. See the sights and whatnot. I'm not flying back to London until Wednesday, Christmas Day. So, if you can reschedule the last sonata concert for some time between now and then, I could still certify it for you and could still offer you that touring contract, as we had previously arranged."

"Oh! That would be wonderful!" I lay my sandwich on its wrapper. "But I'm not sure how—"

"Why don't you talk things over with your manager and Mr. Morales and get back to me later today? Since you completed the other seven concerts, I feel that it would be a shame for you to miss out on the record. I'd like to help you make this happen, if at all possible."

"Thank you."

"Call me back," he says and disconnects.

I drop my phone onto the next chair. Can Aunt Cassie pull together another concert in the next three days? Isn't that asking way too much of her, with all she's been through? She isn't even going to be released from the hospital until tomorrow—Sunday. And then she'll probably have to stay in bed for a few days. Adding a new concert to her plate seems like *way* too much. Unless...

I sit up, take a big swig of coffee, and then eat my sandwich, one carefully considered bite at a time.

Twenty minutes later, I push through the door to Aunt Cassie's room, where I find Dak, Dave, and Mrs. Fox gathered around her bed, laughing. As I enter, they all turn their joy-filled faces toward me, which makes me smile, too. I say, "Dave, I was wondering if the Courthouse Center had any dates available between now and Christmas Day."

In an instant, their faces go from looking joyful to appearing a little perplexed, as if they suspect what I'm up to but are not sure.

Dave says, "There's a theater group doing *A Christmas Carol* there tonight, Sunday, and Monday, but it's not booked for Tuesday, Christmas Eve. Why do you ask?"

Christmas Eve. Mom's favorite day of the year. That seems like more than just a coincidence. "Because I want to reschedule my concert for then," I say before I can change my mind. Then I tell them about my phone conversation with Mr. Thompson. "And he's right. We've come this far—seven concerts. We *have* to finish the eighth one."

Aunt Cassie frowns at the hospital room and her pink cast. "Well, I'll be getting out of here tomorrow, and then I can—"

I hold up my hand. "Aunt Cassie, you don't need to do anything for the concert. Just concentrate on getting better."

Mrs. Fox says, "Well, you and I could get together tomorrow and go over the sonatas again—"

I hold up my hand toward her, too. "Thanks, Mrs. Fox, but I'm okay. You've taught me the pieces very well. I'll be able to practice them by myself to get ready for the show." I look toward Dave. "But I will need some help from you, if you don't mind, to reschedule the Courthouse. I don't know how to switch today's tickets to Tuesday or sell new tickets or whatever needs to be done."

He nods. "No problem, young lady. You and I can get that all straightened out very easily."

Finally, I turn to Dak, who's grinning like the Cheshire Cat, presumably approving of my new plan. To him, I say, "And it would be great if you could help me out with a few rides. For starters, I'll need a lift home tonight and then," I point toward Aunt Cassie, "she'll need a ride home from here in the morning." Look at me—I'm organizing stuff for others. And it feels *good*.

Dak bows low from the waist like a courtier. "Your wish is my command."

I smile at everyone and pull out my phone. "Good. Then I need to call back a man about getting a world record." I stroll out of the room, feeling happy and...*powerful*? It feels good—and a little bit scary—to take charge of my own life. I sure hope I can pull this off.

Master of My Fate, Captain of My Soul

Later that afternoon, Dak drives me home from the hospital in his mother's car. Pulling up to the farmhouse, he doesn't comment about the big, green tractor still attached to the dead fir tree in the driveway—*thank God*. I'm not sure how I'd explain it to him. Instead, he asks, "Are you sure you don't want me to stay for a bit?"

"It's time I start learning how to stand on my own two feet." I get out of the car and make footprints in the fresh snow, which looks like vanilla frosting on the ground, tractor, and house.

He powers down his window. "Want me to help you make dinner before I go?"

Tempting. But I should practice this self-reliance stuff, right? "Nope. I'll figure out something." I smile. "I can always make myself a grilled cheese sandwich and some soup, right?"

"Okay. Shoot me a text or call me if you need anything." He waits until I'm inside the house and then drives away. Nice guy.

I shed my coat and boots and head to the kitchen to make a cup of tea, deliberately ignoring BC, who's sneering at me from the top of the stairs. As I wait for the kettle to boil, Dave Morales phones and we work out the details for rescheduling the eighth concert for three days from now: Tuesday, December 24. The show will be at eight p.m., so it's going to be billed as a Christmas Eve concert of Beethoven's sonatas, numbers 29 through 32. I sure hope people will be willing to come to a concert on Christmas Eve, rather than spending the night at home celebrating their family holiday traditions. On the phone, Dave says he'll take care of contacting the ticket holders from the canceled concert and will advertise the new concert online. No way we'll get a full house with such short notice, but maybe we'll have enough of an audience so Mr. Thompson will be able to certify the concert for the world record.

To do this *master-of-my-fate* stuff, I need to concentrate on one thing at a time. *First*, I have to make it through this concert on Tuesday. Curled up on the parlor sofa, cradling my warm cup of tea, I pray out loud, "Hey, Mom, if you're up there and you can hear me, I'd appreciate your help with this concert. I want to make you proud, but I'm a little freaked out, so whatever you can do to help would be great."

BC stares at me from the cold fireplace and rolls his eyes. "Now you're praying to a *dead* person for help? Sounds like a solid plan to me."

"What do you know? Father Nick always says good people go to heaven, and Mom was a good person. So I believe she's up there with God right now."

"Anything's possible."

I scoop BC up and cuddle him in my lap. "How can I get you to be the sweet kitty I've known my whole life? I mean, you're not actually talking, right? I'm probably just wigging out about all the bad stuff that's happened lately. If I get my act together, I bet I'll stop hearing you and we can go back to the way things used to be. Wouldn't that be *great*?"

"Whatever you say," he mutters unhelpfully. He does purr loudly while I pet him, though, so maybe that's a good sign.

My phone vibrates on the coffee table and a Polish phone number flashes on the display. Someone else from Guinness World Records?

"Hello. This is Rebecca O'Sullivan."

"Hello, Rebecca. This is Krystian Zelinski."

Oh, dear! He was planning on coming to my concert today and then we were supposed to get together to talk afterward. With all the mayhem of Aunt Cassie's accident, I'd forgotten all about him.

"Are you all right, Rebecca?" he asks. "I heard your concert was canceled—something about an automobile accident—and I feared the worst."

"I'm fine, thanks. My aunt's truck slipped off the road and she ended up with a minor concussion and a broken leg but she's coming home from the hospital tomorrow."

"Thank God for that. And what about your concert and your attempt to join the B32 Club? You only have a week or so until the end of the year."

"We've rescheduled it for Tuesday night, Christmas Eve, eight o'clock at the Courthouse Center."

"Wonderful! I'm so glad to hear that. You've worked so hard. Maja and I will be there."

"I'd be honored to have you attend."

"We look forward to it. Also, I'd like to set up a time when we can talk, face-to-face. As you might recall, after you told me of your mother's death—please allow me to offer my condolences to you once again—I mentioned that I have something important I'd like to discuss with you. After your concert. Perhaps early in the new year?"

What does he want to talk to me about? Mom? Concert piano playing? Dear Old Dad? I don't want to deal with any more drama right now, but I also don't want to wait weeks to find out what's on his mind. I might as well get it over with. I say, "I have some time available

tomorrow afternoon or evening if that would be convenient for you.
I don't drive yet, but I could arrange a ride to meet you somewhere.
Or you're welcome to come here to the house."

"Wouldn't you rather wait until after your concert?"

"No thanks. Tomorrow would be fine."

"Okay then. Why don't we plan on meeting at your home tomorrow evening? Let's say six-thirty? Maja will be coming, too, if you
don't mind."

"Sure." I give him our address and hang up.

"What do you think that's about?" I ask BC.

"Maybe they're going to tell you how badly you play and that you
should quit before you tarnish your mom's legacy more than you
already have."

"That was nasty."

"But true."

BC's comments have gone from kind and reassuring to questioning
and doubt-causing to downright caustic and insulting. As I get closer
and closer to my final sonata concert, it's as if he's voicing all of my
doubts and insecurities. *Definitely not helpful.* I dump him off my lap
and go to the piano where I spend the rest of the afternoon practicing
the four sonatas, over and over again. I think they sound good. Am I
wrong? BC offers me no more feedback on my playing. *Thank God.*

⁓

That night, I'm fine being by myself while I take care of the farm animals and feed BC. For my dinner, I undercook the pasta but kind of
like its crunchiness, and my sauce made of random ingredients tastes
pretty good, too. Who knew lima beans and mushrooms go well on
spaghetti? It's not until I finish practicing piano for the evening and
settle down on the sofa with a bowl of popcorn that I notice how

creepy the farmhouse is tonight. Outside, the snow has finally stopped but the wind has picked up, making the trees moan and swirling the snowdrifts high against the trees and barn. Every little noise makes me jump a mile. I make sure all the doors and windows are locked but that doesn't help much. I wish Aunt Cassie was home from the hospital already.

BC is snoozing, curled up on my feet, looking all sweet and innocent. What should I do about him? I'm afraid if I tell Aunt Cassie, Mrs. Fox, or Dak about him, they'll have me locked up somewhere for my own good. Look at how they reacted when I said that *stupid* thing about BC at the hospital this afternoon. But maybe now that I'm taking control of my own life, I won't hear him talking anymore. Let's wait and see what happens after this last concert. Maybe once the pressure is off, everything will go back to normal. Or as normal as things can be without Mom.

Without Mom. I look around the shadowy room and realize how different it would look if she were still alive. Beautiful Christmas lights, ribbons, and decorations would twinkle everywhere, glowing candles would fill the house with the scents of pine and cinnamon, and traditional carols would be played nightly on the piano, embellished differently every time. Mom thoroughly enjoyed the season and said it brought out the best in people.

Grandpa loved Christmas, too. All year long, he built wonderfully crafted wooden toys at his workbench out in the barn—I called it his Santa's Workshop—sculpting and painting toy trucks, airplanes, and doll wagons. Even now, there are still dozens of them out there, all lined up on the shelves. And then on Christmas Day, he would dress up as Santa Claus and go to the Grange to help serve Christmas brunch and distribute the toys to the kids. With his white beard and booming laugh, he made a perfect Santa. I loved to go along with him to see the looks on the kids' faces when they opened their simple gifts. I swore they liked those wooden toys more than any sort of electronic device they could have gotten instead.

At home, Grandpa would sing along with Mom and me as we played carols on the piano, adding his rich baritone to the mix. Christmas had been an especially joyful time with the two of them around. Now they were *both* gone. Sitting in the quiet, unscented, undecorated piano parlor, I miss Mom and Grandpa terribly and feel guilty for not keeping up their holiday traditions.

I give BC a piece of popcorn, which he chews loudly. "I can't do much about Grandpa's toys, but I could make an effort to spruce up the house a bit, especially since Aunt Cassie's going to be laid up here for a few weeks."

"I'm sure some shiny tinsel and twinkly lights will go a long way toward making her broken leg feel *so* much better," he says.

I ignore his sarcasm. "Maybe we could start a new tradition: a family Christmas Eve party for Aunt Cassie, you, and me. And we could invite guests, like Mrs. Fox and Dave Morales...and Dak."

"Definitely make sure that loser comes."

"It'll be nice to get together with everyone. We could have it after the concert. It would be late but that could be a lot of fun—an after-show dinner party. Maybe Dak could help me decorate the house sometime in the next few days. And Aunt Cassie could tell me how to make a nice meal and some desserts, or I could order food from somewhere. And I could ask Mrs. Fox to take me out shopping—maybe Monday—so I could buy gifts for everyone."

"Sounds *wonderful*. I can *hardly wait*." Once again, his comments drip with sarcasm.

"Oh, come on. It *will* be fun. And it will make it feel more like Christmas around here." I'm excited about my plan. As a peace offering, I ask BC, "Want to watch a movie?"

"Why not," he mumbles.

I click on the TV but TCM is showing Hitchcock's *Psycho*, so I quickly shut it off. "*Nope.* Not tonight. How about a fire in the fireplace?"

"Whatever floats your boat."

I've seen Mom, Grandpa, and Aunt Cassie make a fire hundreds of times, but I've never done it myself. "How hard can it be?" I ask BC, but he's sleeping, so no help there. I google it on my phone and follow the directions by piling crumpled newspaper, twigs, bark, small logs, and bigger logs onto the grate. I strike a match and light it, remembering to open the flue at the last minute when a small cloud of smoke puffs into the parlor.

BC makes a snickering sound, but maybe it was a sneeze from the smoke.

After a few minutes of watching the fire burn, I start twitching for something to do. I spy the *Rhode Island Driver's Manual* on the coffee table, my birthday gift from Aunt Cassie. "Why not?" I say and crack open the cover. "Seventy-nine pages. Piece of cake." For the next three hours, I read all about driving, while adding logs to the fire whenever it burns low. By midnight, I've finished the manual—mostly commonsense stuff—and feel sleepy, but the stairs up to the bedrooms look dark and spooky.

"And what do I do about the fireplace?" I ask BC. It would be just my luck to have a log roll out and light the house on fire. I glance again at the creepy dark stairs and decide against going up to bed. "My teeth won't rot from not brushing them for one night," I explain to the sleeping cat, and then wrap myself tighter in another one of Mom's quilts—she made so many beautiful ones. BC snuggles up to me, keeping me warm.

Even though I'm exhausted, the creaks and groans of the old farmhouse remind me every few minutes that I'm all alone here tonight, so I can't sleep. Sometime at around three in the morning, I hear a loud rasping noise that sounds like someone dragging something across the upstairs hallway. "Probably a tree branch scraping the roof," I say to a snoozing BC. I get the poker from the fireplace and prop it against the arm of the sofa, just in case.

By six, the sky has lightened to dove gray, and by seven-thirty, the sun shines on the trees' leafless branches, making the snow sparkle like tiny rhinestones. I'm not going to get any sleep now, so I slip out from under the quilt and head upstairs to change my clothes, taking the fireplace poker with me, just in case. BC tails me on his silent cat feet. Peeking into every room upstairs, there's no evidence of any unwanted visitors. "Must have been a branch on the roof, just like I thought," I tell BC.

"What a *relief*," he says sarcastically.

Aunt Cassie calls at eight to say that she's being discharged from the hospital at ten. Knowing I won't be alone much longer, I immediately feel calmer. I do my chores, shower, and practice my pieces until Dak rolls up to the house with Aunt Cassie.

I am so happy to see both of them. Aunt Cassie looks pale—like she's in pain—but she's still smiling and being nice because she's sober. *Yay!* Dak looks *good*, with his curly hair still damp from his morning shower. He helps me get Aunt Cassie up to her bedroom and gives her his Netflix password so she can watch movies on her laptop. Her doctor told her to keep her broken leg *higher than her heart* for at least two weeks, so she's going to be stuck in bed for a while. I'm bummed that she's hurt but very glad she's back here at the house with me.

In her bedroom, I tell them about my upcoming date with Mr. and Mrs. Zelinski.

"Tonight, huh," Aunt Cassie says. "Do you want me to try to come downstairs to be there with you?"

"No, thanks," I say. "I'll be all right. I plan to mostly listen."

"Sounds like a good plan," Dak says.

I tell them about my Christmas Eve party idea, too, and they both sign on wholeheartedly. "It'll give me something nice to look forward to while I'm lying here," Aunt Cassie says with a grin. "Maybe I'll use my laptop to look up some fun recipes for us to try out."

Looking out her bedroom window, Dak points down to the big green tractor still chained to the dead tree in front of the house. "What happened there?"

Aunt Cassie and I laugh together, which feels good...*really good*. "A little midwinter landscaping," she says. "But one of you should put away the tractor to keep it from rusting."

"Don't look at me," I say. "I don't even know how to drive a car... *yet*." Reading the driver's manual last night did make it seem doable, however. Maybe I could get my license soon. That would change things. I say to Dak, "Speaking of driving, would you be interested in another set of piano slash driving lessons Monday morning? I feel like I'm beginning to get the hang of it and I don't want to lose momentum."

"You sure you have time with the concert coming up on Tuesday?" he asks.

"The last four sonatas were already sounding polished last week, so it's just a matter of keeping them tuned up for Tuesday. That shouldn't be a problem."

"Okay, then we have a date." I like his use of that word. "Ten a.m. on Monday?" he asks.

I nod.

He looks at Aunt Cassie. "So, about the tractor...?"

She gives him a quick primer on how to operate the John Deere and he successfully drags the tree into the woods and then motors the tractor into the barn without incident. He looks good on the tractor—as if he belongs there. *Farmer Dak?* I giggle to myself.

Afterward, he helps me lug in the Christmas decoration boxes from the barn and then settles into a kitchen chair to keep me company while I prepare a lunch tray for Aunt Cassie. I hand him an apple, which he accepts with one of his cute grins. He takes a large bite, tilts his head, and frowns as if he's studying me. "You seem different to me today. Less afraid."

"Of what?" I add a napkin and a can of seltzer to Aunt Cassie's tray. This scene feels so domestic and so *right*.

"Of everything. You just seem surer of yourself: meeting with the Zelinskis, driving lessons, the Christmas Eve party, everything. Like you've figured out what you want."

I laugh. "I don't know about that. But I have decided to try to do more stuff on my own. Like your Henley guy said, I should be the master of my fate, the captain of my soul."

"You've got a good memory."

"Comes in handy when I'm playing an hour-long piece without the sheet music in front of me." I nod toward the tray. "I'm going to take this up to Aunt Cassie, but then do you want something for lunch besides your apple?"

He smiles. "Grilled cheese and soup?"

"What else?"

"Sounds good."

After we eat, we spend an hour planning the food for the Christmas Eve party and ordering prepared platters from Frank's, the grocery store where he works. The food won't be homemade, but it'll taste good and we'll have fun celebrating together after the concert. Then for a couple of hours, Dak and I clean the house and hang garlands, lights, and Christmas decorations in every room on the first floor, even the bathroom. By the time we're done, I feel like Mom would be proud of the way the farmhouse looks. Grandpa, too.

"Want to stay for dinner?" I ask Dak. "I'm not sure what we can make but we should be able to come up with something besides soup."

He laughs. "No, thanks. I'm scheduled to work at the grocery store in an hour, so I'm going to take off. If you'd like, we can talk on the phone later, when I get off work, so you can tell me what happens with the Zelinskis."

"Sounds good." This makes me feel *normal*, like a regular girl planning to talk on the phone with her...friend? Boyfriend? I'm still not sure.

He says, "Okay, we'll talk then, and I'll be back for our lessons at ten tomorrow. Unless you want me to stay for your meeting with the Zelinskis tonight? I mean, I could call in sick, if you want me to."

"Nope. I'm good."

He pauses and looks intently at my face like he's going to say or do something, but then he just smiles and jogs out to his car.

As I watch him drive away, making tracks in the snow, I ask BC, "Was he thinking about kissing me?"

"I certainly hope not because frankly, that would be *disgusting*." He bats his dish, splashing water on the wood floor.

That night, the doorbell chimes precisely at six-thirty, and I open the door to find Mr. and Mrs. Zelinski standing on our snowy porch. We settle in front of the glowing fireplace in the parlor with a tray of tea and cookies I prepared—Aunt Cassie's idea. BC sits upright in his bed atop the piano, staring at us intently, as if he plans to memorize the conversation about to happen.

As I pour cups of tea for all of us, Mrs. Zelinski gestures around the room. "I love your beautiful decorations. They make your home feel so festive."

"Thanks. Mom was a big fan of Christmas and I'm trying to keep up some of her traditions."

"She was a pretty special lady, wasn't she?"

I nod.

"Actually," Mr. Zelinski says, "your mom is why we're here tonight."

Mystery solved. I nod again.

"As you know, when your mother was about your age, she visited Poland with the Juilliard group and played with my orchestra. What you may not know is that during her visit to Warsaw, your mother and I had a brief...*liaison.*"

Wow. He sure gets right to the point. "I didn't know that," I admit. I glance at Mrs. Zelinski but her face remains impassive. I guess this is not news to her. "My mother was very protective of her past, only telling me things if she felt I needed to know them."

He nods. "I suspected as much. At that time, I was a young, up-and-coming pianist and composer who had just won another major competition. I thought I was above the rules of society. Even though I'd recently married Maja, I believed I could be in a relationship with your mother without facing any consequences. I found Maggie fascinating. She was an exceptional pianist, full of life, and beautiful with her fiery red hair. You remind me so much of her at that age."

I smile to acknowledge the compliment.

He says, "Your mother and I only met together one time, at a cottage owned by a friend of mine. After that, we agreed that a relationship would be impossible due to my marital status, our age difference, our countries of residence, etcetera. We parted on friendly terms. Fortunately for me, rather than rejecting me as I deserved, Maja forgave my infidelity. Once I realized how my actions had hurt her and others I loved, I changed my ways and never strayed again." He gently squeezes his wife's hand. Returning his gaze to me, he says, "I wrote to your mother a few times afterward but when she did not reply I stopped trying, believing she preferred that we not keep in touch.

"The next time I heard from Maggie was a few months ago when she contacted me and invited me to attend your seventh Beethoven concert. I was glad to see her and to meet you, her beautiful, talented daughter." Mr. Zelinski pauses and sips his tea. Then he says, "Rebecca, I understand that your mother never told you who your father was. Is this true?"

I nod.

"Up until your mother's email a few months ago, I did not know you existed, but based upon the timing of her relationship with me and your birth, there is a chance I may be your father." He pauses again as if expecting me to say something. When I don't—can't—he continues. "With that possibility in mind, Maja and I wonder what you wish to do about it. I would be happy to take a paternity test, if you'd like me to, and would be very proud to assume whatever role you would like me to have in your life, especially now that you have so tragically lost your mother. Maja and I were not blessed with any children of our own but we both would welcome the opportunity to mentor a young lady, especially one as kind and intelligent as yourself."

Wow. My mind is whirling at a million miles per second. I scoop BC from his piano bed and bring him back to the couch, hugging him tightly.

Mr. Zelinski smiles kindly. "I know this is a lot for you to process. You don't have to make any decisions tonight. Please take your time, consider what you'd like to do, and then let us know."

I nod and squeeze BC even tighter.

"In the meantime, I'd like to present you with two more things to consider. As a concert pianist of some renown, I can provide you with introductions to some of the best orchestras and concert venues in the world, which will advance your career. Let me know where you would like to go and I will be glad to do whatever I can to help make that happen."

"Thank you," I mumble.

"Also, as I mentioned a few weeks ago, as the chair of the music department at URI, I would be proud to recommend you for a full scholarship as a music performance major at the school and would be thrilled to personally mentor you. You would be a much-welcomed addition to our program."

I am quite literally overwhelmed.

Mrs. Zelinski smiles kindly at me. "This is an awful lot for you to take in, isn't it?"

I nod.

She gently squeezes my shoulder. "As Krystian says, please don't feel as if you need to make decisions about any of this tonight. There is no hurry whatsoever. Think it over. Talk to your aunt. Ask your friends for advice. We will be right down the road at the university for the next three years at least, and so will be around whenever you decide what you want to do." She lifts my chin with her finger. "Okay?"

"Yes. Thank you."

She nibbles on a cookie, sips her tea, and clinks the cup back into its saucer. "Come, Krystian. I think we've given this nice young woman a lot to think about. Let's leave her alone now." She smiles at me. "Thank you for your hospitality tonight and we look forward to seeing you at your concert on Christmas Eve."

Carrying BC, I follow them to the door and wave as they drive away.

A few seconds later, I knock on Aunt Cassie's bedroom door.

"Come in."

I creak the door open and peek in.

"Get your butt in here and tell me what they said," she commands. Leaning back against the bed's headboard with her broken leg propped up on three bed pillows, she pats the bed beside her. I sit down gently—careful not to bump her leg—and release my death grip on BC, who immediately hops into Aunt Cassie's lap.

She scratches him behind his ears, prompting him to purr loudly. "Okay. Spill the beans. What did they say?"

I recount my conversation with the Zelinskis, haltingly at first and then with more speed, ending with, "So, I might have just found out who my father is."

"*Wow*," she says. "That's a freaking big deal."

"Yeah, right?"

"What are you going to do about it?"

I shake my head. "At the moment, I don't think I am going to do anything. I'll just concentrate on getting through this performance on Tuesday. After that, maybe you and I can talk about things and figure out what it means if Krystian Zelinski is my Dear Old Dad. But I need to put it out of my mind now, at least for a couple of days."

"That sounds like a good idea to me. So let's change the subject." She nods toward BC, who has fallen asleep in her lap. "I want to ask you about this guy. At the hospital, you said something about him *telling* you that my accident was your fault."

Darn. She remembers that I said that.

"First of all, my accident was nobody's fault. That's why they call them *accidents*. Got that?"

I nod, but I don't agree. If I hadn't pushed her so hard to take care of me, she wouldn't have been rushing home and wouldn't have slid off the road. I may not have put the snow on the road, but I still feel responsible.

"And secondly, what did you mean about BC *talking* to you?"

I fake-laugh. "Oh, I was just kidding—"

She does a traffic cop stop signal with her hand. "No, you weren't, Becca. Don't bullshit me." She looks at me intensely, and I know for sure she's not going to stop until I 'fess up.

How bad will it be if I *do* tell her about BC? I mean, I sure will feel better if I talk to someone about it because I'm sick of worrying. What's the worst that could happen? She'll get me locked up somewhere for being crazy? Then I wouldn't have to worry about the concert or the tour or anything else, right? That might be kind of nice...

"Earth to Becca," she says, eyebrows raised.

I bury my face in my hands. "I'm afraid you're going to think I'm nuts."

She snorts. "Remember you're talking to the lady who used a four-ton farm tractor to rip your mom's favorite fir tree out of our front yard. I'm certainly not in a position to judge anyone."

I smile. "I guess I *do* need to talk to somebody."

"We *are* the only O'Sullivans left standing."

I see Mom and Grandpa's faces and feel their loss with a bone-deep ache. I reach over to scratch BC's tummy, hoping maybe he'll curl up in my lap and give me courage but instead, he scoots closer to Aunt Cassie. I sigh. "That night after Mom d-died, when Mrs. Fox brought me back here...umm...well, BC kind of talked to me."

Aunt Cassie worry-frowns.

"I don't think he was actually talking. I mean, his mouth didn't move or anything. I think I just *imagined* it."

"That must have freaked you out."

I nod. "I googled it and found a site that said I was probably having *auditory hallucinations caused by temporary, stress-induced psychosis.*"

"Did you answer BC? I mean, like did the two of you have a conversation?"

"Kind of. Yes."

"Wow." She's still frowning.

"I don't suppose you've ever heard him speak, have you?" I ask. "I mean, there's no way he is *actually* talking, is there?"

She shrugs. "Stranger things have happened. But, no, I've never heard BC say anything. What kind of stuff did you hear him say?"

"At first, he was pretty nice, saying things that Mom would have said. 'Don't worry.' 'Everything is going to be okay.' Stuff like that. But then, lately, he's been getting nastier, telling me I should quit performing and pointing out all the stuff I'm doing wrong."

"So, he's talked to you more than once?"

I nod. "Pretty regularly since Mom died. But now that I'm starting to do things for myself more—like decorating and cooking and pulling together this last concert—I'm hoping all this cat-speak will stop."

"Why do you think you've been hearing BC talk?"

"I don't know. Maybe I'm having a tough time handling things, just freaking out with Mom and Grandpa being gone."

"And me being a pain-in-the-ass drunk all the time."

I shrug. "You're dealing with all this stuff, too."

"Not very well. And I certainly haven't been much help to you." She reaches out and squeezes my hand. "Maybe it would be a good thing for you to go and talk to someone, about BC and everything."

"Like a shrink?"

Aunt Cassie shrugs. "I figure we could all use a little therapy once in a while."

"Have you ever had any?"

She shakes her head. "But I'm sure it would be good for me, too. All the folks at the AA meeting highly recommend it. Maybe we could get a family rate."

We both laugh.

She says, "But *seriously*... What do you think? It probably would help, right?" She strokes BC's back while he continues to sleep.

"Sounds like a good plan. How about we sign me up for a few sessions after the concert and after Christmas? Next week maybe?"

"Okay. You sure you can make it through the show?"

I nod. "The last four sonatas are sounding good. And the Courthouse is right down the road. Should be a piece of cake."

She smiles. "You sound like your mother." She tucks a curl behind my ear. "And you look like her, too." She draws me in for a big hug and, just for a moment, I feel safe.

When she leans back against her pillows, I notice Aunt Cassie's eyes look pinched—like she's in pain—but at the same time, she looks healthier—as if her body is beginning to recover from all her years of drinking. I sure hope so. Because I want her to be around for a *long* time.

She smirks and asks, "So, have you made any progress with that Dak kid? I got the chance to talk to him on the way home from the hospital this morning, and he seems like a really nice guy. And he had a lot of good things to say about you, too."

I feel my cheeks grow hot.

"Wait! You're blushing! Come on—spill it. What's going on?"

"Nothing yet," I say. "It's just that when he left this afternoon, I got the feeling that he might have been thinking about kissing me."

"And how do you feel about that?"

"I guess it would be *okay*."

"Just *okay*? From that look on your face, I think it might be better than *okay* with you." She hugs me again. "That's awesome, Becca. I'm glad you found someone you like."

"How old were you when you had your first boyfriend?"

"I don't know. Probably around twelve or thirteen." She laughs. "But I started way too early. It's cool that you found someone now. It's perfect timing for you."

I shrug. "He might not be interested in me at all."

"By the way he was talking about you this morning, I think he's interested, but you'll figure that out soon enough." She groans softly and lays her head back on her pillow. "My leg is throbbing. So, I guess it's time for another one of my happy pills and then I should try to sleep."

I get her pain medicine and a glass of water and help her settle in for the night. Carrying a still-snoozing BC over my shoulder, his claws pricking me through my sweater, I turn out Aunt Cassie's bedroom light. "I'm so glad you moved back to the house."

"Me too, kiddo. I love you."

"And I love you, too."

Back in my room, I plunk BC down on my bed and speak with Dak on the phone, filling him in on my conversation with the Zelinskis. He encourages me to find out the truth about my father and is excited about the possibility of both of us attending URI. "We could commute to classes together!"

"Hey, I still haven't made up my mind about whether or not I'm even going to college. And if I do decide to go, I'm not sure I'd go to URI. Mom told me a couple of other schools had contacted her, interested in having me attend their programs. I guess a few of them offered me scholarships, too."

"But none of them would have the added attraction of *me* being one of your fellow students," he says with a chuckle.

BC mumbles, "I think I'm going to puke."

I gasp. "Did you hear that?" I ask Dak.

"Did I hear what?"

Disappointed, I say, "Nothing. See you tomorrow morning."

I've got to remember BC's voice is *probably* a hallucination, no matter how real it seems.

Exploring URI

Monday morning, I do my usual chores, practice my sonatas, get Aunt Cassie fed and set for the day, and then call Mrs. Fox to invite her to our Christmas Eve party. I also ask her to give me a ride to the mall that afternoon to buy presents for everyone. Mrs. Fox sounds excited about the late-night party and shopping with me, saying, "I feel like your *real* grandma!"

Dak arrives for his piano lesson promptly at ten and breezes through his exercises, acing all of them.

"I'm impressed," I say. "You've obviously done a lot of practicing since our last session."

He smiles. "I have a great teacher."

Out of the corner of my eye, I see BC roll his eyes.

I tell Dak, "Keep this up and you'll do just fine at your URI audition this spring."

He says, "Speaking of URI... Since both of us might be going to school there in the fall, I thought we'd take the Goat there this morning to get the feel of the place."

"I'm not ready to drive on actual roads yet!"

He laughs. "I'll drive the car up to campus and then you can practice driving around in one of the big parking lots. The students are away on Christmas break, so the place should be nearly empty."

"Okay. That sounds doable."

~

In the large commuter parking lot at the north end of URI's campus, we spend forty-five minutes with me practicing driving, reversing, and parking. All of the stuff I read in the driver's manual keeps running through my head and helps me remember what I'm supposed to do. By the time we're done, I'm a lot less afraid of the car and of driving in general.

"You know you're doing a great job, right?" Dak asks.

"Am I?" I feel a little proud of myself.

"Yup. You're picking up this driving stuff a lot faster than my sister. But please don't tell her I said that." He smiles.

"Your secret's safe with me."

He asks, "As long as we're here on campus, would you like to go see the music department building?"

"I thought you said the school is closed for Christmas break?"

He nods. "But I happen to have a buddy who arranged for some time in one of the practice rooms this morning. I thought it might be fun to see what it looks like. Want to go?"

I shrug. "Sure. Why not?"

He drives us over to the Fine Arts Center and calls his buddy, Brandon, who lets us in a side door and then gives us a quick tour of the building: classrooms, offices, and performance halls, both large and small. Everything looks clean and state-of-the-art, which Brandon explains is due to a recent total renovation of the building.

224

Finally, he walks us down a hallway to a cluster of small, soundproof practice rooms. I'm surprised to see that most of them are occupied by students.

"I thought the school was on break," I say.

"It is," Brandon says. "But we still need to practice, right? A lot of us are in ensembles together and these rooms are a great place for us to meet. Half of the students here are from Rhode Island, so we don't have far to drive to get here." He waves us toward one of the practice rooms. "Come on. I'll introduce you to my string quartet."

We enter a small white room outfitted with thick carpeting, sound absorption panel walls, and a very nice Steinway K-52 upright piano against one wall. Brandon introduces Dak and me to Tracy, Donna, and Max, the violinists and cellist from his group. He picks up his viola and invites us to listen to the beginning of one of their pieces. "We'd love to get a professional opinion of our work," Brandon says to me.

"Wait," I say. "You know me?" I'm afraid he's someone else I should have remembered from a high school class.

He nods. "I saw you perform with Dak's band a few weeks ago at the Pump House."

"*Oh, dear!* I'd never played rockabilly before. I'm afraid I wasn't very good."

"Actually, you were excellent. When you first started, I could tell that you weren't sure what you were doing, but by the end of the gig, you were digging in and playing up a storm. All your years of classical training were obvious by the way you identified each song's theme and then improvised on it. I learned some good stuff, just listening to you that night."

"Wow. Thanks." I guess BC was wrong when he said that I'd embarrassed myself that night. *Silly cat.* I glance over at Dak and see his face lit up with a smile, looking as if he's proud of me. I like it.

Brandon says, "That's why I hope you'll do us the favor of listening to us play and letting us know how we sound to you."

225

"Sure. I'd be glad to." Dak and I perch on the piano bench as the four musicians launch into a string quartet by Debussy, full of difficult changes in tempo and volume. Seven minutes later, they pause at the end of the first movement and look at me expectantly.

"You nailed it," I say. "*Honestly.* You played perfectly in sync: four distinct voices creating one sound." I smile. "As I was listening, I pictured beautifully colored maple leaves being blown around a sunny brick courtyard on a windy fall day. Well done."

All of them smile and seem truly grateful for my praise.

Back in the Goat on the way home, Dak says, "So...?"

"So, what?"

"What did you think of the Fine Arts Center and Brandon's quartet?"

I nod several times. "The center is nice—very nice. It seems to have a good variety of top-notch performance and practice spaces as well as a lot of well-designed classrooms."

"And...?"

"And...I must admit I was impressed by Brandon and the other musicians. I could tell they are into their music, heart and soul."

"That's good, right?" he asks.

"Yes, and unexpected. It's nice to meet people who care about their music as much as I do."

"So, studying music at URI—or another college—might not be too bad?"

"Maybe not."

He smiles like the cat that ate the canary.

Back at the farm, we park the car and walk to Snowy's stall on the other side of the barn, where we scratch the horse's forehead together in silence. So much has happened in such a short period; I don't know what to think or feel about anything. Some things have been *terrible*, like Mom's death and my utter failure at the Mohegan Sun concert. Some things have been *great*, like building on my relationship with Aunt Cassie and maybe finding out who my father is. And then some things I don't know about yet, like BC's sudden gift of speech and my potential relationship with Dak. Yesterday afternoon Dak looked like he was thinking about kissing me. Standing next to him now, I wonder how that would feel. Would I know what to do with my lips? I've seen hundreds of movie kisses, but I'm sure real ones are different.

Dak points toward Grandpa's Santa's Workshop. "What are all those wooden toys doing over there on those shelves?"

"Grandpa made them by hand. Every year he'd dress up as Santa Claus for the Grange's Christmas Day Brunch and give out the toys to all the kids. Those are the extra ones from last year." I smile as I remember how much Grandpa enjoyed playing Santa.

Dak says, "I bet the kids loved the old-fashioned wooden toys."

"They definitely did."

Snowy nuzzles Dak's hand and nickers quietly.

"She likes you," I say. I wish I was brave enough to tell him I like him too and to ask how he feels about me. I *really* want to know.

"Do you ever ride her?" he asks, nodding toward Snowy.

"A little bit, when the weather is nice. She's eighteen, which is getting old for a horse, so we're pretty gentle with her now, but she's still a great ride—very responsive." I adjust the strap on her blanket, pulling it more snugly across her chest. "Have you ever been on a horse?"

He shakes his head and then grins. "Maybe we could do more lesson swaps this spring: horseback riding lessons in exchange for guitar lessons."

That means he wants to keep seeing me, right? Or, maybe he just views me as his teacher? I ask, "What makes you think I want to learn to play guitar?"

"Everyone should learn. Besides, they're much more portable than a piano."

I laugh. "You've got a point there." I check the time on my phone. "Mrs. Fox is coming over soon, to take me shopping. Would you like to come in for some lunch before she gets here?"

"No thanks. I've got to get to work at the B and G."

We slide the barn door closed and crunch through the snow to his car.

"Still want me to drive you to the sound check at the Courthouse tomorrow afternoon?" he asks.

"If you don't mind."

"Not at all. Around five?"

"Sounds great." I wave as he drives away.

Back in the house, BC glares at me. "I was afraid you two were going to suck face before he left. You're getting way too friendly with that loser."

"You are wrong about Dak. He really is a nice guy."

BC snorts. "Shows what you know."

Shopping with Mrs. Fox

I eat a quick lunch with Aunt Cassie in her room while filling her in on my morning activities and then wait at the front door for Mrs. Fox, who pulls up at one-thirty on the dot. I hop into the passenger seat and kiss her on the cheek. "Thanks for helping me out today."

"No problem. Howard and Roberta were just beginning a game of Monopoly when I left the house, so that should keep him occupied for hours. Alzheimer's is such a funny disease. Half the time Howard can't remember his own name anymore, but he knows all the rules of most board games, even ones we haven't played for years." She shakes her head and smiles at me. "Where would you like to go first?"

"If you don't mind, I'd like to go to the DMV in Cranston. I called them and scheduled an appointment to take the exam for my learner's permit."

"You're working toward getting your driver's license?"

"Yes. I'm eighteen years old, for Pete's sake. It's time I learn to be more self-reliant."

She pats my cheek and puts the car in gear. "While I certainly don't mind driving you places, I'm happy you're getting your license. I know that's what your mother wanted for you. Just a few weeks ago, she was talking to me about giving you her car and signing you up for driver's training classes."

How could that have been just a few weeks ago? I fight against feeling sad and say, "My friend Dak has been teaching me to drive in exchange for piano lessons."

"That's the boy I met at your house the day after the Mohegan Sun concert, right? David Morales's nephew? He seems very friendly... and quite handsome." She smiles mischievously.

I feel my cheeks grow warm as I pretend to look out the car window at the passing scenery. I'm not sure I want to talk to Mrs. Fox about potential boyfriends. It just feels...*weird*.

She says, "I'm glad to hear he's showing you how to drive. And you're giving him piano lessons? My, my, my—your first student. Do you like teaching him?"

"Yes, more than I thought I would. It's fun watching him learn, and he gets more excited about playing piano with each lesson."

"We'll make a piano teacher out of you yet. You know, it can be a great source of income in addition to your performance fees and a wonderful way to pass your knowledge on to children."

"I don't know about teaching children. They seem awfully...*young*."

She laughs. "I must admit, some of them can be a challenge to teach, but that makes it all the more rewarding when you succeed."

"Let's just see how I do with Dak. He has an audition at URI this spring, so I have to teach him how to play decently by then."

"How is he doing so far?"

"Pretty well."

"Because he has a good teacher."

"That's what he says."

We pull into the DMV parking lot and I run in while Mrs. Fox waits in the car with the heater running, knitting a bright red wool scarf. Less than an hour later, I return with a huge smile on my face, waving a piece of paper. "Look, Mrs. Fox! I got my learner's permit!"

"Of course you did, Rebecca. You're such a bright girl." She gently presses my cheeks with both hands. "Your mother would be so proud of you."

"I think she would." I don't feel quite as sad about Mom right now. Is that okay? Or does it mean I'm starting to forget her? I don't *ever* want to do that.

Mrs. Fox tucks her knitting back into her carpetbag purse and asks, "Where to now?"

"To the mall, please. I'd like to buy some Christmas presents...and a gown for tomorrow night's show."

At the mall, I insist on pushing Mrs. Fox around in a wheelchair so she doesn't tire herself out. We have a very enjoyable afternoon, selecting gifts for everyone on our lists and buying a few items for Christmas Eve. I'm looking forward to hosting my first party. The idea of it makes me feel grown-up.

We end the afternoon in the better dresses department of Macy's, looking at gowns for the concert. Before, Mom picked out all of my gowns, which were always black, long, and very demure. Now, I pull out a lace and satin gown that's a beautiful shade of dark purple. It's short-sleeved and comes to just above my knees. Biting my lip, I ask Mrs. Fox, "What do you think of this one?"

She frowns and taps a finger on her lip.

"Bad idea," I say, turning to put the dress back on the rack. "I mean, it's not black, and considering Mom and everything, it should certainly be black, right?"

Mrs. Fox holds up a hand and stops me. "I think your mother would want you to wear the prettiest dress you can find for your last Beethoven concert. With all of the hard work you've done, you deserve it."

"But what about me being in mourning?" I ask. "Aren't there traditions about wearing black for a certain number of months?"

"Pishposh. Your mother was never one to adhere to traditions, was she?"

"No."

"So I wouldn't worry too much about the color. Besides, that gown is a lovely shade of deep purple, certainly dark enough to qualify as a color of mourning, if anybody cares about such things anymore. Why don't you try it on? Let's see what it looks like on you."

I find a salesperson and ask her where the dressing rooms are.

She points behind me. "That's a gorgeous gown. I bet it'll look wonderful on you." Glancing at Mrs. Fox, she says, "We also have a very attractive grandmother-of-the-bride gown in that same shade, if you're interested in trying it on. It's full-length satin with a lace jacket."

"Please try it on," I say to Mrs. Fox. "I'd *love* it if we wore matching dresses."

She frowns. "But that was a tradition with you and your mom—"

"—which I would love to continue with you."

"But what about Cassandra? She's your aunt and your manager now. Shouldn't you match her dress with yours?"

"Unfortunately, with her broken leg, she won't be able to make it to the concert tomorrow night. You could fill in for her. I'm sure she would appreciate it."

Mrs. Fox turns to the saleswoman. "All right. Please bring the other dress to the fitting room. Size ten."

We try on the purple gowns and they look *fantastic*—as if they were custom-made for us with no alterations needed. I figure that's a sign from God...or Mom. I even go over to the men's department and buy BC a bow tie in a matching shade of purple. We're all going to look sharp at the concert.

Mrs. Fox drives me and all of my purchases back to the farmhouse but declines to stay for a dinner of pizza and salad that we pick up on the way home. "I promised Howard I'd watch *Wheel of Fortune* with him," she says. "He thinks Vanna White is the cutest thing on television."

I kiss her goodbye, glad she's part of my life, especially now.

After modeling my gown for Aunt Cassie—she loves it and whole-heartedly agrees with Mrs. Fox's dress matching mine—I bring the pizza and BC's dinner up to her room, and the three of us have a feast together while watching the old-time Christmas movie, *It Happened on 5th Avenue*, on her laptop. I love the story of how strangers come together to form a new family in an empty New York mansion. When the movie ends, I kiss Aunt Cassie and tuck her in for the night, feeling happy and peaceful.

BC pads after me to my bedroom, where he curls into a ball at the foot of my bed as I brush my teeth and get into my cozy pajamas.

"I don't know what you're smiling about," he says.

"Today was a good day." I slide under my quilts and snuggle down into my pillow.

"Tomorrow won't be," he says.

"What do you mean?"

"Honey, if you think you're going to be able to pull off the concert and party and everything else you've got planned for tomorrow, you are fooling yourself—big time."

The pizza suddenly feels like a rock in my stomach. "Everything is going to be fine."

"We'll see about that," he says. He hops down and struts out of the room with his claws clicking on the wood floor.

I pull the quilts up to my chin and try to remember the last time I slept without BC in bed with me.

Getting to the Show

I wake up worried on Tuesday and stumble out to the barn thinking maybe BC is right. Maybe I *have* bitten off more than I can chew. Sure, I've been getting better about doing things for myself, but what makes me think I can handle the concert *and* the party *and* everything else that's been happening in my life right now? That's just *nuts*, right?

I finish my chores and eat breakfast alone in the kitchen. BC doesn't join me. As I wash my dishes, I hear a terrible clattering at the stairs and run over to find one of Aunt Cassie's crutches laying at the bottom and her clinging to the railing halfway down.

"Are you okay?" I ask rushing up to her. "What happened?"

"Oh, I'm fine. I just dropped my stupid crutch trying to stump down the stairs," she says with a laugh.

I retrieve her wayward crutch and help her down the last few steps and into one of the wooden chairs in the kitchen, where I get her settled with a cup of hot coffee. "What are you doing down here anyway?" I ask. "Aren't you supposed to stay in bed with your leg higher than your heart?"

"And leave you by yourself to do all of the prep work for tonight's party? I don't think so."

"You could give me instructions from your bed."

"I'm here now, so let's get organized. What are you planning on serving?"

"I wrote a menu on my laptop. I'll go get it." I jog up the stairs.

BC is preening himself on my bed as I rush into the room. "Why are you looking so chipper?" he asks. "I would think you'd be scared shitless by now, with all of the ridiculous things you're planning to do all by yourself today."

I grab my laptop and yank the power cord out of the wall. "For your information, Aunt Cassie is downstairs right now, waiting to help me get ready for the party."

He snorts. "A lot of help she'll be. She can't even walk."

"Please stop being so nasty. She's going to help me with the menu and food. No walking is required. Dak and I already did the cleaning and decorating."

He sighs. "*Whatever.* It's still going to be a disaster. You'll see." He hops down onto the rug and follows me out of the room. "I may as well come downstairs and watch you, though. It might be entertaining."

In the kitchen, BC stretches out in a spot of sun on the floor near the window. The forecast calls for snow later in the day. *Again.*

I pull up a chair next to Aunt Cassie and open my laptop. "I'm keeping the menu simple, mostly prepared platters I'm having delivered from Frank's Market this afternoon since I'm not much of a cook."

"*Yet.* You will be." She smiles. "All of us O'Sullivan women end up being wizards in the kitchen. It's a tradition, so you—no doubt—will also achieve wizard cooking status very soon. Let's see what you've got planned for tonight." Together, we go through the list of appetizers, entrées, salads, and desserts. "This all looks excellent," she says. "But what do you think about making a cake, too? We never got to eat the one I made for your birthday." After it had sat in the middle of the table for a week, Aunt Cassie threw it away right before the funeral reception, declaring it too stale to serve. I suspect she felt like me and didn't want to eat it without Mom.

I ask, "Do you think we can make a cake today? I mean, I don't know how and you're not able to move around much."

"As your mother would have said, 'Piece of cake.' *Ha-ha.* I'll provide the expertise and you'll do the work." She checks the wall clock. "It's seven a.m. now. What time do you have to leave for the concert?"

"Five."

"Plenty of time. Let's get started."

She pulls up a white snowflake cake recipe for me on my laptop and I gather the necessary tools and ingredients. As I cream the butter and sugar together, she says, "So, you're thinking about going to URI this fall?" She sounds a lot like Mom...and Dak.

"Maybe," I say. "Or some other college. I guess several schools want me to consider them. A few recruiters were supposed to come to my final Beethoven concert before it was rescheduled. I don't know if they'll show up tonight."

"Didn't you say you hate dealing with kids your age because they make fun of you for being so into music?"

I add eggs and flour to the batter. "If those kids I met yesterday at URI are typical college music students, maybe I don't have to worry so much. They were *really* into their music—just as much as I am."

"So you think it might be okay?"

"Yes, maybe. But what about you?" I ask. "Any more thoughts about going to culinary arts school? Grandpa and Mom fixed you up with tuition money, right? All you'd have to do is to apply and get accepted." In my mind, I hear this same discussion taking place right here in the kitchen just a few weeks ago—between Aunt Cassie and Mom—and it makes me miss Mom *terribly.*

"Don't you think I'm a little old to go to college?" Aunt Cassie asks. "I'm twenty-eight years old, for Pete's sake."

"If I'm willing to risk being called a *piano geek*, maybe you could take the chance of being called an *old lady*."

She chuckles. "And a *hick*, too, because I'll bet most J and W students didn't grow up on a farm."

"Hey, I grew up on the same farm you did, but I still got scholarship offers from some of the best music schools in the country. So did Mom."

"Fair enough. I'll think about it." She points to the mixing bowl. "Add a quarter-cup more flour. Your batter is too wet."

"See, you already know a lot more about baking than most of those young'uns you'd be in class with."

"Did you just use the word 'young'uns'?"

"Yes, I did, ma'am."

"Don't you dare *ma'am* me!" she says, and we both crack up.

By 4:45 p.m., I'm standing in our foyer, looking out the door's glass panels, waiting for Dak to pick me up, and feeling pretty good. Upstairs, Aunt Cassie is comfortably tucked back into her bed, binge-watching *The Walking Dead* on her laptop, with snacks and a drink within reach on the nightstand. She's dressed and ready for the party. We managed to find a pair of stretchy yoga pants she could wear over her cast that matched one of Mom's pretty Christmas sweaters. We even did each other's hair (matching French braids) and nails (painted a lovely shade of lavender), and are both wearing simple gold jewelry borrowed from Mom's jewelry box.

Downstairs, everything is ready for the party, too. The snowflake cake turned out *great*, with its sparkling white sugar frosting. It is proudly displayed on the sideboard next to Mom's good china and silverware, which is laid out, ready and waiting to be used. After lunch, a woman delivered the food Dak and I had ordered from

Frank's Market. It made me laugh because we ordered *way* too much for our small event. I hope everyone is *really* hungry after the concert. I plated the various dishes just the way Aunt Cassie told me to and piled them in the fridge, covered in plastic wrap, ready to be served tonight. I know there's only going to be five of us here—Aunt Cassie, Mrs. Fox, Dave, Dak, and me—but I'm still psyched about throwing a party. I wrapped my gifts for everyone while the cake was baking and have them tucked under the piano like Mom and I always did. They look pretty there, in red and green wrapping paper, tied up with silver bows. I can't wait to give them to everyone later.

Peering down the darkening driveway for Dak's car, I see it's not snowing yet, although the clouds look heavy and threatening. What a snowy winter we've had, and it's only December, with February and March usually being the snowiest months in Rhode Island. I hope it doesn't snow too much tonight. I'd hate it if we had to cancel the concert—*again*—along with the party.

At my feet, BC is snoring in his cat carrier. He hasn't talked to me very much today. Of course, I spent most of the day with Aunt Cassie, so he didn't have much of a chance to say anything. He did manage to get in a couple of nasty comments when she left the room, though, once again predicting a total disaster this evening. *God,* I hope he's wrong. I'd love it if tonight's concert turns out to be like hitting a reset button, with everything going back to normal—or at least as normal as things can be without Mom. I don't think I can stand a repeat of my *awful* Mohegan Sun performance.

I feel about as ready for the show tonight as I can be. I've got BC in his carrier and my new purple dress in a garment bag with my portfolio of sheet music, so I can review it right before the concert. My hair is done up nicely, my nails are trimmed and polished, my teeth are brushed, and my stage makeup is already on. As far as I can tell, I'm ready to go.

I see Dak's car coming down the driveway and step out on the snowy porch to greet him. He has the stereo cranked way up and is singing along with Van Morrison about a brown-eyed girl. Even from a distance, I can hear Dak's clear singing voice and talent for harmonizing. He brakes to a stop in front of the house as I tote BC and my bag down the steps.

Dak hops out of the car, music still playing, and says, "My name is Dak Ronen and I will be your Uber driver this evening." His breath forms a cloud in front of his face.

"What's an Uber driver?" I ask.

"You know... Those guys who drive people around for money. Kind of like a taxi service but with their own cars."

"Oh, yes. I've heard of them. How do those drivers get paid?"

"It's all done electronically. I've got a friend who does it and makes a couple of hundred bucks a weekend."

Uh-oh. Is Dak trying to make a point? Nervously, I ask, "Did you want me to pay you to drive me to the theater? It's okay if you do—I'd certainly understand. Especially with me having to be there early, for the sound check and all. But the thing is, I don't have much cash on me. Maybe twenty dollars or so. So, we'd have to stop at a bank. Or I guess I could write you an IOU." Maybe I should have asked Mrs. Fox for a ride to the theater.

Dak smiles. "No worries, Becca. I was just joking."

"Oh." I stare at my boots and feel like an idiot.

He laughs. "You know you're even cuter when you're all embarrassed."

He thinks I'm cute? I search his face for hints of sarcasm but find only a pair of gorgeous, dark brown eyes, looking kindly at me.

He says, "Come on, O'Sullivan, get in the car. We've got a concert to get to."

I deposit BC and my stuff in the backseat and hop in the front. "Thanks for driving me."

He points to the stereo. "Van Morrison and I think it's a marvelous night for a moondance. Do you agree?"

"With all these clouds, we won't be able to see much of the moon."

"Van and I don't quibble about such insignificant details." His smile looks particularly adorable right now.

"Then it's moondance time," I say.

All the way to the theater, we sing along to the CD. Whenever the song ends, he pushes *replay* and we start over again, switching the lead and harmony parts. I *love* it. For a few minutes, I'm not an orphan, I'm not going crazy, and no one's asking me to perform a bunch of ridiculously hard piano pieces. I'm just a girl going for a ride in a car with a good-looking guy, singing along to some classic rock music. And it feels *great*.

⌒~⌒

Way too soon, Dak pulls up to the stage entrance at the Courthouse Center for the Arts. "End of the line, O'Sullivan," he says. "Do you need a hand carrying your stuff?"

"Nope. I've got it. But aren't you coming in? You could hang out while your Uncle Dave and I do the sound check."

"Thanks, but I've got to go back home to pick up Gracie and Mom. All of us are coming to see your show tonight."

"Okay. I hope I get the chance to meet them." I gather my things and place them on the sidewalk as a couple of snowflakes twinkle in the cones of light cast by the parking lot lamps.

Dak rolls down his window. "Well, thanks for singing along with Van and me. I had fun."

I grin. "Yeah. Me too." We lock eyes for what seems like a whole minute. Before I can change my mind, I lean over and kiss him, very gently, just for a fraction of a second, but long enough for me to feel how soft and warm his lips are.

His eyebrows shoot up. "*Wow.* I didn't see that coming."

"Was it a mistake?" I was trying to be the *master of my fate*, but I sure hope I haven't messed up whatever is going on between us.

He smiles brightly. "Not as far as I'm concerned. I've been wanting to kiss you for a while."

"You have?" *Yay!*

"Yup. Maybe we could do a little more of that later, at the party?"

"That sounds nice."

"Good. It's a date then. Speaking of the party, did you want me to give you a lift home, too?"

"Or I could call an Uber driver and meet you there," I say with a little smile. I'm *definitely* flirting with him.

He says, "Consider me your pseudo-Uber driver for the evening. No other mode of transportation necessary."

We smile and lock eyes again. What will it feel like to kiss him again...for longer?

His phone buzzes and he glances at the screen. "Got to go. Mom's holding dinner for me."

I wave as he drives off with snowflakes swirling after his car.

Turning around, I'm struck by the majesty of the two-hundred-year-old building dramatically lit up by spotlights. As its name suggests, it used to be the county's municipal courthouse, but when the state consolidated its legal districts almost thirty years ago, a group of artists adopted the historic stone building and converted it into a display gallery for visual arts and a wood-paneled, 200-seat auditorium, the perfect size for small musical or theater performances, like my piano concerts.

I flex my hands inside my mittens and turn to pick up my gear, only to find Olivia Ravello, my former best friend, standing three feet away from me on the now snowy sidewalk. Where the heck did she come from?

"Hi, Becca," she says.

I nod.

She crouches down and pokes a finger through the bars of BC's carrier. "Hi, boy. How are you doing?"

He rubs his face against her glove and purrs loudly.

"Hey, I think he remembers me." She looks up. "Becca, I've been thinking a lot about calling you. I was *so sorry* to hear about your mom. She was such a nice lady. I wanted to come to her funeral, but I wasn't sure you'd want me to be there."

Why is Olivia talking to me *now*? We used to be BFFs, but it's been a whole year since we last talked in person—at that awful sleepover for my seventeenth birthday.

The night had begun *so well*. Mom had chauffeured Olivia, Hayley, Chelsea, and me to a Mexican restaurant for tacos and then back to our farmhouse to watch a movie and hang out. That was when things got *awful*. The movie was all about some high school girls stealing each other's boyfriends, so naturally, Hayley and Chelsea started talking about the guys they were dating. Olivia joined right in, giving gruesome details about her relationship with Ben Menlo—*yuck*—while I cuddled BC, hoping no one noticed I wasn't contributing to the conversation. No such luck.

"What about you?" Hayley asked me. "Are you seeing anyone?" She knew I wasn't.

I shook my head and offered them the bowl of popcorn.

Chelsea took a handful. "What about Alvin from our music class? Don't you think he's cute?" They all laughed because Alvin was an awkward kid who was picked on relentlessly for playing violin in the state orchestra.

"No," Olivia said. "Becca is too much of a *prima donna* to go out with any of the local boys."

Wow. Why did Olivia say that? She usually stood up for me. Was she mad at me about something? I tried to catch her eye but she wouldn't look at me.

"Well then, why haven't you hooked up with another piano nerd from one of your concerts?" Chelsea asked.

Another piano nerd? Is that what they thought of me? I hugged BC even tighter.

A ruckus at our front door was followed by Aunt Cassie bursting into the parlor, staggering drunk and smelling like weed. She made a big deal of peering around the room and then said to me, "Good! Your mom's not here." She held up two six-packs of beer. "For your birthday present, I brought some beverages."

"Let's get this party started!" Chelsea said. She, Hayley, and Olivia laughed.

"Aunt Cassie, we're only seventeen," I said. "We're not allowed to drink."

She said, "What difference does it make?" She looked at the other girls. "You're sleeping over, right? Brush your teeth before you go home tomorrow and no one will suspect a thing."

"Your aunt knows how to have a good time," Hayley said.

Aunt Cassie laughed. "That's me: a *party animal*. Everything is more fun when I'm around. Right, Becca?"

I was relieved when Mom came into the room carrying a tray of fancy teacups filled with hot chocolate. "I thought you girls might like something warm to drink on this cold night."

Aunt Cassie said, "Nah," and held up the beer. "I brought all the drinks they need. A couple of these and they won't care one bit about the cold."

The girls giggled.

Mom said firmly, "No underage drinking allowed."

The girls groaned.

"Oh, come on, Maggie," Aunt Cassie said. "A couple of beers aren't going to hurt anyone. Hell, they might be good for Becca. Loosen her up a bit."

"She *is* kind of uptight," Hayley said with a snort.

Why were they being so mean to me?

Mom said, "Absolutely not." She frowned at the other girls. "Your parents trust me to take good care of you. Letting you get drunk is not part of the deal." She handed a cup of cocoa to each of us.

"Well fine," Aunt Cassie said. "I'll just drink them myself, then." She opened a beer. "Move over," she said to Olivia and then flopped onto the couch between us. Tipping the bottle to the ceiling, she chugged it down and then belched long and loud. "Better out than in, right?"

The girls laughed again. I cringed with embarrassment.

Mom said, "Cassie, you can't sit here and get smashed. No way." She gently tugged on her sister's arm. "Come on. Let's go to the kitchen."

Aunt Cassie said, "I want to watch the movie with the girls." She jerked her arm away and accidentally whacked me across the mouth with her bottle. Hard. BC scrambled from my lap and fled from the room as I tasted blood from my split lower lip, which immediately began to swell.

Aunt Cassie's hand flew to her face. "Oh my God, Becca. I'm so sorry." She glared at Mom. "Look what you made me do." Standing up quickly, she clenched her stomach and ran out of the room. A few seconds later, we heard her throwing up in the bathroom.

My party was officially a *disaster*.

"We'll be right back," Mom said. She picked up the beer and walked me out to the kitchen where she gently applied an ice pack to my lip.

Silent tears dripped onto my new jeans, the ones I had thought made me look cool. But I was wrong. I was the piano nerd with the puking aunt. Definitely *not cool*.

Mom brushed my hair away from my face. "What do you want to do, hon?"

"Cancel the whole thing."

"The sleepover?"

I nodded.

"Are you sure?"

I nodded again and that was the end of my party. Mom drove Olivia, Chelsea, and Hayley home that night, and I stopped talking to them. I stayed home from school for a few days and then convinced Mom to homeschool me after that. I told her I wanted to work harder on my performance career, but really, I just didn't want to face the kids in school. They didn't understand me and I didn't feel like defending myself to them anymore. Olivia texted me for a few weeks, long after the other girls had stopped, but eventually, she quit, too.

That had all happened more than a year ago, and now, standing in the snow in front of the Courthouse Center, I can't think of a single word to say to Olivia.

"Do you need a hand?" She points toward my pile on the sidewalk.

"No, thanks." I scoop up the carrier and my bag and awkwardly stand there as the snowfall intensifies.

"Oh. Well... I'm supposed to help decorate the lobby for your concert, so..."

"Okay. Bye." I hurry toward the building.

"Let me get that for you." Olivia runs ahead of me, yanks open the red stage door, and holds it for me.

246

"Umm...thanks."

"No problem." She nods toward the main entrance. "I need to go around to the front, but maybe we could talk after the show?" She looks nervous and maybe a little bit scared. Of *me*?

"Sure," I say.

She flashes a little smile. "Great. See you then."

When the door swings shut behind me, I sigh. One minute I'm on top of the world for being brave enough to kiss Dak. And then the next minute, I'm standing there like an idiot, not able to talk to the person who used to be my best friend in the whole world.

"Good going."

Peering inside the cat carrier, I find BC staring back at me with an ugly sneer on his face.

Sound Check

Just inside the stage door, BC moves around restlessly in his carrier, making it bang against my leg. I'm freaked out that he just talked to me. I'd been so sure he wasn't going to say anything anymore, but I don't know why I'd thought that. "Maybe because cats don't really talk," I say out loud. "I'm just imagining it because I'm super stressed."

"Whatever you say, honey," his voice rasps.

The exterior door swings open behind me as Dave Morales walks in, dressed in black jeans and a dark green Jersey Boys sweatshirt, with a few snowflakes clinging to his dark hair. "Hey, Becca," he says with a smile. "Here for your sound check?"

I nod, but I certainly don't feel like going ahead with the performance anymore.

Dave lifts his chin and noisily draws in a deep breath. "Don't you just love the smell of snow? And doesn't it make the Center look beautiful?"

I nod again. Is it too late to cancel the show?

Dave says, "I hear we're expecting six inches or so, but the worst of it isn't due until after midnight, so that shouldn't affect your concert. When I checked our website a few minutes ago, the show was almost sold out—just a few empty seats here and there."

"That's great." A full house. And a talking cat. Nothing to worry about.

"Here. Let me give you a hand with BC." He takes the cat carrier and walks with me down the narrow corridor. At its end, we turn right and then left and then climb a few concrete steps to finally reach the door to my dressing room. The venue's backstage area is such a maze and walking down these twisty hallways tonight just boosts my stress level.

Dave deposits the carrier on the dressing room table. "How's your aunt? Going stir crazy yet, lying around with her foot propped up?"

"She's okay."

"Cassie's nice. Reminds me a lot of your mom. Is she going to make it to the show tonight?"

"No, she's home in bed. But she plans to come downstairs for the party later." I wish we could skip the concert *and* the party.

"I'm looking forward to it." He walks toward the door. "I'll give you a buzz when I'm ready for you onstage for the sound check, probably in about five minutes."

"Sounds good."

"Are you okay?" he asks with a small frown.

"Yes. Why?"

"You seem a little...quiet, which is understandable with such a big concert tonight."

I stare at the concrete floor and wish with all my might that Mom was here with me.

"You're going to do great, Becca," Dave says. "You know that, right?"

I nod, but I'm pretty sure he's wrong.

"Okay. See you in a few minutes." He disappears down the hallway.

I plunk into one of the dressing room chairs and look into the cat carrier to find BC staring back at me. "I know *you* don't think I'm going to do great," I say as I pinch the stainless-steel latch and swing open the door.

He reaches a black paw onto the countertop, then a white one, leans backward and stretches, and then slowly saunters out of the carrier, opening his jaws in a huge yawn. I drop the cat bed in front of him. He settles into it and cleans himself, his long tongue rasping through his short fur while he fixes me with a yellow-eyed stare.

I pick up my portfolio of sheet music, sway back and forth in the chair, and study the first sonata I'm to perform that evening. If I just stick to my normal preshow routine, maybe everything will be fine.

"Make sure you play it slowly, *bonehead*." The voice is clear and loud, not like the raspy whisper I've been hearing from BC for the past few weeks. I look around sharply but find no one else in the dressing room. No one except for the preening cat.

The backstage intercom buzzes loudly making me jump. "Y-yes?" I say.

"Is this a good time for the sound check, or would you like to wait a bit?" Through the speaker, Dave's voice sounds thin and plasticky.

"Let's do it now." Maybe playing the piano will calm me down. I grab my music, BC, and his bed, and follow the twisted corridors to the backstage area and then walk through the wings to the dark stage, all the time trying to shake the feeling that everything is going to go very badly tonight. All week long, and especially today, I've been feeling more independent and more confident. But not now. Now I feel so afraid and alone. And I miss Mom. *A lot.*

On the stage, I look out at the empty seats. With Mom's attitude about Christmas Eve, I had thought tonight would be the perfect night for the rescheduled concert. I'd even asked Dave to make an announcement before the show, letting the audience know the importance of the date to Mom. I'd thought she would appreciate that.

But now, standing here in the middle of the stage, I realize that all of that planning was *stupid*. Because Mom doesn't care about me playing a memorial concert for her. What she wants is to be here with me now and not in a pink-lined wood box in the cemetery down the street, or wherever her soul is now. And I want her to be here, too, more than I've ever wanted anything else in my life.

But that doesn't make any difference. No matter how much I want Mom to be with me, she isn't going to show up. She's *dead*. End of story. No amount of wishing is going to change the fact that Mom is gone from my life. *Forever.*

"It's about time you figured that out," BC mumbles under his breath. He's reading my mind now?

My hands shake as I deposit BC, his bed, and my sheet music on the piano. He immediately curls up and goes to sleep. *Thank God.*

To try to calm myself, I examine the familiar piano: a Steinway Model B. Not the biggest grand piano Steinway and Sons makes but by far my favorite instrument for a small concert hall like the Courthouse, and so much better than that awful white monster I had to play at Mohegan Sun. The Steinway is seven feet of black lacquered maple with a solid Sitka spruce soundboard that sings along with the music and fills the auditorium, especially with the additional sound equipment Dave installed inside it.

Red, blue, and white spotlights flash on suddenly, temporarily blinding me and jolting me into action. My hands naturally find the keyboard and play their warm-up scales in C, C sharp, D, D sharp, etcetera. Up and down the piano without pause, just the way Mom taught me. I've done these same exercises every day for more than ten years now so my fingers don't need me to tell them what to do.

Fifteen minutes later, my warm-ups completed, I shield my eyes with one hand and peer toward the sound booth at the rear of the house. "You ready?" I call out. The sooner we finish this sound check, the sooner I can go back to my dressing room.

"Anytime you are." Dave's deep voice booms from the dozens of speakers.

"Here's the first one, *No. 29*, the *Hammerklavier Sonata*." I launch into the opening movement while picturing a stream spilling over a waterfall. On top of the piano, BC clacks his tongue repeatedly as if he doesn't approve of the way I'm playing the piece. I slow my tempo a little.

Dave adjusts the sound levels, giving the piano's voice more bass and then more volume. "How's that?"

I nod. "Sounds good. But this one is long—forty-five minutes—and it changes tone and tempo quite a bit." I skip to the second movement, then the third, and finally the fourth. Each time, Dave adjusts the sound system and takes note of the levels to be used for the show that evening. Twice BC groans loudly, causing me to slow down even more. Why am I paying attention to the opinion of a cat? Maybe I *am* going crazy.

We do a sound check for the three other sonatas, too. The process takes nearly an hour. By the time we're finished, my sweater is damp with sweat and BC has fallen asleep again.

Dave climbs the stage stairs from the house auditorium. "As long as we're at it, why don't we check the light levels, too?"

I nod, and then give a thumbs-up or -down as he works the lighting board, offstage right, adjusting the various colored stage lights and the main spotlight. He also corrects the scrim lighting, making the curtain across the back of the stage glow red and green with white dots of starlight. He even places two decorated Christmas trees onstage to "give the place some holiday spirit." For each of the sonata shows, he's dressed the stage a little differently, "Just to keep things interesting," he says. Finally, an hour and a half after we began the sound check, we are ready for the show.

Dave leans against the piano and reaches over to pet BC, who sits up abruptly and hisses at him. "*Whoa!*" Dave pulls back his hand.

"Sometimes he's a little shy," I say.

"Or grumpy." Dave chuckles.

BC walks to the edge of the piano and jumps into my lap, so I scratch him behind his ears, hoping to keep him quiet. He doesn't say anything—*thank God*—but he doesn't purr either.

Dave props his chin on one hand. "Hey, I have a question for you. Why do you play the piano professionally? You could be out having fun like most young ladies your age, but instead, you spend hours every day practicing. Why? Is it because you love performing in front of an audience?"

I think about his question for a moment and then slowly nod. "Although it's not as much fun without Mom. Practicing and performing were things she and I shared. Like when I had a new piece to learn, she'd set up a reward—she called it a *carrot*—that she'd give to me once I'd mastered the piece: a DVD of a favorite old-time movie, a new dress, or a pizza dinner. She made playing the piano fun."

"Do you think you are going to keep performing now that she's gone?"

Gone. Yes, Mom is definitely *gone.* The hole she's left in me feels big enough to drive the farm tractor through—especially tonight. "I honestly don't know," I say. "This is the last concert she organized for me. I guess I'll have to see how I feel afterward." The idea of performing more shows without Mom makes me feel exhausted...and so very sad. "Some folks are suggesting I go to URI—or another school—next year, to get a degree in musical performance. Mom seemed to think it would be a good idea, too."

"I can see you going to college. I bet you'd have fun."

BC sinks his claws into my thigh.

"Ow!" I stand up and drop him on the floor. "Why did you do that?" Spots of blood bloom on my jeans.

Dave scoops up BC, carefully holding the cat out in front of him. "Come on, Mr. Grumpy. Let's put you in your cage." He leads the way to my dressing room, deposits BC in his carrier, and shuts the door. Pointing to my legs, he says, "Make sure you clean those scratches."

I nod and slump into a swivel chair but don't bother swiveling.

Dave flashes me a big smile. "I'm looking forward to your Christmas party tonight. It should be a lot of fun."

"I hope it isn't snowing too hard by then."

"It's not supposed to get bad until after midnight, so no worries. And don't worry about the show, either. You sounded great in the sound check."

"Do you think so?"

He nods. "Just keep reminding yourself in a few hours we'll all be hanging out around your fireplace, drinking eggnog, and celebrating your world record."

"I sure hope so."

He smiles and pats me on the shoulder. "I'll scram and let you get ready. One hour until showtime. I'll give you a shout-out at thirty minutes and again at fifteen minutes, as usual." He clicks the door shut behind him as he leaves.

Just a few hours and then I can have my party. Piece of cake, right? So why do I feel like I'm not going to make it?

BC Predicts the Future

I lean back in the red swivel chair and take in some deep breaths, in and out, in an attempt to calm myself. Mom called it *yoga breathing*. When that doesn't work, I go to the sink and splash some cold water on my face—another of Mom's remedies for nerves. When that doesn't work either, I sit back in the chair and just feel overwhelmed.

"Hey you," a human voice calls from the cat carrier, "let me out of here."

"BC?" Why does he sound so different today?

"Who else would it be? The Ghost of Christmas Past? I know it's Christmas Eve and all, but come on, get a grip."

"What do you want?"

"Well, for one thing, you could let me out of this cage." His voice is so clear and so real.

"I don't think so. You scratched my leg."

"You were blabbering to that Morales guy about going to college. I had to stop you."

"Why?"

"For one thing, I don't like you telling that guy our business. He may be smarter than his idiot nephew, but only marginally. And for another thing, what makes you think you'll be able to go to school in the fall?"

"I've been offered scholarships."

He snorts. "It's not the money, stupid. You couldn't handle the pressure of classes and rehearsals, not to mention having to deal with jackass classmates. You'd come home crying in a week. Two weeks tops."

"But the kids I met at URI—"

"You talked to them for all of five minutes. Big deal. You think you could handle being with morons like them twenty-four/seven?" He snorts again. "I don't think so."

"Mr. Zelinski said—"

"Zelinski? As if he cares about you. He'll say anything to keep you from suing him for child support."

"I'm not a child anymore."

"You could have fooled me. Besides, he still owes you for the last eighteen years, right?"

"I don't even know if he's my father." I drop my head into my hands. "I wish you'd stop talking. You're making me feel like I'm going crazy."

"Oh, you *are* crazy, dearie, especially if you think you're going to be able to pull off this show tonight."

"What do you mean?"

"You have so many balls in the air right now, there's no way a klutz like you will ever be able to juggle them all."

"I don't know what you mean."

"*Really?* Then let me spell it out for you. Your Dear Old Mom, who used to do *everything* for you, just died, and you haven't a clue how to handle even a small fraction of all the stuff she did."

"I'm learning—"

"How to make grilled cheese sandwiches. Good job, Becca! Of course, that's not going to help you perform those sonatas tonight, is it? And it's not like the sonatas are your only problem. *Oh, no.* You've got plenty of other things to worry about. Like this guy who all of a sudden is claiming he could be your Dear Old Dad. Don't you wonder why?"

"He didn't know about me before."

"Whatever. Of course, we could also talk about your drunk aunt, who's supposed to be taking care of you but instead is lying in bed while you take care of her."

"I'm glad to help."

"Yeah, right. Should I continue? Because if you want me to, I could talk about how poorly prepared you are for this concert. Mrs. Fox might be a sweet old bag but she's not much of a piano teacher anymore, definitely not up to teaching someone of your caliber."

"Dave just said the pieces sounded good."

"Not so much. And would you like to discuss how you're foolishly risking injury—or death—by taking driving lessons from a creep who's just using you so he can pass his music audition for college?"

"I don't think Dak—"

"You don't know much about boys. Just like you don't know anything about fashion. That grape jelly-colored gown you picked out? Let me spell that out for you, too: U-G-L-Y. And it matches the old bag's dress? How ridiculous can you get?"

"Mrs. Fox is *not* an old bag."

"And then to top it all off, you decide to throw a late-night Christmas Eve party for your pathetically few friends and family members? For Pete's sake, what makes you think you can pull that off? The food is going to taste like shit—especially that disgusting cake you made—and no one is going to have a good time. They'll just smile and pretend because they feel sorry for you."

Tears drip off my chin and soak into my jeans.

BC scoffs. "I'm pretty sure tonight is going to be a disaster of *epic* proportions."

The intercom speaker crackles. "Thirty minutes, Becca," Dave says.

I press the *Respond* button and say, "Thank you." I slip off my jeans.

"Are you going to let me out of here, or what?" BC asks, his voice sounding even clearer and louder than before.

This makes me wonder...I know most cats don't talk. But what if BC does? As unlikely as that is, it would mean that I'm *not* hallucinating and I'm *not* crazy. And it would mean other people can hear him, too.

I wash out my cat scratches, change into my lacy purple gown, slip on my black ballet flats, and press the intercom button. "Dave, would you please come to my dressing room for a minute?"

"Sure. Is something wrong?"

"I want to ask you a favor—in person."

"Okay. I'll be right there."

Thirty seconds later, he taps on the door. I gesture toward the cat carrier. "Would you please check on BC for me?"

Dave bends down and peers through the bars. "He looks fine to me. Maybe a little grumpy still."

"Say something," I prompt.

"Excuse me?"

"I know it seems a little crazy, but would you please say something to him?"

Dave looks baffled but turns toward BC and says, "Hello, good sir. How are you this fine evening?"

The cat blinks his eyes.

Dave straightens up and faces me. "Was that the reaction you were expecting?"

"No. I mean, yes. It's not like he was going to answer you, right?" My laugh sounds fake.

Dave frowns. "Are you feeling all right, Becca? Should I call Mrs. Fox or someone else for you?"

I shake my head rapidly. "No, I'm fine."

He nods slowly.

I hope Dave doesn't think I was trying to play a joke on him by asking him to talk to the cat. "I'm sorry I bothered you about BC."

"No harm done." He pulls out his phone. "Fifteen minutes to showtime, four sonatas, and then we party. Right?" He smiles kindly and points at my gown. "That's some dress you've got on there. It's different from your usual style. Shorter."

"Mrs. Fox helped me pick it out yesterday. Do you think it looks okay?"

"Better than okay. It looks great. Good choice." He nods toward BC. "Do you want me to take Godzilla out to the piano for you? Help you to avoid more bloodshed?"

Inside his carrier, BC hisses.

"No. I'd better take care of him," I say.

"All right. See you onstage."

Dave leaves and I collapse into a chair. "What a mess," I mumble.

"You're telling me," BC says.

"*Now* you talk! Why didn't you say anything when Dave was here?"

He cackles. "Because I enjoy seeing you worry about going bonkers."

I drop my head into my hands.

"You are, you know?"

I look up. "Are what?"

"Going bonkers. Because—if you hadn't noticed—you're hearing voices. Or actually, just one voice: mine."

"You're a hallucination."

"Am I?" He displays his fang teeth.

I want to get away from him and his nasty comments. *Now*. I bang open the dressing room door, startling a kid who's standing in the corridor, holding a bouquet. "Shit!" he says and then laughs. "Are you Rebecca O'Sullivan?"

"Yes."

261

"Then these are for you." He thrusts a plastic-wrapped bouquet of red roses toward me.

"Thanks," I say, grabbing the flowers and closing the door in his face. As I listen to his retreating footsteps, I realize I was rude to him. I groan.

"Smooth," BC says.

"Oh, shut up." I drop the flowers onto the dressing room table and pat my hair with shaking fingers. To my mirrored reflection, I say, "This will all be over in a couple of hours, and then I'll be at a party with Dak." I'm dangling a carrot in front of my nose to help get me through the concert, just as Mom would have done.

"If Dak even bothers to show up," BC says.

"He'll be here." I point toward the flowers. "These are probably from him." I pull out the card from the roses. "Dear Rebecca," it reads, "I'm afraid I am going to miss your show tonight. Roberta is sick and I can't find anyone else to stay with Howard. I am terribly sorry! Please know that I am there with you in spirit and wish you every success. Much love, Mrs. Fox. P.S. Your mother would be very proud of you tonight."

"Not from your *boyfriend*, are they?" BC asks snidely.

"Whatever. It's time to go." My pale face in the mirror looks panicked. I pull BC from his carrier, strap on his purple bow tie, and head for the stage.

The Eighth Beethoven Sonata Concert–Again

As I walk on stage at the Courthouse Center for my final Beethoven sonata concert, carefully holding BC so that his claws face away from me and my new gown, I can hear the murmur of the audience on the other side of the blue velvet curtain. Dave, now dressed in a tuxedo, smiles at me from the lighting board and loudly whispers, "You've got a full house."

Great. There's a whole theater full of people waiting to hear me play while I'm wishing I could forget about the entire show. I drop BC into his fleece bed on the piano and take my seat on the padded bench.

BC snickers.

Ever since I arrived at the theater, *nothing* has felt right. Mom isn't here. Neither is Grandpa or Aunt Cassie or even Mrs. Fox. After a year-long silence, Olivia is talking to me. So is BC—my *cat*—and he's saying very nasty things. With all of this going on, how can I *possibly* concentrate on Beethoven's sonatas? And why bother?

Dave walks over, his black dress shoes sparkling under the stage lights. "How're you doing?"

I try to smile but my lips stick to my teeth. "I'm fine."

"You sure? Because I can make an announcement and say you aren't feeling well. We could cancel this whole thing right now, no problem."

I shake my head emphatically. "I have to do this."

"Are you sure?"

I nod.

As Dave goes back to the lighting board, Dak slips through the stage door. "Hey, Becca, how's it going?" he asks, flashing one of his trademark lopsided grins. "That's some dress you've got on. Purple, huh? I like it."

"You look pretty nice yourself," I say shyly. He's wearing a vintage three-piece dark blue suit with a tweed vest, which looks *great* on him.

"Thanks." He deliberately bumps me with his hip as he sits beside me on the bench. "So, how're you feeling? You ready for this?"

I struggle against the sudden urge to cry.

"You look stressed. Normal preshow jitters—or is it something else?"

From his bed, BC is glaring daggers at Dak and me.

Dak follows my gaze. "I see you brought BC along for the show."

"Of course."

"Is he helping you stay calm like he's supposed to?"

I try to chuckle but it comes out sounding like a cough. "Not so much."

BC narrows his eyes at me.

"But he'll be fine," I add quickly. "He always falls asleep as soon as I start playing."

"So, you've got this?" Dak asks.

"Sure."

"How long's the show?"

"Around two and a half hours with the intermission."

"So, in three hours, we'll be on our way back to your house for the party."

"Sounds good." I wish we were headed there now.

He starts to walk away and then turns back. "I almost forgot... *Merde!*"

I smile. "Thanks."

Dave pats Dak's shoulder as he passes and then he smiles at me. "You ready?"

"In just a minute." I turn toward BC. "Where's middle-C?"

"Oh, find it yourself." He yawns and closes his eyes.

Shaken, I stand and do my dress-smoothing ritual. It feels different with a shorter dress, as if there's not enough fabric to cover me. Seated back on the bench, I signal my readiness to Dave with a nod. I want to get this show over with.

And then what? What happens after tonight? Mom and I—mostly Mom—always had my life planned out so carefully before. But now I have *no idea* what I'm going to do tomorrow. Or the next day. Talk to a shrink like Aunt Cassie suggested? Will that really help? Mr. and Mrs. Zelinski offered to help me in any way they could, but that seems wrong, as if I'd be taking advantage of them, just because Mr. Zelinski *might* be my biological father, even though he didn't even know about me until a few weeks ago. So, as far as my future goes, I'm standing on the edge of a big, dark chasm with no bridge in sight.

Why am I thinking about this stuff now? I need to concentrate on the sonatas.

"Okay. Here we go," Dave says. Beneath the curtain, I see the house lights flicker on and off.

"By the way," BC hisses in my ear, "you sounded *terrible* during the sound check."

"Be quiet," I mutter.

"Especially *Sonata 32.* Sloppy and uninspired."

"Shut up!" I hiss.

"Are you sure you're ready, Becca?" Dave whispers loudly.

Why does he keep asking me that? I nod and shoot a murderous look at BC, hoping to scare him into silence.

"Good thing your mother's not here to hear this," he says and turns his back on me.

My eyes fill with tears.

Dave straightens his black bow tie and steps through the curtain. A moment later, his deep voice booms out over the house speakers, "Ladies and gentlemen, the Courthouse Center for the Arts is proud to present this evening's concert. This is the eighth and final concert in a series by Rebecca O'Sullivan, a local pianist, who is presenting all thirty-two of Ludwig van Beethoven's sonatas in one season. This is a difficult feat for any musician to perform, having been accomplished by only a handful of the most accomplished pianists in the years since 1822, when Beethoven finished writing the final piece. But tonight's performance is especially noteworthy because, at its conclusion, Ms. O'Sullivan will become the youngest pianist ever to have done so. That accomplishment will be verified by Mr. Nigel Thompson from Guinness World Records who is here tonight to witness history in the making. Mr. Thompson, would you please take a bow?"

As the audience applauds, I hurriedly pull out my lace hankie, wipe my eyes, and then tuck it back into my sleeve. "Mom, I'll make you proud," I whisper.

"Not very likely," BC mutters.

"Thank you for being here, Mr. Thompson," Dave says from the other side of the curtain. "As many of you know, Rebecca lost her mother quite suddenly last month."

I wish that was true—that Mom is simply *lost* and will be *found* very soon.

"As you also know," Dave says, "Margaret O'Sullivan was not only Rebecca's mother, she was also her piano teacher and manager. Her customary seat—front and center—has been left vacant tonight, in her honor."

I hear clapping and picture the big vase of holly and red roses on her chair. A few days ago, it seemed like such a good idea, but now it seems sappy and stupid.

Dave continues, "What you may not know is that Margaret *loved* Christmas—especially Christmas Eve—and went out of her way to make it a special time of year for everyone around her. In honor of her mother and her love for this season, Rebecca plans to donate all of her proceeds from tonight's concert to the Exeter Grange's Christmas Fund, a charity that was very important to her mother."

A murmur runs through the audience.

"If you wish to make an additional donation to their Christmas Fund in Margaret O'Sullivan's honor, envelopes will be available in the lobby at intermission."

I cringe, afraid the audience will think I'm trying to milk them for more money by asking them to give to Mom's favorite charity. *Another* stupid idea of mine.

Dave concludes, "And now, ladies and gentlemen, it gives me great honor to present Beethoven's sonatas, numbers 29, 30, 31, and 32, played by our very own Rebecca O'Sullivan."

Sonata No. 29 and No. 30

The applause is loud and then—as the curtain opens—it becomes even louder. *Too loud.* I feel like putting my hands over my ears and running offstage. But I can't. I've promised to perform. My word is my bond. So, instead of running, I sit at the piano and let the applause bury me, clogging my ears, nose, and lungs like dirt, making it hard for me to breathe.

The clapping dies down and is followed by dead silence in the auditorium, which is even *worse* than the suffocating applause had been. All these people are waiting for me to play my pieces. Or to screw them up.

Dave smiles and nods at me from the wing, encouraging me to start.

I glance toward the middle seat of the front row, hoping with all my heart that Mom will be there—that these past weeks have just been a nightmare. But no one is there. With just the vase of flowers in it, the seat looks empty, like the gap of a missing tooth.

I close my eyes and take a deep breath. You know these pieces. You've been practicing them beautifully all week. Playing them now will be a *piece of cake*. Right, Mom? I smile weakly, place my hands on the keys, and begin.

I start quietly, just a few notes at a time, and then I let the piece grow and build. As I play, I picture waterfalls. I imagine the sun peeking out from behind rain-filled clouds. I picture birds and bears and other creatures capering along to Ludwig van Beethoven's music. When I reach the end of the first movement, I pause for a moment, my fingers still resting lightly on the piano keys, my head bowed, beads of sweat haloing my face, sparkling around the edges of my vision. Again, the audience waits soundlessly. But this time, it's all right. This time, I don't feel like they are waiting for me to screw up. This time I believe they're looking forward to what I'm going to play next, and their silence gives me strength. I confidently play the second movement, the Scherzo; then boldly perform the Adagio; and finally dive headfirst into the fourth movement, the Introduzione, putting my love for Mom and the music into my playing for all the audience to hear.

And then, forty-seven minutes after I began playing *Sonata No. 29*, I finish and sit with my head bowed and my hands on my knees.

The applause is thunderous.

I smile, rise, and bow. Withdrawing my hankie, I wipe my face and hands and then reseat myself.

As the audience quiets, BC startles me by standing up. He turns a circle in his bed and then reaches his white paw out onto the top of the piano. *Oh, no.* Is he going to walk around while I play? Instead, he sits again in his bed but doesn't lie down. He scratches his neck with a back paw, twisting his bow tie to one side.

The audience grows silent, awaiting *Sonata No. 30*. It's the shortest of the four pieces I am to play this evening, but it's packed with emotion. I place my hands back on the keys, which feel hot under my fingers—as if they've heated up from me playing the first piece.

I depress the first key, then the second, and then strike the opening chord, gradually allowing the melody to reveal itself, too.

This one's for you, Mom.

I end the first movement as gently as I began it. All is going well. Then, as I start to play the second movement, I hear a very quiet voice singsonging, "Dak and Bec went up the hill to fetch a pail of water—"

I look up to find BC, still sitting up in his bed, staring at me with his yellow eyes.

"Dak fell down and broke his crown and Bec came tumbling after." He shakes his head violently, fixes his stare on me once again, and then repeats more loudly, "Dak and Bec went up the hill to fetch a pail of water—"

Can the audience hear him? I stumble over a difficult passage of the Prestissimo but continue playing, hoping no one will notice my mistake...or the cat talking.

"Dak fell down and broke his crown and Bec came tumbling after." BC stands up and arches his back, looking like an evil Halloween kitty. He hisses loudly and then repeats again, "Dak and Bec went up the hill to fetch a pail of water—"

My playing falters, but I'm able to pick up the end of the phrase without stopping altogether.

BC snickers and says even louder, "Dak fell down and broke his crown and Bec came tumbling after."

"*Shhh!*" I say. I finish the second movement, playing it at a much quicker tempo than I'd intended.

"You're rushing," he hisses. "Your mom would be so disappointed."

"Be quiet!" I whisper. I blunder into the third and final movement without pausing adequately, but that's not important right now. I just need to get to intermission.

"Dak and Bec went up the hill!" BC is screaming now.

I glance at the lighting board and see Dave standing next to it, one hand grasping the cord for the curtain. Is he going to close it on me? Am I playing that badly?

The third movement is a theme with six variations. I rush through the theme and the first variation.

"To fetch a pail of water!"

I play the second, third, and fourth variations poorly, but I get through them.

"Dak fell down and broke his crown!"

I skip the fifth variation altogether and jump into the middle of the sixth with an obvious break in the rhythm of the piece.

A murmur runs through the audience.

"And Bec came tumbling after!"

I slam down the final chord of the sonata, stand, and bow.

The audience claps politely, Dave yanks the curtain closed, and the applause dies almost immediately.

Standing next to the piano, sweating and shaking from head to toe, I have *no idea* how I'm going to make it through the second half of the concert.

Intermission

Five seconds after the Courthouse curtain closes for intermission, I snatch up Beethoven the Cat and hold him out in front of me like a furry bag of toxic garbage. He hisses and swipes his sharp claws toward my face.

"He sure is being a pain tonight," Dave says as he approaches the piano.

"Did you hear him?

"Hissing? Yeah, I heard that."

"But did you hear anything else? 'Dak and Bec went up the hill.' Did you hear that?"

Dave slowly shakes his head. "Was someone in the audience talking? Because I could make an announcement after intermission, reminding folks not to talk. I did forget to ask people to turn off their phones. Maybe that's what you heard."

I bite my lip. I know I *must* be imagining BC talking, but he sounds so much louder and clearer now, even more so than in the dressing room.

Dave says, "You'd better get him into his carrier before he does any more damage. And leave him there. He'll be fine until your concert is over." He checks the time. "Fifteen-minute intermission?"

I nod, still staring at the writhing cat.

Dave says, "Go put him away and then put your feet up. I'll call you with a five-minute warning."

I hurry down the twisted corridors to my dressing room, stuff BC into his carrier, and slam its door.

"Aren't you the *big lady*, now?" he says in a mocking tone. "Locking the poor little kitty up in his cage."

"You aren't a *poor little kitty*—you're *awful!*" I say, turning the carrier around so its door faces the wall. "Be quiet. I needed to calm down. I have two more pieces to perform and I need to play them a whole lot better than I did that last one."

"Yeah, that one sucked," BC sneers.

"Because of you!"

"Sure. Blame me if it'll make you feel better."

"Just shut up."

A knock sounds on the dressing room door.

I open it to find Dak standing there. I smile at him, feeling both glad to see him and embarrassed that he witnessed my train crash of a performance.

"Who were you talking to just now?" He peers into the room. "I thought I heard someone else's voice, too."

"*Really?*" Can he hear BC? I turn the carrier around again so that Dak can see him. Talk to him, you stupid cat. Prove that I'm not losing my mind.

Dak crouches down and sticks his finger through the bars of the carrier's door. "How're you doing, little man?"

BC slashes at him, cutting a gash in his fingertip.

"Ow!" He sticks his finger in his mouth. "Why did he do that?"

274

I turn the carrier back to face the wall. "I'm sorry. He's being a jerk tonight."

Dak rinses the cut under running water and wraps his finger in a paper towel. Then he sits in the other swivel chair. "Are you all right?" he asks. "I mean, your first piece was great—*amazing*, actually—but during that second one you seemed a little distracted."

I laugh. "Yeah. It stunk."

"I wouldn't go quite that far."

"You don't have to be nice. I know it was bad. BC was bothering me and I lost my concentration."

"What was he doing? I heard him hiss at you. Is he freaked out by the audience or something?"

"You heard him hiss but did you hear anything else?"

"Like what?"

"Oh, I don't know. Like a nursery rhyme or something..." With my polished fingernails, I pick at brown paint splatters on the makeup table.

"No. Why? Did you?"

I shake my head.

"Becca, you seem stressed, big time." Dak touches my arm, his fingers feeling hot on my skin. "Why don't you call off the rest of the concert? Just have Uncle Dave make an announcement."

I brush off his hand. "Why is everyone trying to make me cancel this concert tonight?" I press my fingers into my eyeballs. "It's like you all think I can't handle the pressure or something."

"We're just worried about you, Becca."

"Well, don't be. I'm *fine*."

"You don't seem *fine*. And you didn't play that second sonata *fine*."

"As I said, BC distracted me."

"You're blaming your performance on your cat?"

Is Dak mad at me? Disappointed? I hope not. "I'm leaving him here in the dressing room for the second half. That should solve the problem."

The intercom crackles. "Five minutes, Becca," Dave's voice says.

I push the button. "Thanks." I spritz my hair with hairspray and blot my face with my hankie. Catching Dak's eye in the mirror, I ask, "So are we still on for the party later?"

"Yup."

I smile with relief.

He laughs. "You're such a *goof*. Come on. You're going to be late for the second half of your own concert."

We step out into the corridor and shut the door behind us. As we walk away, we hear loud yowling coming from the dressing room. Both of us burst back through the door to find BC clawing frantically at the latch of his carrier. One of his paws is bleeding.

"Stop that!" I say.

BC struggles even more violently.

I tear open the door to his crate, grab him, and hold him up in front of my face. "What is wrong with you tonight?"

He hangs limply in my hands.

Dak reaches out to pet BC but he swipes at him again, claws extended. "What are you going to do with him?" Dak asks me.

I shake BC gently. "You are driving me crazy."

He meows piteously.

I close my eyes and sigh. "I can't leave him here in his carrier; he'll hurt himself more. And I can't give him to you or Dave; he'll rip you to shreds. So, I'll just have to bring him with me onstage again and hope for the best."

"Becca, are you on your way?" Dave asks over the intercom.

"Yes. Sorry. Be right there."

"Two more sonatas. Then you get a Guinness World Record and we get some chicken marsala...or eggplant parmesan, for you vegetarians,"

Dak says, mentioning two of the catered dishes we ordered from his market.

I smile. "I honestly don't care about the world record thing but the party with you sounds great." I tuck BC under one arm and gesture toward the corridor. "Shall we?"

Dak nods and the three of us head toward the stage.

Sonata No. 31 and Half of No. 32

At the edge of the stage, Dak grins at me and then slips through the stage door to go sit in the audience, while I stand in the wings, holding BC.

"Hey, I thought you were going to leave that monster in the dressing room," Dave says.

"He was clawing at the door to his carrier so much that he hurt himself." I hold up BC's bloody paw.

"Do you want me to take care of him for you?" He reaches toward BC, who squirms and hisses loudly. "Never mind," Dave says, chuckling.

"I think there's something wrong with him tonight."

BC fixes me with a squinty-eyed glare.

Dave asks me, "You ready for the second half?"

"In a minute." I plunk BC into his piano bed, bend down, and whisper in his furry ear, "I've had enough of your nonsense this evening. From here on out, you are *going* to stay in this cat bed and you are *going* to be a good little kitty. You are *not* going to move, you are *not* going to hiss, and—most especially—you are *not* going to talk. Do you understand me?"

BC blinks slowly and twitches his tail.

"Because if you do any of those things, I swear I will take you back to the dressing room and leave you there. If you bash yourself up inside the carrier"—I do a palms-up—"not my fault." Does he know I'd never be able to follow through with my threat?

He twitches his tail again but says nothing.

"Good." I give a thumbs-up to Dave, who flickers the house lights in the auditorium.

I tuck my dress underneath me on the bench and perch on the edge of the cushion, pulling my shoulders back and sitting up ram-rod straight, the way Mom taught me. Closing my eyes, I visualize the opening bars of *Sonata No. 31.* "I can do this," I whisper. I hear a snicker, but when I open my eyes, BC appears to be sleeping.

I nod to Dave, who clicks on his microphone. "And now, ladies and gentlemen, the Courthouse Center for the Arts is proud to present the second half of Rebecca O'Sullivan's record-breaking concert of Beethoven sonatas." He pulls the thick cord and the velvet curtain opens to polite applause, revealing a pumpkin patch of glowing faces, all looking up at me.

I close my eyes. Before the applause completely dies, I lift my hands a half-foot above the keyboard and then pounce on the first chord of the piece, beginning the Moderato with the "appropriate amount of vigor," as Mom would have said. If you're here, Mom, please help me.

I finish the first movement without making any major mistakes. I pause briefly and then leap into the double-quick Scherzo of the second movement. Up and down the keyboard, my fingers run, seeming to find the correct notes all on their own. I smile and nod to the rhythms of the piece.

The final movement alternates between two slow sections and two faster fugues. Beethoven—the composer, not the cat—wrote instructions that the pianist is to use the soft pedal on the slow sections, which I do. Slow, fast, slow, fast. And then I am done with my third piece of the evening. The audience claps as wildly as they did for *Sonata No. 29. All right.*

I take my bow and then sit for the fourth and final piece. This performance is almost over—*thank God.* Maybe I should take some time off before signing on to do any more concerts. Or maybe I should go to college? I have to decide my future...*soon.*

Ludwig van Beethoven wrote *Sonata No. 32* in 1822. Unlike most other sonatas, this one has only two parts to it: a Maestoso, which takes ten minutes to perform, and an Arietta, which takes twenty. Some music historians suggest the piece has just two movements because Beethoven lost interest in it, or became ill when he was writing it, while others feel that the two movements are perfectly balanced, making a third movement unnecessary. Whatever the reason, I am within a half-hour of my first real date with Dak.

I smile and light into the first movement. It starts well, but then a minute into the piece, I miss a downward leap of a seventh with my left hand.

"Becca, I told you to practice that section more," Mom says loudly and clearly.

I gasp, stop, and look around. No one is anywhere near me and BC appears to be sleeping.

I turn toward the audience. "I apologize. I will begin again."

"Oh, Rebecca! You should never stop in the middle of a performance. Don't you remember what I taught you?" Mom says, even louder and more distinctly.

I snap my head, looking left and right and then behind me. No one else is on the stage.

Dave smiles encouragingly at me from the wing, but his eyes look worried.

I *know* I'm just imagining things.

Mom says, "No you're not."

I turn back toward the piano and catch BC fixing me with an evil stare.

"It's you, isn't it?" I ask aloud.

An uneasy murmur rumbles through the audience.

Embarrassed, I smile apologetically and refocus on the piano keyboard. One more piece. I can do this. I place my right thumb on middle-C, my left pinkie on the C an octave lower, and begin the piece again, playing the first chord firmly but not percussively. I keep going. This time, I hit the seventh perfectly with my left hand, and smile.

"Don't get cocky," Mom says.

It's the *cat*. Ignore him. It's all in your head.

"Becca, concentrate!" Mom scolds.

"I'm trying," I growl under my breath. I continue with the Maestoso, my hands flying up and down the keyboard, crossing over each other.

BC walks to the piano's music stand, stretching his neck toward me, putting his furry face only inches from my nose. He says, "You're terrible. Such a disappointment," in a perfect imitation of Mom's voice.

A cold draft blows across my naked arms and legs. I can't think about that. I must *concentrate!* I close my eyes and keep playing. BC can't talk. I'm just imagining it because of the stress. If I pull myself together and finish this last sonata, I'll get to go to the party. That's my carrot: a party with Dak.

"You and your stupid *carrots*," Mom says. "I always hated having to offer you bribes just to get you to do your job. Do you think Sviatoslav Richter's mother had to buy him an ice cream cone every time he performed well? Did Alfred Brendel's mom pat him on the head like a puppy? And what about Vladimir Horowitz? He was crazy—like you—but no one had to give him lollipops to get him to perform to his potential."

"I'm not crazy!" I cry, glaring at BC.

I hear gasps from the auditorium, but I don't care anymore. I just want to finish this piece and get out of here. So I keep playing. Out of the corner of my eye, I see someone approach the lighting booth. I turn to find Dave in earnest conversation with Aunt Cassie, standing next to him on crutches. What is she doing here? She's supposed to be home in bed. And what are she and Dave talking about?

Mom/BC says, "You're pathetic. I am so disappointed in you."

"Be quiet," I plead.

"And you know you killed me," she says.

"What?" I gasp.

"I had to spend so much of my energy taking care of you that I didn't have anything left to take care of myself. I got sick and died because you're such a baby!"

"That's not true!" I cry.

The auditorium speaker system crackles and then cuts out altogether. I stop playing.

Dave walks onto the stage. "Ladies and gentlemen," he says calmly, "we are experiencing some difficulties with our sound system. However, I believe we will be able to fix the problem quickly and bring you the rest of Rebecca O'Sullivan's record-setting performance. Please remain seated and the show will continue momentarily." He bows slightly, steps back, and Aunt Cassie, balancing on one foot, pulls the chord and drops the curtain.

I whisper to Dave, "What's wrong with the sound system?"

He smiles kindly. "Nothing." Pointing to Aunt Cassie, he says, "But this nice lady thought you might need a moment or two to compose yourself."

"Oh!" I drop my face into my hands and sob.

Interruption

Behind the closed curtain at the Courthouse Center for the Arts, Aunt Cassie hobbles over to me on her crutches and lowers herself onto the piano bench. Still crying, I lean my head against her shoulder.

Dak bursts through the stage door and follows Dave over to the piano. Kneeling in front of me, Dak says, "Hey, Becca. How's it going?"

"Not too well, actually." I sniffle and pull out my hankie.

"I can see that."

The stage door opens again and Mrs. Fox appears, a major frown creasing her forehead. "Rebecca, my dear girl, are you all right?"

"You're here?" I'm surprised, happy, and embarrassed, all at the same time. "The note with your flowers said you couldn't make it."

"I was able to find a friend to stay with Howard." She squeezes me with a grandmotherly hug.

Dak gets a chair for Mrs. Fox and sets it next to the piano bench so she can sit with Aunt Cassie, Dave, Dak, and BC, all huddled around me—*the crazy girl*.

"So, what's up?" Aunt Cassie asks. "At the house this afternoon, you seemed psyched for the show. I saw you leave with Dak, singing and having fun. But, now... Maybe not so much?"

"Everything fell apart in a hurry."

"Tell us about it," Dak says.

I look around at their concerned faces. What will they think of me if I tell them the truth? I start sobbing again.

"Oh, honey," Mrs. Fox sighs, "whatever it is, we can help you. I promise. Just tell us." She pats my hand.

Aunt Cassie nods emphatically.

I close my eyes, completely exhausted. The horrible events of the past few weeks are pressing down upon me so hard, I can barely breathe. And a huge abyss of nothingness is in front of me, making me feel disoriented and lost. I can't cope with it all by myself anymore. Like it or not, I need to tell them what's been going on. I wipe my eyes and blow my nose, searching for the right words.

"Does this have something to do with BC?" Aunt Cassie asks.

I nod.

"BC?" Dak asks.

Aunt Cassie says, "Becca mentioned to me the other day, that she's been kind of stressed out and—"

I hold up a shaking hand. "Aunt Cassie, please let me tell it." Keeping my eyes on my hankie in my lap, I say, "On the night that Mom died, I was pretty upset."

"Of course you were," Mrs. Fox says and pats my hand again.

I smile weakly at her. "That night, I heard BC speak to me."

"Oh!" Mrs. Fox exclaims. "That's what was happening up in your room that night, wasn't it—when you said the cat called you an orphan?"

"And he's been talking to me ever since."

"But you know he's not *actually* talking. Right?" Dak asks.

"His mouth never moves, and he never says anything when anyone else can hear him. I googled it and found out that I'm probably having *temporary stress-induced auditory hallucinations*. I was hoping they'd go away if I got my act together."

"But that hasn't happened yet?" Dave asks.

I shake my head. "No. And it's worse than ever today. He's saying some awful things."

Aunt Cassie asks, "Like what?"

"He viciously criticized all of you and told me I was insane because I heard him talking." I laugh sadly. "I even called Dave down to my dressing room before the show, hoping he could hear BC too because that would mean BC actually *was* talking and I *wasn't* going nuts." I smile sheepishly. "Saying that out loud, now, I can hear how crazy it sounds."

Mrs. Fox pats my hands some more. "Dear, I think you are doing remarkably well considering all that has happened recently: your mother's passing, and your grandfather's just a year before that, Cassandra's accident, your two final concerts..."

I laugh again. "When you put it like that, it seems almost reasonable for me to be hearing a talking cat." I reach out and scratch BC's chin, who immediately purrs loudly.

Dave says, "That's a lot for anyone to deal with."

Mrs. Fox smiles kindly. "But despite all that, you played the first piece very well."

"And then I completely messed up the second one."

"What happened there?" Dave asks.

"I imagined BC saying a nursery rhyme over and over. It completely distracted me. I lost concentration and played poorly."

"Parts of it were lovely," Mrs. Fox says.

"I got through it. Then during intermission, Dak was kind enough to speak with me and help me calm down." I shoot him a grateful smile.

He nods. "You played *Sonata No. 31* beautifully, even better than the first one."

"Thanks."

"But, what about that last sonata, *No. 32*?" Aunt Cassie asks. "Why did you stop playing?"

"I imagined BC yelling at me—in Mom's voice, no less—telling me how disappointing I was."

"That must have been rather unpleasant," Mrs. Fox says.

"You can say that again." I shake my head sadly. "So, I *am* going crazy, right?"

"No, Becca," Dave says. "I think your brain is just trying to help you cope with your stress overload."

"Really?"

He shrugs. "I'm not saying that you wouldn't benefit from some sessions with a therapist, because I think we all need someone to talk to when things get tough. And you have a lot of tough things happening to you right now."

"But you don't think I'm nuts?" I look at all four faces.

As one, they shake their heads and embrace me in a group hug, making me feel the best I've felt in weeks.

I hear grumbly voices on the other side of the curtain. "The audience is getting restless," I say. "I'd better finish this concert."

Dak frowns. "You sure you want to do that?"

"I've come this far. I might as well finish it, right?"

Aunt Cassie nods toward BC, who is sound asleep. "Why don't we lock him up in your dressing room?"

"I tried that at intermission. He clawed at the carrier door and made one of his paws bleed."

"Maybe he'd be calm if I sat in the dressing room with him," she says.

I smile. "Thanks for offering, but I want to finish the concert with BC here at the piano, just to show myself I can do it."

She frowns. "What if you start hearing him talk again?"

"I'll deal with it. The way I see it, I have to play *No. 32* with him here. Otherwise, I let the stress win, and I don't want that. So, I'll just play it as well as I can and be done with it, if only to prove to myself I can."

All week, I've been thinking I need to learn how to take care of everything by myself, but now I realize there's nothing wrong with counting on other people, too. These folks surrounding me right now love me and want to help me. They are my new posse; my *family*. Smiling at the four of them, I say, "Get out of here. I've got an auditorium full of people expecting to hear one more piece of music tonight."

"You sure?" Aunt Cassie asks.

"Sure enough. If I hold things together for thirty more minutes, I can move on with my life." I laugh. "Of course, I'm not sure what I'll move on to. After my performance here tonight, I doubt anyone will want to book me to play any more concerts." I shake my head. "At this point, that doesn't even matter. I just need to finish this thing."

Dak points to BC. "You sure about him?"

The cat is snoozing in his bed with his black tail covering his pink nose. "Let sleeping cats lie, right?" I look at Dave. "Please tell the audience we're ready to finish the show."

"Will do," he says with a wink. "And Becca, I know one thing for sure: Your mom would be *very* proud of you right now."

"Definitely," Mrs. Fox says and kisses my cheek with her soft lips.

Dak says, "No doubt," and smiles.

I smile back at him, Dave, Mrs. Fox, and Aunt Cassie. "Thanks. To all of you."

Aunt Cassie squeezes me tightly. "You are a very special young lady, Becca. You know that, right? You're going to get through this tonight and come out on the other side even stronger than you were before."

"I hope you're right."

"I'd bet the farm on it," she says with a grin.

And with that, my *family* strides off the stage and back to their seats to hear me finish performing my final Beethoven sonata.

Sonata No. 32

Once again, Dave's deep voice booms over the Courthouse Center's PA system. "Ladies and gentlemen, if you will please retake your seats, we've made the necessary repairs to the sound system and will now bring you the conclusion of tonight's performance." He clicks off the microphone. "You sure about this, Becca?"

I nod.

"Then here we go." He slides the rockers for the house lights down, the ones for the stage lights up, and then slowly raises the curtain. It sways back and forth a few times and then settles.

Center stage, I sit at the beautiful black piano, blinking in the bright spotlight. I am going to finish the concert. No hallucinations of a talking cat are going to stop me. I've given my word and we O'Sullivans *always* keep our word. Unfortunately, however, I can't remember a single note of the piece.

The audience is silent for a few moments. Then someone claps. Someone else joins in. Then another. And another. Soon, the whole audience is clapping steadily. Mrs. Endicott, my first-grade teacher, stands and raises her hands above her head, clapping wildly. The people next to her and behind her stand and clap, too. Then everyone in the auditorium rises and gives me a standing ovation.

Sitting on the piano bench with tears streaming down my cheeks and splashing onto my purple dress, I watch as Dak helps Mrs. Fox climb the stage steps, each carrying a bouquet of red roses, which they hand to me. Dave comes over from the lighting board and gives me another bouquet, this one a mix of red and white roses. Aunt Cassie stumps up on stage, crutches and all, and envelops me in a monster hug while the audience continues to clap.

"I sure do love you, Becca," she says.

"I love you, too."

Mrs. Frederick, my third-grade teacher, climbs the stage stairs, her cane thumping on every step, and gives me a bunch of white carnations and another kiss on the cheek. And then, one by one, dozens of people come up and present me with bouquets of beautiful flowers until the floor around the piano becomes a carpet of blooms of all colors. And during all of this, everyone in the audience stays on their feet, clapping thunderously.

But this time, I don't feel like running away from the applause. Even though it's twice as loud as it was earlier, I don't feel attacked by the noise. Instead, the clapping becomes arms, wrapping around my body, enfolding me in a hug. Yes, Mom died a few weeks ago, and, yes, I might have a few mental health issues I need to deal with, but I also have a whole community of people who love and support me and are here to help when I need them. I close my eyes. Thank you, God, for everyone in my life.

I rise to my feet.

The audience quiets.

"I've never been a great public speaker," I say and then chuckle. "Mrs. Timpson, my seventh-grade English teacher, can verify that. I was supposed to give a short book report in her class but managed to get myself so worked up about it that I threw up in her garbage can."

Everyone laughs with me.

I shield my eyes from the stage lights and locate a middle-aged woman in the eighth row. "Sorry about that, Mrs. Timpson."

She calls out, "As I recall, after you washed your face and we cleaned out the garbage can, you gave a very nice report on *Huckleberry Finn.*"

Everyone laughs again.

"Well, ever since then, I've tried to do as little public speaking as possible and instead let my music talk for me. What you all have done for me here tonight is simply *amazing*—something I will *never* forget." I take a breath. "As you can imagine, these past few weeks have been difficult for me." I pause again, unable to continue.

"We love you, Rebecca," someone calls out.

"Yes, we do," other voices say.

"And I love you, too," I reply. "*All* of you. And to thank you for your love and support, I would like to finish my performance. So, if you'll please retake your seats, I will play the final piece scheduled for this evening: Beethoven's *Sonata No. 32.*"

Everyone sits and a warm hush falls over the hall.

I perch on the edge of the padded piano bench, place my fingers on the keys, and play as I've never played before. I play for my new family and for everyone else in the auditorium that night. I play for Mom and Grandpa, who I *know* are together somewhere, watching me. I even play for BC, my sweet kitty who loves me, and who didn't say any of the terrible things I imagined him saying during these past awful weeks.

But mostly, I play for *myself.*

When I finish the piece, the applause is thunderous. I stand and bow, over and over again, tears streaming. No one leaves the theater. They stand and clap on and on. *For me.*

After a long time, Dave Morales hands a microphone to a tall, thin man in a dark green suit, who joins me center stage. "May I have your attention, please," he says, in a strong British accent.

The room falls silent.

"Rebecca O'Sullivan..." He pulls a scroll of paper from his briefcase and ceremoniously holds it out to me. "I am Nigel Thompson, and on behalf of Guinness World Records, I hereby bestow upon you this certificate, acknowledging you as the youngest pianist ever to perform all thirty-two of Beethoven's sonatas by memory in one year." He shakes my hand and gives me the scroll as everyone claps loudly once more. Cell phone cameras flash from all corners of the room.

Mr. Thompson holds up his hand for silence. "When Rebecca's mother—God rest her soul—first made arrangements with Guinness to document Rebecca's record-breaking accomplishment, this series of concerts was supposed to culminate with her being awarded the world record and given a contract for a twelve-city North American tour. But then, a few days ago, Rebecca called me and asked if she could modify the terms of the contract."

Dak flashes me a puzzled look.

"It seems her Aunt Cassandra recently had an automobile accident and needed surgery, but lacked medical insurance, so Rebecca asked if she could trade in her concert tour for a check to pay her aunt's medical expenses."

A murmur runs through the audience.

Mr. Thompson continues, "I called the Guinness home office and they agreed to Rebecca's new terms."

A few people clap, but Mr. Thompson silences them quickly with another raised hand. "Then, this morning, the home office called back and said they didn't feel it was appropriate that Rebecca's accomplishment be celebrated with a check used to pay medical expenses."

A few people groan.

"That's not fair!" someone calls out.

"Not if Guinness already agreed to the deal," someone else says.

I'm crushed. I was counting on giving that money to Aunt Cassie as a sign of my growing up at least a little, and as a contribution to our new life together. But now... How are we going to pay the hospital bill?

Mr. Thompson raises his hand for silence one more time. "Please allow me to finish. This morning, the home office told me they had decided to stick to their original agreement to send Rebecca on the concert tour and *also* to give her this check for forty thousand US dollars to pay for her aunt's medical bills." He hands me a large envelope while sporting an even larger smile.

The audience at the Courthouse Center for the Arts explodes into a new wave of deafening applause. Meanwhile, it takes me several seconds to process what Mr. Thompson said: a concert tour *and* medical expenses, all paid for by Guinness! I look at the vase of holly and roses in the front row center seat. "Merry Christmas Eve, Mom," I say and feel her smile at me in return.

One after another, people I know but haven't spoken to in years come up to me onstage and congratulate me on my performance and my upcoming concert tour, making me wonder why I've spent so much time over the past few years hiding behind Mom and my career. What was I afraid of? How much have I missed because of my shyness or cowardice, or whatever it was that kept me from venturing out of my small world on the farm?

Several parents of Mom's former students shake my hand and then ask me if I'd teach piano to their children. The idea of teaching them feels *right*—as if I'll be carrying on a tradition handed down from Mrs. Fox to Mom and now to me. I smile and nod as the parents say they'll call me in the coming weeks to schedule lessons. I've enjoyed teaching Dak and I think I'll have fun teaching other students—even squiggly kids.

Dak comes up on stage with an attractive woman and a pretty girl at his side.

I say, "These must be your mom and sister."

"This is Angela," he nods toward the woman, "and this is Grace," he says, indicating the girl who looks like a feminine version of him.

I squeeze their hands. "I'm so glad to meet you both."

"I hope you know you were *awesome*!" Grace gushes. "The way you made the parts of the songs sound so different from each other was incredible. Loud, soft, fast, slow, in-your-face, whispering... Who knew one piano could have so many different voices? Now I want to learn to play piano, too."

I smile at her. "I'm really glad you enjoyed the show. It seems I'm going to be taking on some more students—besides just your brother. I'd be very happy to teach you, too."

Mrs. Ronen smiles at me. "When Grace decides she wants to do something, there is no stopping her, so I'm sure we'll be calling you soon."

"That would be great." I look at Grace. "And maybe we can practice driving together, too."

"Cool."

Mrs. Ronen leans in toward me and slips me a business card. Quietly she says, "Without going into any details, Dak mentioned that you might be looking for a good therapist to help you deal with the loss of your mother. Although I can't treat you because of a definite conflict of interest," she smiles at Dak, "my partner, Theresa Siller, is an *excellent* therapist. She's a former professional ballet dancer, so she might understand some of what you're going through as a performer, too."

"Thanks." I take the card. "I'll call her."

Dak flashes me one of his signature lopsided smiles. "I'm going to drop off Mom and Gracie and then I'll be right back to take you home to the party."

"Unless they'd like to come, too?" I say. "As you know, we have plenty of food."

"Thanks for the invitation," Mrs. Ronen says, "but Gracie is singing in our church's choir at midnight mass tonight, so Dak is driving us there."

"A dancer and a singer?" I ask Grace. "You are a talented woman. Have fun singing tonight, and *Merde!*"

She giggles as they leave.

Right behind them, Olivia Ravello appears. "You were *incredible*," she says with a smile.

"Thanks."

"And how about that standing ovation? Hometown girl makes good and scores a world record, right?"

"I can't believe how many people came out to support me. It blows me away."

She hands me two stuffed animals: a large black-and-white bear and a matching mini bear.

"One for me and one for BC?" I ask.

"Of course. It's a tradition, right?"

"This is sweet of you. Thanks."

She says, "I know this probably isn't the right time for us to talk about stuff, but I want you to know that I've really missed you this last year, in school and...everywhere. I'm so sorry for the stupid way I acted at your sleepover party that day and I'd like to talk to you about it, to see if there's any way we could possibly be friends again."

Looking into her earnest face, I realize how much I've missed her, too. With Mom gone now, I could certainly use a best friend again...or *any* friend. I smile. "Sounds good. Do you still have the same phone number?"

She nods.

"I'll call you this week, right after Christmas."

She reaches over and gives me a tight hug. "I'd like that. A lot."

As she starts to walk away, a thought occurs to me. "Hey Olivia," I say, "are you doing anything tonight—like right now?"

She looks confused. "Tonight? No..."

"We're having a little Christmas Eve party at the farmhouse as soon as we get out of here and I'd love it if you'd stop by." I add, "Maybe we could talk a little."

"That sounds great," she says. "I'll be there."

I smile hopefully as she walks up the aisle.

A short, friendly-looking guy in a nice suit offers me a business card. "Hi, Rebecca, I'm Russell Newton from Berklee College of Music in Boston. I'd like to speak to you about our excellent classical music program and let you know about some generous scholarship opportunities available to you."

"Not so fast," another guy says, holding out *his* business card. He wears a royal blue sweater with "The Juilliard School" embroidered on it. "New York City is where it's at if you want to be a professional musician, and we can offer you a free ride if you come to Juilliard. I believe your mother once attended our fine institution."

I am surprised they both showed up for the rescheduled concert and even more surprised they still are interested in me, considering my rocky performance tonight. I have no idea what to say to them and am very glad when Aunt Cassie quickly crutches over to us.

"Gentlemen, thanks for coming to the show," she says, collecting their business cards and shaking their hands. "I will call both of you in the next few days to discuss your programs and your offers for Becca."

"And you are...?" Mr. Newton asks.

"Cassandra O'Sullivan, Becca's *manager*." She says it with confidence and pride.

"Wonderful," he says. "Do you have a card so we may reach you?"

"A card?" She giggles. "No. But don't worry; I'll be in touch."

I give Aunt Cassie a one-armed squeeze of thanks as the men walk away.

"Hello, Rebecca." I turn to find Mr. and Mrs. Zelinski standing next to me. He kisses me on both cheeks and Mrs. Zelinski does the same. Mr. Zelinski says, "Please allow us to congratulate you on becoming the newest—and youngest—member of the B32 Club."

"Thank you." I grimace. "I'm sorry I didn't play better. I had some...er...difficulties."

Mrs. Zelinski smiles kindly. "My dear, in the end, you played *brilliantly*. I can only imagine how proud your mother would be of you right now."

"I loved your phrasing on *No. 32*," Mr. Zelinski says. "Very original. As I was listening, I kept envisioning a couple of swashbucklers participating in an epic swordfight."

I gasp. "That's amazing! Because while I play, I picture scenes in my head, similar to providing a soundtrack to a silent movie."

"I do the same thing!" he says.

"Really?"

"Yes. I find it helps me remember the pieces better."

"Exactly!" I say. "And for the two movements of *No. 32*, my mental images were scenes from *The Three Musketeers*—"

"—by Alexandre Dumas," he says. "That's one of my favorite classic novels."

"Mine, too. It seems we have a lot in common." I smile at them. "Do the two of you have plans for this evening?"

"We don't know many people in Rhode Island," he says, "so, alas, we have no plans for Christmas Eve."

"My aunt and I are throwing a small party at the farmhouse tonight, to celebrate the holiday season and the world record and...everything. We're having a late-night dinner and then we'll probably sing some Christmas carols. Would the two of you like to join us?"

They look at each other and then nod simultaneously. "We'd love to," Mrs. Zelinski says.

"Wonderful. And Mr. Zelinski, maybe you could do us the honor of playing one or two Polish Christmas carols for us."

"I'd be delighted."

299

They both kiss my cheeks and leave.

Regardless of whether or not he's my father, Mr. and Mrs. Zelinski are very nice people.

After the Show

An hour after the show ends, the last audience member finally leaves the concert hall. Dave turns off the stage lights and locks the house doors. Still dressed in my lacy purple gown, I slip off my ballet flats and sit on the edge of the flower-strewn stage between Dave in his tuxedo and Dak—returned from dropping off his mother and sister at church—dressed in his handsome suit and vest, our legs dangling over the stage apron. BC, who hasn't spoken a word since his interruption of *Sonata No. 32*—and who I hope will *never* speak again—snoozes peacefully in his bed behind me, his purple satin bow tie askew. He looks like the adorable, sweet kitty I've always known and loved.

Aunt Cassie and Mrs. Fox sit in the front row of seats, on either side of Mom's Christmas vase. Aunt Cassie is wearing Mom's gown again, but this time it looks *good* on her—as if she's grown into it. Mrs. Fox is looking quite elegant in the purple grandmother-of-the-bride gown we bought together at Macy's, which matches the new purple highlights she's had added to her gray hair. How in the world did she find a hairdresser open on Christmas Eve Day?

"What a night!" Mrs. Fox says with a tired laugh.

"I'm glad you were able to make it," I say to her, and then look around at everyone still there. "Actually, I'm glad you all made it. This was the toughest concert I've *ever* had to perform—without a doubt. There's no way I could have done it without every one of you being here with me."

Aunt Cassie smiles at me. "You were fabulous, Becca. We're soooo proud of you."

Everyone murmurs their agreement.

"Thanks," I say. "It was one for the record books."

Aunt Cassie snorts at my bad joke. "Pretty cool about Guinness paying the hospital bill for me. Thanks for arranging that."

I shrug. "It's the least I can do, considering how much you do for me."

"And you get the concert tour, too," she says. "That's *awesome*. Do you know the dates and locations of the shows? After all, as your manager, I need to keep track of that sort of information." She flashes me a goofy smile.

For the first time, I can see her being my manager—and a good one, too. "I found a proposed schedule on Mom's desk. I have two concerts each month from March to August—twelve in all—beginning on the West Coast and ending up in New York City at Carnegie Hall."

"My old stomping ground," Dave says with a laugh.

"Yup. The last concert is on August 20," I say, "just before the start of fall college classes."

"Are you going to apply to schools—like maybe URI?" Dak asks.

"We'll see," I say with a devious smile. I look at Aunt Cassie. "Are you going to apply to Johnson and Wales?"

"We'll see," she says with a matching grin. We do look a lot alike. More like sisters than aunt and niece.

"How's the leg?" I ask her.

She raps her knuckles on her pink cast. "I must admit, it's aching a bit. I should probably get home and get an ice pack on it."

"How'd you get here?" I ask.

"I called an Uber. Pretty cool service."

I smile at Dak. "I know all about Uber."

Dave says to Aunt Cassie, "I seem to remember hearing something about a Christmas Eve party at your house. I think I'll go check it out. Would you like a lift?"

"Sure. Sounds great," she says.

Dave bows slightly to Mrs. Fox. "Jean, I'm afraid I've neglected to tell you how beautiful you look in that gown. What a stunning shade of purple."

She grins and blushes like a schoolgirl. "Rebecca thought it would be appropriate if we wore matching gowns in honor of Margaret."

"She was right. You look lovely," he says. "I understand you will be joining us at the party. May I offer you a ride?"

"I have my car here. But if you don't mind, I'll follow you to the farm, just in case I have any difficulty with the snow. It was falling pretty heavily before the show."

"That sounds like a good idea." Dave picks up Aunt Cassie's crutches and helps her to her feet. Waving his hand toward me, he asks Dak, "Are you escorting this beautiful young lady to the party?"

"I am," he says, "as her assigned pseudo-Uber driver for the evening."

"Unless you'd like me to drive," I say.

"Do you feel ready to drive on the road?" Dak asks.

"The State of Rhode Island says I am. I got my learner's permit yesterday."

"What? How?" he asks.

I wink at Mrs. Fox. "A nice lady took me to the DMV before we went dress shopping."

Everyone congratulates me.

I slip on my shoes, scoop up BC, hop down from the stage, and pick up the vase of holly and roses. "I know this sounds like a cliché, but I honestly believe Mom is here with us now. Does anyone else feel that, too?"

"I do," Aunt Cassie says and gathers BC and me into a hug.

"Certainly," Mrs. Fox says and joins our embrace.

Dave says, "Without a doubt," and wraps his arms around all of us, too.

Dak says, "I didn't know your mom very well, but I feel her here with us. And your grandpa, too. I mean, you're the ones they loved most in the whole world. They've got to be here, right?"

Aunt Cassie and I each reach out an arm and pull Dak into our group hug. I realize I'm crying, but there's a lot of joy mixed with my sadness. For several moments, all I hear is the rhythmic vibration of BC purring.

We gradually break from the huddle.

Looking at Dave, I point to the bouquets covering the stage. "What should we do with these?"

"Good question," he says.

"I have an idea," Dak says. "Becca, why don't you and I pick them up tomorrow morning and take them to that hospice center near your house? We can give them out to people who don't have anyone to visit them for the holidays."

"That's the place where Grandpa stayed," I say. "That seems very appropriate."

"And while we're at it, let's deliver those wooden toys he made to the Grange. The kids there would love them."

"You don't mind doing all that on Christmas morning?" I ask.

He smiles. "It sounds like fun to me."

"Me, too." And I'll get to spend some more time with Dak. *Good deal.*

I look around at everyone. "Are you ready to go? I want you all to see the gorgeous cake I made with instructions from a talented pastry chef I know." I smile at Aunt Cassie.

"Sounds good. I'm starving," Dak says.

"Then let's go." I tuck BC inside my coat and follow Aunt Cassie and the rest of my family outside into the fluffy falling snow.

Acknowledgments

While working on this novel, I have been blessed with the support of many amazing people:

- The wonderful folks at Woodhall Press, who have polished and published my last three books. Your hard work and dedication have brought my stories to life on the printed page. Thank you.
- Faculty and fellow alumni of Fairfield University's MFA program. You continue to teach and inspire me. I offer a special thanks—with lots of love—to Jill Ross and Barbara Wanamaker for reading through multiple versions of this manuscript and offering excellent advice on how to improve it. I treasure you both.
- My colleagues and clients in the book coaching/editing world. I am awed by your talents, honored to be in your company, and thankful for all that I learn from you every day. I am especially grateful to award-winning book coach Lisa Tener for her invaluable assistance and sage advice generously offered over many years. Thanks.
- My dear friends and family. Thank you for your steadfast support and encouragement. I send a special shout-out to Jayna White for always being willing to talk books and for joining me at nearly every one of my author events. You're the best.
- And especially to Chris, Julia, Laura, and Mom—my inner posse. Your love makes this all possible. I thank you from the bottom of my heart.

About the Author

Growing up, Lynne Heinzmann (LynneHeinzmann.com) was a ballerina nerd, taking dance classes up to seven days a week. This sometimes made her feel like an outsider—especially in high school—so she appreciated and relied on the support of her family and close friends. In college, Lynne switched majors from ballet to architecture, and then, after a 30-year career as an architect, she went back to school and is now an author, book coach, editor, and teacher/lecturer—which she loves. *But Cats Don't Talk* is her fourth published book. In addition to writing, Lynne still enjoys dancing whenever and wherever she can and spending time at her home in Rhode Island with friends and family, including her wonderful husband, Chris, her amazing adult daughters, Julia and Laura, her loving mom, Marilyn, and her sweet beagle, Fred.